GREAT
BRITAIN
1942

SCOTLAND

IRELAND

Bramhope

WALES

ENGLAND

Garlingston

RAF Rochford
Southend-on-Sea

LONDON

White Cliffs
of Dover

Warfield Hall

English Channel

OCCUPIED
FRANCE

Foxford Press, Asheville, NC

First American Edition, July, 2018

Library of Congress Control Number: 2018950613

ISBN-13: 978-1-948907-03-3

Printed in the United States of America

MESSAGE FOR HITLER

ALSO BY CATE M. RUANE:

Telegram For Mrs. Mooney

Letter Via Paris

Ticket to Manhattan

MESSAGE FOR HITLER

Cate M. Ruane

Foxford Press

To Glenda.

PROLOGUE

Somewhere in The English Channel

A FISHING BOAT BOBS ON CHOPPY WATERS, as its captain scans the horizon with a spyglass. He tilts his wrist and moonlight illuminates the crystal on his watch.

"They're late," he says.

Inside the cabin, a radio operator taps out a message —the same message he's been sending for more than an hour. He adjusts his headset, as though that will help, then shakes his head, "Negative," he says.

A crewman cranes his neck out the porthole and shouts, "Still no contact, Captain."

Just then, a whitecap rocks the boat, almost capsizing it. The radio operator is thrown against a pile of nets, but manages to hold onto the radio set.

"We have contact!" he yells.

The crewman shouts, "Contact, sir."

"Obviously, you idiots," says the captain as he watches a thousand tons of steel rise from the waters. He waits until the submarine has surfaced, then orders the crew to come up as close as they dare. When the forward hatch swings open, two figures emerge from the belly of the submarine. The crew helps them aboard the fishing boat.

The captain turns toward his new passengers. "Welcome aboard," he says. Noticing their uniforms for the first time, he begins to laugh. He straightens his back and executes a fast and sharp salute, "It is always a pleasure to be of service to the Royal Air Force."

Both passengers turn toward the submarine, bidding its crew farewell. They raise their right arms, palms perfectly flat. "*Heil Hitler,*" they shout in unison. The salute is returned and the hatch shut.

The German U-Boat vanishes below the waters of the English Channel.

The captain says, "Back to England, boys. Nice and slow now."

CHAPTER ONE

London, England

I was warm and toasty in the back seat of the Rolls, on my way to meet my brother Jack in London, when Lord Sopwith—my guardian for the duration—said, "Duncan here will drop me at the Air Ministry, then take you around to the Eagle Club. Will that suit, old boy?"

"Boy oh boy, sir. Does it ever!" I said.

My mouth began watering. The American Eagle Club was a joint to boost the morale of Americans serving in the British Armed Forces. They dished up peanut butter and jelly sandwiches on real Wonder bread, and cheeseburgers with fries and a Coke. With any luck, we'd get s'mores for dessert—toasted marshmallows and Hershey bars squashed between two crisp graham crackers. Washed down with a Yoo-hoo, it was the perfect meal.

I'd been to the Eagle Club before, a special guest of my brother Jack, who joined up to fly with the Royal Air Force before we Americans had the sense to start fighting off Adolf Hitler. Except for the squadron leader, who was British, all the pilots in my brother's squadron were Yanks. Winston Churchill used the Eagle Squadron pilots to get America off the fence. He made sure their photographs appeared in *Life* magazine and *Colliers*, looking dashing in their flight suits, with parachutes strapped on their backs in case they had to jump from a burning airplane. They showed up in Pathé newsreels, dogfighting in their Spitfires against the German Luftwaffe. Getting medals pinned to their chests by the King and Queen of England. A Kansas girl, on a movie date with her Joe Shmoe boyfriend, took one look at them pilots and started swooning. Because of this, every man from sea to shining sea wanted to fight the Nazis. Ma called it propaganda, but it worked.

"I'll be back Sunday night, sir," I told Lord Sopwith. "My brother will take me back to Warfield Hall on a Triumph motorcycle filled up with high-octane aircraft fuel."

"Then you'll be back in time for supper, no doubt," said Lord Sopwith, adjusting his 14-karat gold wire frame glasses. "Invite your brother to join Lady Sopwith and me, will you? Just the thing—a good chat with a flyboy. Puts everything into perspective. Can't have too much theory, what?"

Lord Sopwith was an aviation pioneer. His company, Hawker Aircraft, made the Hurricane, the fighter plane my brother was flying when he shot down his first German plane. My guess was Lord Sopwith was headed to the Air Ministry to discuss his latest invention. He was working on top secret airplane designs, very hush-

hush.

"And you'll be billeted with the squadron?" he asked. "Should be jolly good fun being so close to the action."

We were passing by Downing Street. I rolled down the window, getting ready to wave if I caught sight of the prime minister, Winston Churchill. If you ask me, he got gyped. His house was smaller than the White House pantry.

"Close that window, boy, before we catch our deaths," said Lord Sopwith, shivering. He buttoned up his coat and pulled a scarf tight around his neck. Then, to drive home his point, he pulled a handkerchief from his pocket and sneezed into it. I rolled up the window fast. Lord Sopwith is a real gentleman, so he didn't take a look at the booger that came out of his nose. Instead, he folded the handkerchief back into a perfect triangle and tucked it into his pocket.

I said, "I've already sat in a Spitfire, sir. I am learning how to fly one."

Lord Sopwith blew out a puff of air. "It's come to that, has it? God preserve us." He wasn't taking me seriously. It happened all the time, even though I was a hero of the Belgian and French Resistance after rescuing my brother from the Nazis when his plane went down in German-occupied Europe.

"Really, sir," I said. "I've started my training, just the same way Jack did. He put me in his Spitfire with a blindfold around my head. Had to feel for the instruments and name them one by one. Once I get that right, he'll let me fly the girl. The fellas call it 'feeling the tits and bits.'"

"Rather risqué for a twelve-year-old, what?"

I knew he was dead right, and that my ma wouldn't like Jack using colorful language to refer to the thing that fit into a lady's brassiere. She wouldn't like him teaching me to fly either. Ma wanted me home to East Hempstead, New York, because she was missing me something awful. Problem was that with the war full-on, there was no way for me to cross the Atlantic without getting torpedoed by U-Boats. Last week a German submarine sank the British freighter *Goolistan*. Every living soul on board was now on the bottom of the ocean floor being eaten by catfish.

I was sure grateful to the Sopwiths. While I waited for a safe passage home, they were letting me hole up at Warfield Hall. "It's the thing to do," said Lady Sop. Everyone lucky enough to own a grand country estate was expected to take in stray children—save them from the German bombs dropping on London. Lady Sop was in cahoots with my ma. Every single day she made me write a letter home, even if all it said was "I'm still alive and kicking." She'd always check the spelling and grammar and make me rewrite the whole letter over if there was one mistake. "Mind your P's and Q's," she'd say. Which was strange, seeing that I hardly ever used words with the letter Q. I wrote my letters at a special desk made for letter writing. Lady Sop called the desk by its French name, *escritoire*. It had built-in letter slots, inkwells, pen stands and matching blotters. There were also secret drawers, designed to confuse thieves. That was where you were supposed to keep the jewels and treasure maps. I checked, but the drawers contained nothing but rubber bands and paperclips. Turned out Lady Sop kept her diamonds in a safe-deposit box at the bank, which was probably a good idea.

If a day came when a letter didn't arrive to East Hempstead, my ma would know I'd been killed in action. Ma knew the Germans were dropping bombs on Southampton, England, near where the Sopwiths lived. There was no hiding the fact—she'd seen it in a newsreel. The Supermarine Aviation Works had factories around Southampton making Spitfires. A Spitfire can go 400 miles an hour and push 600 in a nosedive. That's so fast it will make the pilot black out. When a Luftwaffe pilot sees a Spitfire coming he starts praying. Living at Warfield Hall, it being so close to the Supermarine factory, meant my life was in grave peril. Ma was lighting so many candles for me, she said Saint Brendan's Catholic Church looked like the Consolidated Edison power plant.

Duncan, the chauffeur, slid open the glass divider and said, "Whitehall, your lordship." Lord Sopwith pressed a bowler hat to his head, put on a pair of kidskin gloves, and waited for Duncan to open the back door.

"Toodle-oo, sir," I said as he exited the Rolls.

The door slammed behind him. He knocked on the glass to get my attention, motioning for me to crank down the window. I figured he'd forgot his attaché case containing top secrets but then I seen he had it in his hand.

"Promise me you'll stay out of mischief, Tommy," he said. "Remember, you're *my* responsibility. And I must answer the American ambassador for your conduct. So be a good chap and no tomfoolery. Consider this an order from Ambassador Winant himself. On second thought, make that F.D.R."

"Oh, don't you worry, sir. My brother will keep a tight rein on me." I yanked an invisible leash wrapped around my neck, choking with my tongue hanging out.

Lord Sopwith took off his glasses, rubbing at his temples. Him and Lady Sopwith were against me visiting my brother for the weekend. It took all my powers of persuasion to convince them to let me go. Last time I left their house unattended, their Chris-Craft powerboat ended up over in German-occupied Belgium where it was still sitting. Docked next to a German submarine base.

Lord Sopwith hesitated before entering the Air Ministry building. He turned around and looked at the Rolls, troubled-like. I knocked on the glass divider.

"Step on it!" I said. As Duncan pulled away from the curb, I added, "Sir." I was the low man on the totem pole at the Sopwith residence, and boy, did I know it.

"Yes, me lord," said Duncan. When I looked into the rearview mirror he winked.

We were stuck in traffic, which was making me fidgety. I was looking forward to this weekend with my brother. Jack was so busy fighting Nazis I hardly got to see him. We had big plans: after lunch at the Eagle Club, he was taking me to see the Crown Jewels, which they kept in the Tower of London. St. Edward's crown alone contained 444 precious stones and had emeralds the size of Milk Duds. They also had the 105-karat Koh-i-Noor diamond, which had come from India. It was the size of a marshmallow Easter egg, the kind with sugar stuck to it. The Koh-i-Noor diamond came with a curse, which worked only on men. Every fella who ever owned it met with disaster. Queen Victoria, on the other hand, was able to wear the rock and go on to become the longest reigning queen since Cleopatra— make that the Queen of Sheba. The curse now applied to King George VI, whose older brother would've been king if he hadn't ditched the throne to marry a twice divorced Yank. The curse: maybe that explained the war. If someone didn't take that diamond off King George's hands, the next monarch would be King Adolf. My fingers started twitching.

Finally, the Rolls pulled up in front of the Eagle Club on Charring Cross Road and I let myself out, tipping my tweed cap to Duncan. I looked around for Jack and didn't see him, so I started toward the front door where a pack of American airmen were smoking cigarettes and boasting to each other. One bragged, "I was flying so close to his tail, could smell the sauerkraut on his breath—"

"Excuse me," I said interrupting them, because I knew this sort of one-upping could go on until Miami froze over. "Have you seen my brother Jack Mooney?"

"Eagle Squadron, right?" said a gunner. "Heard their leaves got canceled. Heard it from Reade Tilley's girl, who was just here looking for him."

"You mean that woman you just tried to make a date with?" asked an airman. "Ain't right, nosing in on another feller's gal."

"Mind your own business, Bill, if you know what's good for you," said the gunner.

You could tell they were itching for a fistfight. They had that look that tough guys get right before they throw a punch, shifting their weight from one foot to the other, clinching their jaws and widening their eyes so the white showed around the eyeballs. I was scared just being in the vicinity. Innocent bystanders end up with black eyes exactly this way.

Just then, Daphne—Jack's British fiancée, my future sister-in-law—ran up, out of breath. Her cheeks were pink from the exertion, her hair wild and wind tossed. Like the cover of an *Action Comic*. Gee, was she a knock-out. "Thank goodness," she said to me. "I was afraid I'd missed you. Jack's leave has been canceled, worse luck."

I looked down at my sneakers and kicked the ground, "We were going to see the Crown Jewels in the Tower of London."

"Well, you would have been disappointed in any event, because the jewels were moved to a hidden location in '39. Can't let Hitler's girlfriend, Eva Braun, get her hands on them."

"But we could've at least seen where Henry VIII's wife, Anne Boleyn, had her head chopped off. They've got the actual block with her dried blood on it. And I know you won't take me, because you faint at the sight of blood."

"Hey, doll," said the gunner, interrupting and making googly eyes at Daphne. "How's about you and me go for a hot toddy?"

Daphne sneered like a Doberman. Bill grabbed the gunner by the shoulder, spun him around and socked him in the nose. "That's Jack Mooney's fiancée," he said. The gunner was flat out on the pavement, blood gushing from his left nostril.

"Thanks, William, but you needn't have," said Daphne, pulling me back. "I'm capable of defending myself."

When, really, she was about to faint.

"My pleasure, miss," said Bill, clutching his aching knuckles.

Daphne wrapped her arm around mine, so's she wouldn't fall down. "See here," she said, "let's go back to my place. I've already rung Lady Sopwith and you have her permission to stay the weekend with me. And you don't have to look like such a sourpuss. If the Luftwaffe takes a break, Jack might be able squeeze in lunch tomorrow—a sandwich on the airfield with one eye on his Spitfire. We'll take the train and cross our fingers the whole way. Mum's got a nice wicker picnic basket and then there's the tartan blanket we can sit on." She stopped short, took a little notebook from her coat pocket and added to a list she'd already started. "Do you like vegetable pasties? Mind you, they'll have to be eaten cold," she said. "But we shouldn't get our hopes up, because he might be flying." Her face fell, like she'd just said the saddest thing imaginable.

The airmen were now on top of each other, landing fists left and right and yelling out nasty names. Daphne put her hands over my ears. Even so, I was pretty sure I'd heard a jaw crack.

"My goodness," she said, "why do we need the Germans, anyway?"

I heard a whistle blow and saw a cop—the kind wearing one of them foot-tall hats—rush up swinging a nightstick. I wanted to stick around, but Daphne grabbed my hand and pulled me in the direction of a subway station.

"Boys will be boys," she said, shaking her head.

CHAPTER TWO

In London, the subway is called *The Tube*. Stations double as bomb shelters, with canteens and bunk beds built into the walls. So while the Germans drop bombs, English folks go on drinking tea, playing cricket, and having a good night's sleep.

Our train was at the bottom of a flight of stairs that took you so deep underground, it was amazing there was still oxygen. Daphne walked down the slow way—one step at a time—but I used the railing. Gaining uncontrollable speed, I let out a scream. A lady carrying a shopping bag marked *Harrods* jumped in fright, tripping a stair but with enough time to grab my passing body. Posh she was, with a fox stole around her neck, complete with beady eyes and razor teeth. The two of them glared at me.

"Where is your mother?" she snapped. She had that look we Catholics call *self-righteous*. But if she wanted to rat on me, boy, was she in for a crushing disappointment.

"New York," I said, pulling loose and picking up speed as my sneakers got in the right position for a landing.

"Liar!" echoed off the tiled walls.

"*Really*, Thomas," said Daphne when she joined me at the bottom.

Our train was loaded and about to pull from the station, a two-wheeled shopping cart the only thing holding the door open. A grandma-type pulled at the rubber handle, trying to get the wheels out of the gap. From the opposite side, I held onto the wire frame, keeping the cart in place long enough for Daphne to catch up. We got in and the train rocketed toward the Leytonstone station.

"So why was Jack's leave canceled?" I asked once we found seats.

"Seems there's been some sort of an accident. A number of the boys are out of commission while they heal and now Jack has to fly in their place. He's exhausted, dear man. Twenty days in a row and sometimes three ops a day. Yesterday he fell asleep in the cockpit after he'd landed, too knackered to make it to a cot."

"What kind of accident? You mean a crash?"

"Well, yes, actually. But not an airplane crash, thank God." She chuckled with relief. "Jimmy tripped running down the stairs this morning and then quite a few of the other chaps tripped over him. There were broken bones, even. Sel was nearly blinded by a telephone directory. You know how it is when the air-raid siren goes—the mad rush to get into the airplanes. It's a wonder that something like this doesn't happen every day."

I narrowed my eyes and said, "How'd Jimmy trip is what I want to know."

"Oh, Thomas," said Daphne laughing harder, "I

know how your mind works. Why I can see the gears spinning. It was just clumsiness, plain and simple."

She was proving my point: English people were too trusting. That's what got them into this mess in the first place. While Hitler was building Panzer tanks and Messerschmitts, teaching kids to goose-step and getting ready to march into Poland, their prime minister was flying to Berlin for tea parties. New Yorkers, on the other hand, are born suspicious. We don't trust nobody— not policemen, not politicians, and especially not Nazis. Good thing our president is a New Yorker. Hitler wasn't going to pull the wool over Roosevelt's eyes.

"First we'll join Mum and Dad for dinner. She's making Wartime Vegetable Turnovers with Wartime Dipping…from a recipe she found in *Woman's Own* magazine. Doesn't that sound scrummy?"

"Just delicious!" I said, in a way that any New Yorker knows means just the opposite but fools the English every time. Recipes with the word "wartime" are supposed to make you feel patriotic while eating cardboard. It always worked out to this: hold the sugar, skip the cream, forget the meat, and hide the butter.

"And now we should make our plan for the week's end," said Daphne. "After dinner, how about taking in a picture show!" She took a folded newspaper from the big pocket on her wool coat and opened to the movie section. Her red lacquered fingernail began hovering dangerously above an advert for *Hold Back the Dawn*, one of them tearjerkers girls love but men fall asleep watching.

"How's about *The First of The Few*," I said, snapping my fingers like the idea just came to me. It starred Leslie Howard, the British actor who'd pretended to be a Confederate soldier in *Gone With The Wind*. Scanning down the movie timetable, I could see it was playing at the Leicester Square Theatre.

"Haven't you seen that ten times already?" said Daphne. "I know I have. Jack can't get enough of it."

Ten was too low a number. Once, when I'd gone to see it with Jack, we stayed for three shows in a row. Lord Sopwith and me already been eight times. I didn't mind seeing it a million times, it being about the invention of the Spitfire. There'd been only one teary bit where the inventor gets cancer and dies. That was my cue to visit the refreshment stand and buy myself some of what the British called *candy floss* but is the exact same thing as cotton candy. I'd get back in my seat for the spine-tingling dogfight ending. Jack would whisper in my ear, explaining every maneuver. It was all part of my ground training.

"How about *The Goose Steps Out*?" I said. It featured Nazi spies. I'd learn how *Abwehr* secret agents worked. There were spies all over London, which was why they had to paste posters everywhere warning people to keep their lips buttoned.

I looked around the train car. Across the aisle from us sat the grandma-type with the shopping cart, a case in point. Pinned to her lapel was a *Bundles For Britain* button with a red *V* in the center that stood for victory. She was knitting a pair of men's socks with green wool. By the look of it, a real patriot. Yes, siree, this was the perfect cover: secret agents, armed with bayonet-sharp knitting needles—sending those socks to the German Wehrmacht. And who knew what lurked in the shopping cart?

But Daphne wasn't going for *The Goose Steps Out*. "I'm living in a war film," she said. "What I need right now is escapism. Anything wrong with that?"

We landed on *Jungle Book*, which wasn't a war film or a romance. The book wasn't half bad and the advert showed a roaring, man-eating tiger. I knew the tiger was going to eat one of the bit players. Coming out of the theater later that night, I said, "Technicolor. They oughta make all the pictures with the stuff. Blood is so much more bloody when it's red."

"I prefer black and white, actually," said Daphne. She was looking a little queasy, so I changed the subject:

"So Sel's eye got knocked out by a telephone book, that right? He'll probably have to get a glass eye."

"I didn't say knocked out. He's not blinded but his eye is scratched and bruised and he can't fly."

"Which phone book exactly?" Details are important to good detecting.

Daphne sighed. "How should I know? Southend-on-Sea. London. Why does it matter?"

Los Angeles, I thought. Some of the Eagle Squadron pilots had Hollywood starlet girlfriends and would need their numbers handy. For sure, it wasn't the Southend-on-Sea directory. Too thin. "What caused Jimmy to trip?" I asked.

"Honestly, Thomas. I wasn't there. And if you want

to know, my guess is that he had one too many at the pub last night and woke with a hangover. The boys are under enormous pressure these days and they do like to let off steam. Or perhaps he was bone-tired from all the flying he's had to do."

"I'm not buying it," I said. I knew these pilots. They had reflexes like cats. Could take a plane up to 15,000 feet, dive at 500 miles an hour, and level out so close to the ground they got grass stains.

Daphne yawned. "Well, Sherlock, if you *must* mount an investigation, you can ask Sel yourself. We'll bring him flowers and a get well card. That is, if Jack can free himself long enough to make the trip worthwhile. Otherwise I'll take you to the British Museum. We can see the mummies. You'll like that, won't you?"

"Nah," I said. I'd already been and it was a gigantic letdown. All the real treasures had been moved from the museum for safekeeping. Good thing too, because a German bomb destroyed the room where they'd kept the ancient Parthenon frieze. All they had on display now were cat mummies, a dime-a-dozen. Rumor was, some of the treasures were kept in the basement and others in an unused Tube station. I'd been asking around. My plan was to become America's answer to Howard Carter— the Egyptologist who uncovered King Tutankhamen's tomb. The problem was that fighting around Malta was preventing me from getting to Egypt. But for now I had other things to think about.

"We've got to go to RAF Rochford tomorrow," I said. "I suspect there's a ring of—"

Daphne rolled her eyes. They were so pretty, what with them long lashes. I couldn't finish the sentence. "Oh, get on," she said. "You just want to see your brother, and I shan't argue with that." She got that glazed look in her eye I knew all too well—daydreaming about her wedding. Once that started, there was no use discussing anything serious. We were back on the train again, heading to her house. I took the paper from her pocket without her noticing and turned to the comics: *Addy and Hermy. The Nasty Nazis*: my favorite British cartoon, featuring Adolf Hitler and Hermann Göring. Daphne yawned and her eyelashes lowered. Before I knew what happened, her head was resting on my shoulder. If Jack were in my place he would've leaned over and kissed her cheek. I was puckering my lips when I heard his voice in my head. "Stop right there!" he said. My lips went slack and I shook my shoulder until Daphne bolted upright.

"Are we there yet?" she said, not suspecting a thing.

CHAPTER THREE

I WAS SLEEPING ON A FOLDAWAY COT with a mattress that made my body feel like it'd been pressed in a waffle iron. I'd gotten soft sleeping on a feather bed at the Sopwith's place. It didn't take much for Daphne to wake me.

"Jack just rang up and said that we might be in luck," she said, flattening my cowlick with her spit-dripping fingers. "Things are quiet thus far. I say we head to the base before the Luftwaffe change their minds. We can pick up breakfast rolls in the refreshment room at Liverpool station. You can get a currant bun if you'd rather."

"Currant?" I said yawning, propping my head on my elbow. "What's a currant?"

"They resemble cherries." She was trying to lore me into getting up, taking advantage of my passion for maraschino cherries. Daphne was still in her nightgown with her hair in curlers. I'd get another hour of shut-eye while she prettied herself up. That's what I thought anyway. Not fifteen minutes later and she was poking me again, dolled up and dragging me from the cot. "Get up already!" she said in a begging voice. "If we miss the next train, it shall be an hour wait for another."

I thought: *An hour wait—while Jack sits there all lonely.* Good thing I'd slept in my clothes, making it possible to move directly from the cot to the front door. Daphne was having trouble catching up in those clickety-clack high heels of hers.

While she locked the door, an air-raid siren went off. We ran for the Leytonstone Tube station. A Dornier Do-17 flew overhead, its engines shaking the ground under us and rattling the fillings in our mouths. Daphne held the picnic basket in one hand and put the other over her head. I stopped short, taking a compass from of my pocket. The German bomber was coming from the southeast and heading toward downtown London, aiming for Buckingham Palace where King George was drinking his breakfast tea: Earl Grey, same as the Sopwiths drank.

Daphne made her way down the stairs ahead of me and didn't see a squadron of Spitfires chasing after the bomber. *Drats*, I thought, knowing that one might be my brother's. But I wasn't about to say anything. It was a good idea to get out of town even if Jack wasn't there to greet us. At any minute bombs would start raining down. If one dropped on you, it was goodbye Charlie. The force alone could suck your eyeballs out. The Home Guard was teaching people to press tight over their eyes.

We made it to Liverpool station in the nick of time, slowed down by the wicker picnic basket which we were taking turns carrying. Rain was pounding on the greenhouse roof in the main terminal, water pouring through glass shattered during the Blitz. Lucky for us, Daphne brought along an umbrella. The Southend-on-Sea bound train whistle blew and we made a beeline for the first car. A sailor grabbed Daphne by the waist, making like he was helping her in. She said, "Thank you very much, but I'm perfectly capable of entering a train unaided." We made our way through three packed cars before finding seats next to the lavatory, where no one wanted to sit because of the stink.

Daphne was talking nonstop, filling me in on her wedding plans. If I was still stuck in England when the big day came, I was slated to be best man. Some of my duties, I was learning, belonged to the maid of honor. Sophie, Daphne's best friend, should've got the part, only she lived in occupied Paris and the Nazis wouldn't issue her a travel permit.

The train left the station and I began scanning the horizon for one of them barrage balloons—fake helium blimps tethered to steel wires, which the RAF knew to fly around but everybody hoped the Germans would crash into. The Luftwaffe was now equipping bombers with wire cutting explosives and that was something I desperately wanted to see. My eyes were on the window with an ear pointed toward Daphne.

She was explaining that as best man *and* man of honor, it would be my job to help her make *hors d'œuvres*. From what I gathered this involved Spam and biscuits. Only I didn't have a clue what that word meant, not knowing big-letter French words. I'm fluent in Latin, thanks to the nuns at Saint Brendan's Catholic School in East Hempstead, New York, where I was once a student. If you ask me, Latin is pretty much a waste of time. What with it being a dead language, fluency is useless. The lingo—or *lingua*, I should say—died out when the Barbarian's plundered Rome starting in 363 AD, forcing Roman citizens to speak Proto-Germanic. From that sprung Yiddish, a language still used in Brooklyn. I had a neighbor back in East Hempstead who'd emigrated from Germany via Brooklyn and spoke German and Yiddish, but not a word of Latin. You don't need Latin unless you plan on taking your orders and becoming a priest, which I didn't. Hieroglyphs was what I needed.

Meanwhile I was having a hard enough time with my English, which according to Lady Sop was "atrocious." So I figured I'd try out some real English on Daphne: "What shall we dine on whilst traveling?" I said. "Dare say, we've forgotten to stop off for the cherry buns, what?"

"Listen to you!" she said, laughing so hard I could see her molars. "Speaking like a Peer of the Realm. Jack will hardly recognize you."

That had me worried. If Jack even hinted to Ma that I was turning into an Englishman, she'd disown me. Ma and Da were straight-off-the-boat Irish immigrants and didn't like the British none. When a boy came rolling down the aisle with a food wagon, I said, "Whatta ya got, bub?"

An hour later, we exited the Southend-on-Sea Victoria station. It always reminded me of something out of "Hansel and Gretel."

"Call it Tudor," Daphne said, correcting me. "Hansel and Gretel were German."

We walked miles before we got to the gate leading into RAF Rochford. Every time a Spitfire flew over our heads we waved, hoping it was Jack. One flew so low, it messed with my hair. The pilot tipped his wing and waved back from his open cockpit. He got one look at Daphne and spun the Spitfire like a gyroscope. By the time we arrived at the guardhouse, my feet were blistered.

The soldier said he couldn't let us in without clearance. Daphne asked him to call into the dispersal hut, hoping Jack was there. A minute later, he stuck his head out the window, "Line's busy, miss."

"Can you try again, Corporal?" said Daphne, batting her eyelashes. "Keep at it and someone is bound to pick up." The corporal got right back on the horn.

A minute later: "Warrant Officer Noble picked up. She's comin' out to get you. She'll authorize you and sign you in, right and tidy."

While we waited, Daphne explained that Geraldine Noble was stepping out with another pilot in the squadron. The four of them had been out on the town, double dating. Geraldine was in the Woman's Auxiliary Air Force, abbreviated WAAF, which rhymed with calf. They had the important job of plotting the course of bomber and fighter squadrons, giving radio instructions to airmen, and operating the radar. They were the envy of every dame in the kingdom, seeing that they had first dibs on handsome pilots and were issued an endless supply of black nylon stockings.

Me and Geraldine were already acquainted. She might be going steady with a pilot, but I knew she was sweet on me. "Tommy!" she squealed as she came to the gate. I had to back away before she could smear lipstick on me. "Aren't I your best girl?" she asked.

"No going," I said. "Where's my brother, anyway?"

"Out, I'm afraid. He asked that I entertain you until he gets back." She took a clipboard from the corporal and signed us into the base. As she handed the clipboard back, she doubled over and groaned. Her whole face went ghost white and she fell to the ground, landing hard on her backside.

Daphne ran over to help. She was a nursing school dropout. "Corporal," she shouted, "Quick! Ring the medics!"

"Ruddy 'ell! I feel like a double-decker hit my stomach," said Geraldine.

"What did you eat for breakfast?" I asked.

"Eggs and kidneys. Toast with a little margarine and Marmite, same as everyone. And would you look at that—I have a ladder in my stocking!"

I knew my brother didn't like Marmite on his toast. It was yeast paste. "What else did you eat?" I asked.

"Tea without sugar," she said, twisting her stocking until the rip faced backwards.

Before I could continue the investigation, the corporal interrupted with: " 'fraid the medics are occupied. Seems 'alf the base is sick. Guess um lucky I 'aven't 'ad me breakfast yet. Been on duty."

Just as he said the word *sick* Geraldine threw up on

herself. All over the good stocking, too. I backed away, gagging. She obviously liked Marmite.

"Any German POWs working in the kitchen?" I asked.

"As if we'd let Nazis prepare our food!" said Geraldine, a bit dazed.

Daphne rolled her eyes. Little did *she* know. I'd heard it on the radio: some numbskull in Washington D.C. was hatching a plan to make German POWs work at military base commissaries—washing dishes, cooking and mopping floors. According to Geneva Convention rules these POWs had to get American military wages, 80 whole cents an hour! Didn't matter, said one politician: better the Germans do the grunt work and the Americans get sent to fight Hitler. I was meaning to write President Roosevelt and warn him of the risks. I'd met Nazis and knew how shifty they were.

While Daphne and me helped Geraldine to the infirmary, I used my free hand to hold my nostrils shut. People were throwing up into buckets or anything they could find. One soldier vomited into his tin helmet. Fellas who fought for a living called out for their mums. There were only two nurses and one doctor on duty. Normally, their job was patching up pilots: burns, bullet wounds or broken bones. Every squadron had an ambulance waiting near the airstrip, just in case. But they weren't trained to handle an outbreak of food poisoning.

I spotted Sel Edner laid out in a hospital bed, laughing his head off. Sel was my brother's best friend in the squadron. Understudy for the best man job, should

I get sent home before the wedding. He was from California and had seen more than his fair share of Hollywood starlets—doing ordinary things like walking their dogs, taking out the garbage or shopping. In his cockpit, he kept an autographed press photo of Deanna Durbin.

"Hey, Sel," I said. He waved to me with his bandaged wrist. "How's the eye?"

I didn't have to ask. I could see for myself. The eye was crusty with blood and swollen shut, black and blue. It looked like his nose might be broke too.

"At least I skipped breakfast," he said. "Took the rare opportunity to sleep in and missed it, see?" He handed me a pen so I could sign his cast. "And to think—a few minutes ago I was fantasizing about crispy bacon and fried eggs."

"Glad to hear you won't lose the eye," I said, punching his one good arm and returning the pen to a metal side table, next to a bunch of flowers. "Knew a kid once with a glass eye—Kenneth Backer was his name. It looked real enough to fool you. He'd pop it in and out to scare the girls. Worked every time." Scared me too, if I'm honest.

"No joke," said Sel, focusing on a nurse with his good eye. "Woulda been the end of my flying days. They say I have a mild concussion, though. So I'm stuck in this bed with the nurses shining a flashlight in my eye every hour on the dot. Lets them know my brain is functioning right. Can't say I mind—they've got some pretty nurses." He let me feel the bump on his head. It was the size of a softball. "Doc says I'm out of commission for at least a coupla weeks, and that's hard luck for the other fellers."

"I'm sure the Third Reich is happy about that," I said winking.

Sel didn't get my drift. "Thanks for the compliment," he said.

"So give me the lowdown on the *so called* accident," I said. "We'll need the facts before ruling out foul play."

"Who? You and Scotland Yard?"

"Just give me the blow-by-blow."

His one eye widened, the other fused shut. It was starting to dawn on him that something was fishy. He said, "It was like this, see? I came flying down the stairs, taking two at a time, thinking I'd beat the other fellers to the john. It gets mighty crowded in there, see? Didn't notice Jimmy lying at the bottom of the stairs, unconscious-like. Tripped right over him and crashed into a table—bang! Well, on that table was a telephone, one of those of Bakelite models weighs at least ten pounds. Collides with my head—whack! Gave me the concussion." He pointed to his bump. "Then a London phone book hits me square in the eye—bam! I tried to stand up, but my foot got caught in the telephone cord."

"Boom. Sounds like a vaudeville skit. Go on," I said.

"Yeah, except no one was laughing. Jimmy, see, he comes to and lets loose a howl that sounded like a siren. Woke the fellers up. Everyone scrambling to get to their Spitfires. One minute later and a stack of bodies that looked like a football pileup—kind where everybody leaves the field on stretchers."

"How'd Jimmy trip?" I asked.

"He don't know. Can't remember a thing, what with having a concussion too."

I was getting ready to ask another question, when in walked Squadron Leader Hugh Kennard, Jack's superior officer. He was wearing a leather fleece-lined flight jacket and a Mae West inflatable life jacket. His goggles were pushed up onto his leather flight helmet and he was still wearing his flight gloves. I looked behind him hoping to see my brother, but there was no sign of him.

"Tommy, old chap," he said. Kennard was British. The only Brit in the squadron of American pilots. "Jolly good to see you."

"Where's Jack, sir?"

Kennard turned his eyes heavenward. For a second there, I went stiff.

"Jack?" he said, "at the moment, I suppose, he's floating somewhere above Slough. Unless the wind has blown his brolly a bit further east." A brolly, I knew, was an English way to say umbrella, but in the RAF it could also mean parachute. Kennard consulted his military issue Omega watch. "Actually, by now he ought to have his feet on the ground. Dare say he's sitting in a tavern with a Guinness in his hand as we speak."

"He had to bail out?" I asked, my eyes bulging from their sockets.

"His Spitfire caught fire. A group of bandits had gone after him—mighty cheesed-off after we'd shot down a Do. That's a Dornier bomber, as you undoubtably know. Must have hit his fuel tank. We were over a rural area, so I ordered him to get out of the plane. No worries though—I circled back and saw that your brother was tip-top. Gave me the thumbs up as his parachute opened. Looked well enough—not even a scorched eyebrow, from what I could see. He'll be back before long. Well, off for another sweep. Just thought I'd check in on you, Sel. Then get a bite to eat. I'm famished."

"I'd order out for a pizza, if I were you, sir," I said, forcing myself to add, "Daphne packed a picnic lunch and you could have half of my vegetable pastie, sir. The biggest half."

"No kidding, sir," said Sel. "Looks like the food's gone off in the canteen."

Kennard turned down my offer to share a pastie, but he took a stick of chewing gum. I couldn't do enough for the man. He was one of my heroes. He'd flown in the Battle of Britain. Awarded the Distinguished Flying Cross.

CHAPTER FOUR

It smelled God-awful in the infirmary, so I went for some fresh air. It would be a long wait for my brother to get back and I had plenty of time to poke around in the mess halls. Jack and the other Eagle Squadron pilots bunked and ate their meals at their own mess. That's what they called it, but it was really an elephant of a mansion, requisitioned for war use. They ate under a crystal chandelier covered in a burlap bag, to protect it during food fights. Jack's mess was off base, a couple of miles away, and so I headed first for the warrant officers' and sergeants' mess, since that's where Geraldine would've eaten. And I'd seen at least two stricken sergeants in the infirmary.

The building was what you call a Nissen hut: a corrugated steel contraption shaped like a tunnel. Wasn't anybody inside, which figured. It was going to be a while before people got their appetites back. I jumped over a stainless steel counter used to slide trays while you picked your food. The sinks were stacked with dirty dishes, probably because the crew was sick too. In warming trays I found greasy slices of the ham they'd served for breakfast. It smelled so good made my stomach start rumbling, but I wasn't fool enough to eat it. There were fried eggs with the yolks broken and cooked. Toast cut into quarters and lined up like dominoes. And beans. English people ate them with eggs—instead of with frankfurters like you're supposed to. They'd also served kidneys in gravy. Not kidney beans, mind you, but the actual bodily organ.

Disgusting, I thought.

There was a gallon of Marmite, enough to feed an army—or in this case, an air force. In the Great War, British soldiers were issued the stuff in their rations. Daphne loved Marmite, even though it was made from yeast, first used to brew beer. Jack hated Marmite, said he'd rather get his yeast in a frosted glass. I preferred mine in a chocolate layer cake.

While I was examining the Marmite, a blindfold came down over my eyes. I figured it must be my brother, pulling a gag. I began squealing, squiggling, giggling, expecting Jack to start tickling me.

I stopped laughing when I was dragged backwards into a walk-in Frigidaire.

Before I could scream, the door slammed shut and I was trapped, impossible to open the door from the inside. It was pitch dark in the fridge. I felt around for a weapon and hit upon a stack of potatoes, filling my pockets with spuds. If only I'd remembered to bring my slingshot. Carrots were the only thing with a point.

Nazis had Lugers. I had a carrot.

As tight as I pressed my ear to the ice-cold stainless steel door, it was almost impossible to hear anything outside the refrigerator. If Daphne hadn't come to my rescue, I might've suffocated. When I heard her shouting my name, I banged my fists against the door. Yelled at the top of my lungs, too. Opening the latch, she said, "What on earth? You were looking for cake, weren't you?"

The nerve, I thought. I ignored her and ran toward the leftovers. The kidneys were gone. The warming tray was cleaned out and set on the drying rack.

"Someone's been tampering with the food. The kidneys, as a matter of fact," I said.

Daphne paused for a beat, "Odd that you say…because we were just observing that only we British are sick. The American pilots eat at the officer's mess, but a few were in the infirmary this morning and ate the food from this kitchen. Yet we noticed that none of the Americans are sick…and Americans *do* hate kidneys. We'd been wondering if maybe the tea was spoiled, but you could be right."

"Is Squadron Leader Kennard still here? I have to warn him."

"Re—ally, Thomas. But since you mention it, he wants a word with you. That's why I've been searching high and low."

I rushed over to the dispersal hut, hoping I'd find Kennard before he left for another mission. He was sitting in a wicker chair, placed out on the grass. In front of him was a low table with a chess set on top. I figured that while he waited for another battle with the Luftwaffe, he wanted me to play a game with him. I usually lost, which made me the perfect opponent.

"Look here, old boy," said Kennard as I walked up. "Have a favor to ask of you."

"Happy to oblige," I said, taking a seat opposite him.

"Jolly good of you," he said, putting two fingers into his mouth and making a whistling noise before shouting, "Here girl!" A scrawny black and white mutt came tearing toward us, stopped short, backed up until her legs straddled my foot, and then saturated my sneaker. "Daphne has volunteered to help with the sick—good sport that she is—and it's been proposed that you two might bunk here rather than heading back to London. We're terribly understaffed, you see." He reached into his pocket and handed me a key. "Sel has suggested that you bunk in his and Jack's room. Daphne will bunk with that gal Geraldine. Sel asked that you feed his goldfish. Not too much fish-food, mind you, just a sprinkle. And then there's Ringo to see to. As I said, we're short staffed with all these casualties. You've met Ringo, I'm sure. The squadron mascot?" The mutt growled at me. I kept myself from barking back.

"Happy to oblige, sir." I had an aversion to dogs— more like a phobia—but I was no fool. If I ever wanted a place in the RAF, I'd have to follow orders without grumbling.

"Well, then that's settled," said Kennard.

The phone rang in the dispersal hut and he answered while adjusting his Mae West inflatable vest and parachute harness. "Off for another Rhubarb," he said after hanging up the phone. He didn't mean a slice of pie. A Rhubarb was what they called a sweep over occupied Europe: two pilots hunting for German depots, supply trains, air traffic control towers, and armament factories.

Another pilot was napping on a chair inside the hut and Kennard shook him awake. "Off we go into the wild blue yonder," he said, quoting the brand-new U.S. Army Air Forces song. Kennard was always trying to make the fellas feel at home. He'd once bought a tub of peanut butter for the squadron. Had to be special ordered from Fortnum & Mason in London.

A mechanic from the ground crew, an Englishman named Wilson, came up to Kennard. "Everything's ready to go, sir. We've rearmed and the kites are shipshape. Have you had a chance to think through—"

"I'm afraid this isn't the time to discuss it, Wilson. And what you are suggesting is against regulations. End of conversation, I'm afraid." Kennard leaned down and patted the dog on the head.

"Best of luck, sir," I said. "Give it to them good."

"Try to walk Ringo every couple of hours, would you? She's got an active bladder."

"I noticed, sir," was all I said, and then saluted.

Kennard ran to his Spitfire. The ground crew rolled away the trolley accumulator and removed the chocks out from in front of the airplane's wheels. Kennard jumped into the cockpit and slid the Plexiglas hatch shut. When the propeller began turning, my heart started racing. The plane began moving toward the airstrip—*trundling*, you call it. As the wheels left the ground and then retracted, I waved goodbye. There was always the chance he wouldn't come back. Ringo must've been thinking the same thing. She took a big gulp of air and then let out a sigh.

I reached into my pocket and threw a potato. Ringo went racing to fetch it.

Darn, I thought. I tried to warn Kennard, but my voice was drowned out by the Spitfire propellers. Here he was, flying off to France to fight Nazis when there were some right here at the base.

CHAPTER FIVE

Somewhere in London

THE CLOCK ON HIS DESK reads four minutes to nine, and Brigadier A.W.A. Harker, Deputy Director General of MI5, the British Security Service, puts down his fountain pen, listening for the chime of Big Ben, not a quarter mile away, wishing that he could work from home more often. Since the beginning of the conflict, MI5 has had its headquarters over in Wormwood Scrubs, a Victorian prison in West London; depressing as all hell. This study of his—with its embossed leather wallpaper, dark oak bookcases, Turkey carpet, and windows overlooking the Thames River—is much more conducive to problem solving.

Intelligence, he thinks. How is one to use it with the rat-a-tat-tat of typewriters in the background, and the heels of women's shoes, and their chattering gossip whenever they think he's not listening?

And Agent Ellis, his biggest nuisance at the office. How many times that day were his thoughts interrupted by the man, wanting to relay a report from some busybody claiming to have seen a Nazi spy—at the grocery buying chipped beef, checking out a book from the library, watching Pathé newsreels at a local cinema? It is Ellis's job to sort through these reports, but why can't the man leave it at that?

When was the last time a citizen actually caught a German spy? thinks Harker, tapping his chin. Best leave these things to the professionals.

His wife calls, "Jasper, I'm off to bed. Will you be joining me?"

"In a minute, dear," he says.

"All because of that Mabel Somebody-Or-Other," he says to himself, looking at a small desk calendar in a silver frame.

Two years ago, almost to the day: Carl Meier, Charles van den Kieboom, Sjoerd Pons—he can't remember the name of the fourth one. Dutch born Nazi party members, most of them. Sent in by the Abwehr in advance of the feared invasion, equipped with radio transmitters and supplies for a week or so: corned beef, baked beans, and chocolate. Spotted by a tavern keeper—*Rising Moon, was it? Mabel Something-Or-Other*—who thought it odd when Carl Meier, with his guttural accent, requested a cider at nine o'clock in the morning. And then he'd gone and bumped his head on the doorpost. When any Englishman would know to duck.

"A cider for breakfast!" says Harker. And now this ridiculous campaign to put citizens on their guard against Nazi spies. Posters plastered on every wall in England. Busybodies with nothing better to do than spy on their neighbors and then report the slightest change of habits.

He remembers Ellis bothering him with a report from Bristol. A veteran of the First World War, claiming that there were Nazi spies selling oil paintings from door-to-door. They wasted valuable time uncovering a ring of amateur copyists, selling "original" Van Goghs to anyone foolish enough to part with five bob. Why, one of the confiscated sunflower paintings is sitting beside Harker's rubbish bin at the office. If it's there in the morning, he'll burn it himself.

"That settles it!" he says aloud, pulling the chain on his desk lamp. "I'm going to have to have a word with Petrie, put an end to this nonsense. Time we got down to the real business of fighting this war." He smiles, thinking about the success they've had recently by turning enemy aliens into double agents and sending false intelligence back to Berlin.

"The Double-Cross!" he says as he mounts the stairs to his bedroom.

"What was that, Jasper?" says his wife.

He sucks his lips in and then pulls back the coverlet.

"That's right," says his wife. "Like the poster says, *Loose Lips Sink Ships*."

CHAPTER SIX

CIRCLING BACK TO THE INFIRMARY, I went straight to Sel Edner's bed. The only thing laying on it was a rubber hot-water bottle. The invalid in the next bed pulled back the curtain that separated us. He said, "They rushed 'im to the 'ospital—a big one in London where they've got neurosurgeons."

"What! Why would he need a neurosurgeon?"

"'E passed out cold. Bleedin' in the brain."

This was a life-threatening predicament. I remembered the time I crashed my tricycle into a milk truck, hit my head on the hubcap and started seeing stars, just like in the cartoons. After a few minutes, everything seemed fine. I'd broken a collarbone, was all. Jack and Ma rushed me to the emergency room. After the doctor put my arm in a sling, he gave me a lollipop and we headed back to the pickup truck. Then Ma asked if I wanted to stop off at the five-and-dime for an ice-cream soda and I said, "Nope." Right then and there she knew something was wrong. Turned out I had bleeding on the brain and my life was in jeopardy. Jack carried me back into the emergency room piggyback. The doctor said, "What's your name, son?" But for the life of me, I couldn't remember. I was four-years-old at the time and my ma already taught me some numbers, none of which came out in the right order. I stayed overnight, meaning I missed out on a trip to the soda fountain. But a candy striper brought me an extra portion of green Jell-O with fruit cocktail floating inside, which helped make up for it. Lucky for me, the hemorrhage stopped all on its own and they didn't have to cut open my head.

Daphne came up to me with a mop in her hand. Her hair was in a sloppy bun, beads of sweat dripped from the tip of her nose. She blew hair from her face. "I *do* so hate nursing," she said.

"Looks more like maid's work to me."

"It might look that way, but I'll have you know— sanitation is the most important aspect of modern nursing." She didn't look convinced. "Truth be told, that's one of the reasons I gave up on the profession. I so hated cleaning bedpans."

"Then put the mop down and help me uncover a plot to undermine the Royal Air Force."

She looked at me cockeyed, about to make a wisecrack. But just then, Ringo squatted down and left a puddle on the floor. We watched as the yellow stream moved across the floor Daphne'd just mopped, puddling against the wall.

"That does it," she said, resting the mop against the bed. "Let me powder my nose first."

I waited on Sel's empty bed, thinking about recent events and hitting immediately upon two clues:

1. The blindfold was white.

2. It was made of silk.

It was just a flash of memory, but I was sure about these two details. The scarf must've slipped from my face as I struggled to break out of the Frigidaire. Come to think of it, it might be there still.

Daphne returned looking like a pinup poster; amazing what a little powder can do. She was counting on Jack arriving at any minute. Her hair was rolled to the back of her neck the way my brother liked it: a Victory roll, it's called. She said, "I've earned a lunch break. Let's find a spot of grass and have our picnic. I'd wait for Jack to return, only—" She rubbed her tummy. We agreed to save Jack's vegetable pastie, plus a pickle, an apple, and a bottle of homemade ginger beer.

"Let's return to the scene of the crime," I said once we finished eating. Daphne kicked my shoe. She wasn't taking me seriously, thinking it was all a hoot. She sounded like a radio laugh track. As we made our way to the mess hall, Geraldine came running up to us. Recovered from food poisoning from the look of it.

"Lieutenant Mooney is on the line wanting to speak with you," she said, "Jack, I mean."

We hurried over to a brick building, the one used for headquarters. It was on top of an underground room housing the RAF station Sector Control plotting department. That's where the WAAFs received messages from radar operators and then moved blocks around a gigantic map of Europe. The blocks stood for squadrons of German bombers headed over the English Channel. RAF Command would then figure out where to intercept with fighter squadrons. I tried to get into the room once, but was stopped by MPs. Sad to say, but everything I knew about plotting came from watching *The First of The Few*.

Geraldine took us into an office where a phone sat on a desk, the receiver next to the base. I ran for it. "Jack!" I shouted into the phone.

Daphne came next to me and pressed her ear to mine. "Darling, are you safe?"

"What's the meaning of this?" said a voice oddly like Winston Churchill's.

"Is this the prime minister?" I asked.

"I say, is this some sort of prank?" said the voice. "To whom am I speaking? Is this RAF Rochford on the line?"

Another WAAF came into the room and took the receiver from my hands. "Sir, I'm sorry, sir, there's been some sort of mix-up with the telephone."

Geraldine bit her lower lip and apologized to us. "Lieutenant Mooney *was* on the phone," she said. "Someone must have rung off by mistake. Or maybe Jack ended the call. He *did* say he was calling from a phone booth. He might have run out of coins." She tut-tuted: "One would think the operator would have placed a call at no charge, given the circumstances."

I knew that when pilots went on missions they took along a kit with French francs and Reichsmarks in it, in case they crash landed in occupied Europe. But francs wouldn't fit into an English coin slot.

"Good God," said Geraldine. "I ought to have

asked for his exact location. Had I been, well…I might have sent around a driver to fetch him. He first asked to get patched over to Squadron Leader Kennard, but we knew that he was out on a Rhubarb. After that, Lieutenant Mooney insisted upon speaking with *you*."

"Me or her?" I asked, looking a Daphne.

"Daphne," said Geraldine. "I'd mentioned that she was here."

"What else did he say? Details are important," I explained.

She bit her lip again and said, "He'd bailed out of his plane, then walked some distance to a small village. Near Oxford, I remember his saying. Let me think—he'd mentioned the name…"

"Geraldine," I said, "don't fail us now."

"Garsington, that was it! He wanted to find his Spitfire." She tapped her fingers against the desk, her pink lacquered nails. "I remember now! Jack said that he *hadn't* been hit by enemy aircraft. He made a point of that. He said, 'They didn't get me this time, Gerl, no siree, it's all hunky-dory,' and a host of other Americanisms. 'No Jerry's gonna paint a little Union Jack on his fuselage today,' and other such sentiments. Seemed pleased about that, but worried about something else."

Geraldine left the office in search of a map. The other WAAF finished the phone call with the irate Churchill impersonator and introduced herself to Daphne. "I take it you're Flight Lieutenant Mooney's fiancée?"

"That's right," said Daphne, puffing her chest out a little. "We're getting married in January, as a matter of fact." They shook hands and Daphne said, "I've not seen you before, have I? You must be new to Rochford."

"My name's Alice. Just came over from RAF North Weald."

"Jack was at North Weald," said Daphne. "I know another WAAF named Alice who's stationed there. Alice Skinner—know her?

"Common name. Wish my mum had given me something more exotic. Like Felicity or Josephine, or perhaps—"

Before Alice could finish with her wish list, Geraldine returned with a map. She opened it, laying it flat out on the desk. We searched for a small dot and the word *Garsington*. My extra sharp eyes were the first to locate it. I consulted the scale chart and used my finger to measure the distance: at least a hundred miles from Southend-on-Sea. Turned out we'd taken the train in the wrong direction. Garsington was near Oxford University. Rumor was they had a set of coffins excavated from the burial site of Theban priests at the temple of Queen Hatshepsut at Deir el-Bahri. Howard Carter himself worked at the site.

"Do you have a car we can borrow, Geraldine?" I asked.

"I wish. I have a rusty bicycle I can loan you. The front tire needs pumping, but it's otherwise serviceable."

"Thomas, neither of us can drive," said Daphne, incorrectly. "Besides, haven't you promised to babysit a goldfish and this dog?" Ringo licked the tips of her fingers.

Geraldine said, "I'll ring up the Home Guard and ask them to find Jack. I dare say his Spitfire might have crashed miles from where he landed. And why ever does he want to find it? It will be a pile of burning metal. We can only hope it didn't land on someone's house."

I could only hope that it didn't land on the exhibition from Queen Hatshepsut's tomb from Deir el-Bahri.

"Have to push off," said Alice. "Good to make your acquaintance, Daphne. Cheerio!" She'd been sorting through a file cabinet and was holding a stack of manila folders under one arm with another stack against her chest.

"Oh, Alice, you're invited to the wedding," said Daphne. "Everyone is—that is, everyone who isn't on duty that day. I only hope Jack is free. We're getting married in Leytonstone." She took a whiff. "That's a heavenly perfume you're wearing, may I ask what it is?"

Girl talk. I tuned them out and turned my ears toward Geraldine, who was placing a call to the Home Guard headquarters in Oxford. "That's right—Garsington—I said, Garsington—sorry, bad connection—G.A.R—S.I.N.G.—exactly right. You'll send someone around straightaway? Shouldn't be hard to find: flight uniform, leather fleece-lined coat, about six foot, about twelve stones, black hair, blue eyes, Irish good looking sort of chap. And the Spitfire? What's that?" Her mouth formed a perfect circle. "You don't say!" She put her hand to her heart, "That *is* a relief."

She hung up the phone and sighed, "Well, that's good news at least. They've found the Spitfire and no one was hurt when it crashed. It went down frightfully close to a 12th century church, very nearly hitting it. They were having choir practice at the time, so thank goodness the Spitfire didn't crash into it. Unfortunately, it took down quite a few tombstones in the church graveyard. The parishioners will be dreadfully upset."

"Why? All the victims were dead already," I pointed out.

"True," laughed Geraldine.

We stepped out of HQ and I reminded Daphne that she'd promised to come with me to the mess hall. She was one step behind me, blurting out something about a promise she'd made to Jack to keep an eye on me. By then, the kitchen crew was back on duty and in the middle of preparing supper. One man chopped carrots and another sat on a stool with a crate of potatoes in front of him, peeling away. I felt sorry for him. So many ways to serve in the war effort and he was stuck with the spuds.

I'd borrowed a spiral notebook and pen from the administration supply closet. I tapped the pen on the cover of the notebook, opening to a blank page.

"Mind answering a few questions?" I said.

"What are you, BBC?" asked the potato peeler.

"Seen any suspicious characters around this morning? Anyone Aryan looking? You know the sort: blond, blue eyes."

"Since you mention it, there was a bloke sneaking around earlier. But he had dark hair, nearer to black." He paused to think, and I made a notation in my notebook.

"Little black mustache, brown shirt with a red armband, swastika in the middle. Asked if we wanted him to autograph a copy of *Mein Kampf*."

"Okay, wise guy," I said, closing the notebook. "Mind if I take a look in the walk-in refrigerator?" I looked over at the huge stainless steel fridge, my former prison. It looked like any other industrial fridge.

"My apologies," said Daphne, gesturing to the crew. "You know how it is. Too many Hollywood films. Too many comic books. He gets excited over nothing. Please, go on with your work."

In the Frigidaire, I found what I was looking for. Behind a crate of turnips was a long white silk scarf, the kind pilots wear. Jack had one like it. Fighter pilots had to keep swinging their necks around, always on the lookout for enemy aircraft. So the RAF allowed them to wear a scarf instead of a tie, which rubbed their necks raw. I wondered why one of the pilots would throw me in the refrigerator, why a pilot would want to poison everyone at the base. It didn't make sense. Pilots were fiercely loyal and dedicated to the cause.

Unless I could trace the scarf to its owner, I'd be out of luck. Fingerprints didn't stick to silk. I shoved the scarf into my trouser pocket and told Daphne it was time to go. Once outside, I pulled the scarf from my pocket and showed it to her. "The culprit blindfolded me with this," I said.

"It's one of the pilot's scarves," she said, dittoing my thoughts. "Nice quality, that." She rubbed the fabric between her fingers: "Very fine herringbone weave in a hundred-percent silk… Yes, says here right on the tag. Hand wash in cold water." She flipped the label, "Dunhill of London, a very posh shop. We'll have to return it to its owner. I suppose we might put up a notice in the commissary."

Dunhill of London. I'd been to the place with Lord Sopwith. He let me pick out a polka dot bow tie. Looking at the price tag knocked the wind out of me. You could've bought a Lionel caboose and a couple of boxcars with that much money.

"It couldn't belong to any of the men in Jack's squadron," said Daphne. "They're all tight. You know how little the RAF pays them, and few of them come from wealth. Squadron Leader Kennard might be the one exception."

Kennard. I considered him as a suspect, but then ruled him out. For one thing, he'd been out on a mission all morning and wasn't around to poison the kidneys. For another thing, he was one of my heroes.

"So, whose scarf could it be?" I asked.

"I'd say it belongs to a pilot from the Millionaire Squadron."

The Millionaire Squadron! I knew all about them: RAF Squadron Number 601. It was made up of rich kids. England's top of the heap. Or, as Lady Sop would put it, "the cream of the crop." One Squadron 601 pilot was so rich, he bought a local gas station just so's he'd have an endless supply of petrol for his supercharged Alvis Silver Crest. They had their uniforms lined with red silk. Lady Sop said they were a hit at Ascot, that horse race. She went wearing a hat that made her look like the base of a lamp.

There was once an American pilot in the squadron, a fella named Billy Fiske. He was a two time Olympic gold medal bobsledder and then a New York stockbroker before joining up. He married a girl listed in a book called *Burke's Peerage*. Lord and Lady Sopwith had a copy of the book in their library and I'd looked her up. In a dogfight over the Channel, a Messerschmitt shot up Billy's fuel tank and his Hurricane caught fire. He stayed with plane long enough to land it on English soil. Billy was so burnt his flight gloves were fused to his hands. His obituary was splashed all over the front pages in America, his being the first American flyer killed in the war. He was another one of my heroes.

"Is the Millionaire Squadron stationed at RAF Rochford?" I asked.

"Not as far as I know," said Daphne. "But they move the squadrons around so often, maybe they are here and I just don't know it. We can ask Jack when he gets back. Meanwhile, Geraldine has invited us to have dinner. She and some of the other WAAFs will be cooking up something back at their billet. The rule is no men allowed. But since you're under thirteen, they're able to make an exception."

I stood up straight. "Maybe I don't wanta be an exception. I'll eat back at Jack's mess with the other pilots. With the men, that is."

"Oh, get on. It will be great fun. And most men would die for a chance to get inside that house." (She *did* have a point. I'd have something to brag about.) I let her go on: "The house is quite far, but we can ride over on Jimmy's bicycle. He has a broken leg and says he won't be needing it for a while."

"Only if I'm at the controls and you sit on the fender." I looked down at Ringo. "What do we do with her?"

"The basket, of course."

CHAPTER SEVEN

WE WERE SEATED around a large dinner table. The ladies insisted I take the head. Man of honor, so to speak.

"It's not every day we have a gentleman over for supper," said one of the WAAFs. Her name was Blanche. She wore thick glasses that kept slipping down her nose. Her tweed jacket was too tight around the armpits, so that she had to hold her arms out like a penguin. She turned to Geraldine, "Pass the margarine, would you, dear?"

I wanted to know what each of them did. Blanche was a bit cagey, I thought: "Can't say. Official Secrets Act and all that."

"I'm in charge of food requisitions," said Corporal Elizabeth Herbert, who everyone called Beetle. "Top secret stuff. Can't let the Germans know how much marmalade we consume, might tip the scales against us."

"If the Jerries win the war, there shan't be any jam. It will be bread and water for us, and the workhouse," said Blanche, who sat at the opposite end of the table.

Alice, who we'd met already, joined the dinner party late and took the seat next to mine. She said, "So sorry. Just off duty." She'd changed into a green wool sweater and a pair of wool trousers. Herringbone, I noticed, just like the pilot's scarf. She was wearing a string of pearls, but I could tell they were fakes—the shiny paint was clipping off the beads.

"Your turn," I said looking at her. "Whatta you do in the WAAFs?"

"This and that. Nothing that would interest you. Secretarial pool mostly."

"And all this time I thought you were a plotter," said Beetle. "Or, rather, liaison assigned from… Oh, I suppose I shouldn't say." She put a hand over her mouth, but then went on, "To be a plotter seems ever so exciting! Dread as German bombers head towards us, and then relief when they've been turned back. I heard that during the Battle of Britain, Sir Winston Churchill sat in a plotting room with tears welling in his eyes"—she brushed a tear from her own eye, she was so emotional—"realizing that the RAF had averted an invasion."

"That's right," said Geraldine. "It was then he said those immortal words…"

" 'Never was so much owed by so many to so few,' " said Daphne, doing an imitation of the prime minister. Everyone laughed.

"It does make one proud to be working with the RAF," said Beetle, "Even if all one does is help nourish the aircrews."

"Hear, hear," said Blanche, and everyone joined in, lifting their water glasses and clashing them against each other. Alice was a beat behind. She looked like her head was about to fall into her plate, she was so bushed. I figured plotting was an exhausting job. During the Blitz, she'd probably been on her feet night and day.

"Makes me proud to be marrying a Spitfire pilot," said Daphne with that dreamy look in her eye. Her eyelashes fluttered, thinking about Jack in his dress blues and her in a white silk dress. She began hyperventilating.

"When is the wedding, dear?" asked Blanche. "I do so want to be there to cheer you two on. There's nothing I like better than a wedding. Don't neglect to provide a box of tissues for each pew, for those of us who get teary-eyed."

Before they got deeper into oblivion, I said: "Any of you know if the 601 Squadron is stationed here?"

"The Millionaires? Oh, how I wish!" said Blanche, her cheeks reddening.

"Overseas at the moment," said Geraldine. "I recall having read something about that in the paper. Malta, I think, or some such place. You can ask Dot—she's been stepping out with one of the pilots. Come to think of it, she just had a letter from him."

"Lucky girl," said Blanche. "Oh, what I wouldn't do to be dating a Millionaire. They take girls for supper and cabaret shows at the Savoy, afterwards for dancing at the Hammersmith Palais de Dance in Mayfair. Then they escort you home in a chauffeur driven limousine. And the chauffeur is often a French refugee, waiting with a bottle of Champagne chilling in an ice bucket."

I decided to let the ball roll: "So, this Dot—you say she's dating one of the Millionaires? Any chance he gave her his silk scarf to remember him by? You know—a token of his affection?" They were loving it. Their forks hovered midair as they fantasized.

"As a matter of fact, he did," said Geraldine. "She wears it everywhere."

"And this Dot character—she bunks here?"

"Right again," said Geraldine. "She's on duty at the moment, otherwise she'd be here. By the way, we ought to save something for Dot to warm later." She looked at the other girls, but the message was probably meant for me. Everyone had finished eating, but I was shoveling third helpings onto my plate.

Blanche said: "Daphne, *do* tell us all about your wedding dress. We want details! Don't skip anything. Will there be lace?"

"Do tell!" shouted Beetle.

Now was my chance to scope out the place. Standing up, I bowed and excused myself, saying I had to use the bathroom, not that anyone cared. They kept going on about toile veils, garter belts, and elbow length gloves. Daphne's dress was being made from a Luftwaffe silk parachute her ma fought the whole block to get her hands on. The WAAFs were oohing and ahhing about how lucky she was. Silk was rarer than jade, now that the Japanese occupied China. Daphne mentioned that they'd be married by a rabbi *and* a priest, she being half -Jewish on her mother's side.

Alice said, "That's so interesting," as I headed past a bathroom and up the stairs to the second level where the bedrooms would be. Each door was marked with two names. I scanned the doors until I found the right one. In the top slot was a piece of bowed cardboard. Block letters read: DOROTHY DOUGLAS-HOME. The bottom slot was empty. The door was jarred open. I slipped in, closing it behind me.

The closet was the double door kind, divided into two sections and shared between the two girls. One side was packed tight with clothing, the other side practically empty. I began there.

My aim was to check labels, see if anything had been made in Germany. A navy blue Shetland sweater was hand-knit in Scotland, where they kept most of the sheep. I skipped anything RAF military issued, but read the labels in dress necks: Selfridges, Debenhams, and M&S—all English sounding. Although I happened to know that the Selfridge fella was originally American. On a high shelf, I found a felt hat with a blue jay feather. Behind that a cardboard box full of spark plugs, and a small metal tool box with nothing but screwdrivers, wrenches, and a few nuts and bolts. My deduction was that someone had a car.

I moved over to the crowded side and found more stuffy English clothing, and a few clingy sequin evening gowns—the kind worn by the German actress, Marlene Dietrich. They must've cost a pretty penny. None of them had labels. Either they were tailor made or the labels had been removed. I looked for tiny holes where the stitches might've been, but couldn't find one.

I headed for a dresser drawer. Just as I feared, the top drawer held undergarments. I forced myself to examine the labels anyway. If I was caught just then, I'd never live it down. I moved lightening-fast. Brassieres and underpants. A garter belt that looked like an instrument of torture. Handkerchiefs. Nothing out of order: all the labels English. Most of the underwear was made of cotton or nylon.

The other dresser was a different story all together: silk, and lace—the kind made by Belgian Benedictine nuns. The Sopwiths had table linen made by them same nuns. I liked the idea of nuns making lace; much safer than letting them teach kids. I noticed that some of the labels were from high-class department stores. Like Harrods, for one. And a store named Fenwick of Bond Street. Lord Sopwith had a personal tailor on Bond Street, with an account, so that all he had to do was sign his name and walk out with the goods. The street was very hoity-toity.

My conclusion was that one WAAF was rich and one poor.

One or two labels in rich WAAF's drawer were French, the names ended with *elle* and *ette*. I had a friend in Paris named Juliette, so I knew. That had me wondering: France was occupied by the Nazis. It could mean something. I spotted a stack of letters held together with a rubber band. Pulling out the bottom envelope, I slipped it into my pocket.

Then, in a bottom drawer, hidden under sweaters, I found a box of bonbons, the kind fellas give their sweethearts on Valentine's day. Inside the box top was a diagram showing the contents of each bonbon. I picked the one filled with a cherry, popping it into my mouth. I made sure to put the box back exactly where I found it.

Standing up, I noticed that both dresser tops were a cluttered mess. On the rich WAAF's dresser was a stack of *British Vogue* magazines and a silver framed photograph: a group of gals out on the town with a few airmen. The background was London. I knew from a double-decker in the left hand corner, blurry but recognizable. The poor WAAF had only a small red book. At first I suspected it might be Mao's *Little Red Book*, not that I'd ever seen one. But it turned out to be *Baedeker Great Britain*, a guidebook. A ribbon marked the beginning of the London section. If I could find a diary, all the secrets would come pouring out. Most girls keep diaries—my sister Mary, for one. I kept my eye out, coming up empty-handed.

A glass ashtray sat on a low table between the two beds. I poked around finding nothing but burnt out matches, crumpled cellophane wrappers and lipstick stained butts. One girl smoked Benson & Hedges and other smoked India Kings. I brushed ash from my hands. Next I planned to look under the beds.

Lifting a ruffle, I peeked under the one nearest to the door and found a battered suitcase, the kind carried by Fuller brush door-to-door salesmen. Only this one was covered with souvenir travel stickers. From what I gathered, all the destinations were British colonies: Canada, India, New Zealand, Australia, Bermuda, South Africa, Singapore, Palestine, Rhodesia, and Ceylon. The suitcase had two latches, both locked.

I headed back to the dressers looking for a hairpin, finding one next to a matching sterling silver hair-brush, comb and mirror set. The initials D. D. H. were engraved on the backs of the brush and mirror. The silver was .925—the good stuff. Dot had expensive taste. Explained why she was dating a Millionaire pilot. The French silk underwear belonged to her.

Grabbing the hairpin, I returned to the bed and placed the suitcase on the *chenille* cover. They had bedspreads like that in France; the word meant caterpillar. The suitcase weighed a ton of bricks. Daphne knew how to pick locks, but we never got around to a lesson. As hard as I tried, the latch stayed locked. Breaking the lock would alert the owner to tampering. As I slid the suitcase back under the bed, my eyes were drawn to three small initials stamped in gold near the handle. F.C.R. Almost identical to the American president's: F.D.R. All I found under the other bed was a pair of quilted slippers and dust balls. Before I could stop myself, I let out a earth-shattering sneeze.

The door flung open. Alice glared.

"What are you doing in here?" she asked rapid-fire, putting her hands on her hips.

"I was looking for the bathroom."

"That couldn't be true. You passed the toilet and marched right up the stairs." She flew at me, grabbing my chin and prying open my mouth before I had a chance to swallow. "You've been into my chocolates, haven't you? There's evidence stuck between your teeth." She sniffed and growled, "You ate my brandied cherry chocolates, you rotten boy!"

"Okay, you caught me," I said, thinking fast. "Everybody knows that ladies keep chocolate hidden in their dresser drawers. My ma hides chocolate mints in hers." I tried to look shamedfaced. "I'm begging you not to rat on me."

Alice bought it lock, stock, and barrel. Sitting on the opposite bed she said, "I have half a mind to call the MPs. Where are you from, anyway? You're not British, obviously."

"Irish," I said. "Irish-American. Both my ma and da were born in Ireland and then immigrated to New York. But my grandparents still live in the old country. I've never met them, but they send me presents. Once my grandma sent me a four-leaf clover, glued to a card."

"Aren't you lucky," she said snidely. "Ireland... They're not fond of we English, are they?"

"That would be an understatement. My brother Jack is an exception. He likes them so much he's marrying one. Fighting for them, too. Ma had a fit. So can I get another chocolate or not?" I had to keep the game going.

She went to the dresser, the one containing cotton underwear. Deep in the bottom drawer was the box of bonbons. She opened the lid and scanned the rows saying, "At least you didn't eat the toffee. They're my favorite." She straightened her back, prim-like. "Very English of me, I suppose."

I waited for her to offer me another chocolate, but it didn't happen. She lifted a toffee bonbon and slowly dropped it into her mouth. Then she closed the box and retied the red ribbon that held the lid on. She sucked on the chocolate loudly, rolling the chunk of toffee around her mouth slowly, crunching it in slow-motion, ending with a sigh. We stayed eye to eye the whole time, neither one of us blinking.

"You won't rat on me?" I asked.

"I haven't decided yet," she said.

I asked where she was from. Turned out to be a small village somewhere up north. One that no one had heard of, she said.

"Try me," I said. "I aced geography."

"Near Leeds," she said, waving a hand in the direction, I figured, of Leeds. I asked her to be more specific. I was about to pull out my mountaineer compass.

"Tiny place called Bramhope, if you must know. Got out of there as fast as I could. Nothing but cows and hay-chewing farmers. Spinsters with stockings bagging around their ankles, their highest ambition to be librarians. Couldn't stand the place. So provincial." Her nose went up. She untied the chocolate box and took the last toffee, closing the box without offering me a second. Then she returning it to the bottom drawer.

"So you've traveled a lot, have you?" I asked, wondering if the suitcase belonged to her, but not wanting to give away that I'd seen it. Balance was needed, like in Olympic bobsledding.

"You might say I'm an intrepid traveler," she said. This explained the stickers.

"Have you been to the Vatican?" I asked, wanting to get in my real question gradually. Leading up to it, in other words.

"Never," she said. "Although I might go one day, if only to see the Sistine Chapel. But with Mussolini—"

"Germany, maybe?"

"Of course not. What do you take me for?" She huffed a little, insulted. These days, no one admitted liking Germany. Even saying you loved German Chocolate Cake—which I did—could get you in trouble.

"You aren't Catholic?" I asked.

"No, Lutheran," she said. "I mean, my mother was Lutheran but she converted to the Anglican Church when she married father—so that they could marry out of his family church in Bramhope. To tell the truth, I'm not particularly religious myself."

"Name of the church?" I asked.

"St. Nicholas', if you must know. I say, you *are* nosy. What's with all the questions?"

"Just chitchat. I was raised Catholic myself. Christened at seven days old. Confirmed at age seven. Parochial school, the whole nine yards. I even played the part of Saint Simon of Cyrene in the Easter pageant. He's the one who helped carry Jesus' cross."

"Well, bully for you," said Alice. She had a mean streak, that much was clear. And she didn't like Catholics. But most English people didn't. Not since Henry VIII converted, anyway. Alice stood up, signaling that she was finished with the interrogation. "Let's join the others downstairs. They're about to serve pudding," she said.

Before we left the room, she went over to Dot's

dresser, took the silver hairbrush and ran it through her dishwater blonde hair. I could see by the way she admired herself in the matching mirror: vain, through and through. Pride is one of the seven deadly sins. If she'd been raised Catholic, she would have known that. Reaching over to her own dresser, she lifted a bottle of perfume, squeezing a large silk ball attached to the top and spraying herself and half the room both. My brother kept Daphne supplied with Yardley English Lavender. Alice's perfume was stronger, more like whiskey. Almost identical to the stuff my sister Mary bought at Woolworths: *Evening in Paris*, it was called. It came in a blue bottle and set you back a quarter.

Alice walked out the door first and started down the hall. I pretended to tie a shoelace. She didn't see me jump over to the dresser and glance at the perfume bottle. No label, but I turned the bottle over and saw the brand name etched in the glass: *Chanel No. 5*. Never heard of the stuff.

Suddenly, she was hovering over me. "You aren't back into my chocolates, are you?" she said, her lips stretched tight against her teeth.

I meant to quiz her about the roommate, Dot. The one with the Millionaire boyfriend. And about the silk scarf he'd given as a memento of his unflagging love. But I could see that Alice wasn't in the mood to answer more questions. She had a sweet tooth, like me, and didn't want to miss pudding. I came out of her room and she locked the door behind me, using a skeleton key.

CHAPTER EIGHT

ONCE DESSERT WAS FINISHED, I wanted to bolt. The WAAFs were starting up a game of charades. Beetle was pantomiming a mouse, crouched on the rug with her nose twitching. I explained that I was fine on my own, but Daphne insisted on shadowing me and Ringo back to Jack's mess where I'd be sleeping. She had to keep an eye on me, is what she said, when the real reason was she hoped Jack was back. It was near impossible to keep the bicycle straight, what with her on the fender and the dog in the basket.

"That was lovely, didn't you think, Thomas? They're all such great fun."

"All except Alice, that is," I said while trying to concentrate on my pedaling.

"Don't tell me you think she's a Nazi!" Daphne laughed and the bike wobbled.

"I didn't say she was a Nazi, only that I didn't like her. She reminded me of my sister Mary, your future sister-in-law. Who's going to make you wish that you married into a different family."

"Alice seemed nice enough. Quiet, but sweet. What could you possibly have had against her?"

"She's stingy with the chocolates, for one thing. And she blasphemed."

Daphne began shaking the bicycle with her belly laughing, causing us to veer close to a ditch. I managed to bring us back under control. The extra weight on the back fender made it near impossible to pedal, and I had to stand on the pedals to get the bicycle moving forward. We might've made better time walking. By then, it was pitch dark and none of the street lamps were lit due to the blackout, making it tricky to navigate potholes, railroad tracks, and those metal grids the English put in the middle of the roads to keep cows from crossing.

"Blasphemed? You can't be serious?" said Daphne, getting control of herself.

"I am too. She blasphemed the blessed memory of Saint Simon of Cyrene, as a matter of fact."

"Who in God's name is Saint Simon of Cyrene?"

"He's the one who helped carry the cross when Jesus fell down. Don't they teach you anything in the Anglican Church? Don't you do the Stations of the Cross?" Daphne might be half-Jewish, but her father was Church of England. Even I knew about mezuzahs and menorahs, macaroons and yarmulkes. I knew a few Yiddish words, to boot.

Daphne kept laughing. I wondered if they'd broke out a bottle of Scotch while I'd been snooping upstairs. She said, "You didn't try to inveigle Alice out of her chocolates, did you?"

"Try and keep still, for Pete's sake, or we'll crash," I said.

We arrived at Jack's mess, a fancy-schmancy mansion requisitioned for war use. The place had columns that looked like something you'd see Julius Caesar standing under. Windows arched at the top and had diamond shaped panes, some made of stained glass shaped like family crests. Ma would be proud if she could see where her son slept. The pilots made the place homey by moving the antiques to the cellar and bringing in cushy couches and rattan armchairs. They put up dartboards where oil paintings used to hang. A big map of Germany served as another dart board, Berlin being the bull's-eye. RAF recruiting posters were tacked up to fill in the blank spaces.

"I can't come in," said Daphne. "Regulations. The boys might be walking about half-clothed. You go in and see if Jack is back. Send him out if he is."

I took Ringo out of the basket and shoved the leash into Daphne's hand, ordering her to take the dog for a walk. I was still full of righteous indignation over Saint Simon of Cyrene. She leaned the bicycle against the house and started down the circular driveway, Ringo leaping behind her.

I stuck my head into the main parlor where a pilot lounged on the couch listening to the radio. Bing Crosby—my sister Nancy's favorite actor—sang a love song, along with Dorothy Lamour. It was from one of them *Road* films with Bob Hope, the funniest actor ever. I seen the first two: *Road to Singapore* and *Road to Zanzibar,* and was dying to see *Road to Morocco*. It'd already opened in New York. Ma wrote to tell me that her, Mary, and my older sister Nancy, already seen it. For some reason, it wasn't playing in England—the Germans probably sunk the ship carrying the film reels. When the song ended, I said: "Excuse me, sir, is my brother Jack back yet?" I'd never met this particular pilot.

He came out of his daydreaming, surprised to find me in the living room. "Jack Mooney? Not that I know of, bud. Check in his room, why don't ya. Upstairs, first door on the left. Maybe he came in and I didn't hear him what with the radio being on and all, ya know?"

"You from New York, too?" I asked, playing up my accent.

"Yonkers, ya know?" He turned his ears back to the radio. Dorothy Lamour was starting in on a solo number. The pilot looked like a man in love.

I went up the curlicue staircase, to the room that Jack shared with Sel. My heart started beating out of my chest when I glanced at the fishbowl. I ran to it, relieved to see that the goldfish was still kicking. *Phew!*—I'd forgotten all about it. The fish was starved by then; its fins moved in slow-motion. I found a box marked *fish food* and poured what was left in the bowl. The fish swam to the top and began gobbling. Squadron Leader Kennard's instructions came back to me just then: *Not too much food, mind you, just a sprinkle.* Using a fish net, I scooped out most of the fish food and some turds too. Goldfish will eat themselves to death if given half a chance. The thought of death, made me think of Sel. I hoped his brain had stopped bleeding. I said a quick prayer, invoking the name of Saint Simon of Cyrene.

That done, I looked around the room for a sign of my brother, thinking maybe he came back and then went out again. The officers shared a batman: five officers to one batman. Not batman, as in *Batman and Robin*, but a *batman*—as in a British soldier who does the dirty work. He made Jack's bed, shined his shoes, pressed his uniform, and ran errands. Jack had come up in the world.. Not bad for the son of a drunk, out-of-work, Irish immigrant. The room was neat as a pin, meaning Jack hadn't come home. The first thing Jack would've done was to get into civvies. He would've sat on the bed to take off his flight boots. But the bed didn't have a wrinkle on it and his beat-around shoes were next to his dresser, not a spot of dirt on them.

Jack wasn't back from Garsington.

To be sure, I searched around the house, knocking on every door, including the bathroom. I went back outside to break the news to Daphne.

"Odd, that," she said, looking at her watch, which was pinned to her jacket. The dial faced upside down so that it could be read just by lifting it. "It's been hours since he called the base. In the worst case scenario, he would have taken a train and made it back by now."

"I smell a rat," I said.

She started biting her nails, something she always did when she was nervous.

"I'll cycle back over to the dispersal hut," she said. "He's probably there playing chess with his chums. Or poker—they love poker. Perhaps they're at a game of *Monopoly*. One of the pilots brought one over from the

States. A match can go on for a fortnight." She paused to nibble on a thumbnail. "It could be he had to go on another op. I hope not. He's so knackered, dear love. In any event, I should pop into the infirmary and see if they need a hand. I've been negligent in my volunteer duties." She remembered I was standing there. "Look, you go to bed. It's well past your bedtime."

"I don't have a bedtime. It's the weekend."

"Then go read a book or something. Just stay out of trouble, would you?"

Before I could argue, she mounted the bicycle and was halfway down the driveway, pedaling like she was in the Tour de France.

CHAPTER NINE

WITHOUT WHEELS, I was stuck out there at the officer's mess. Yonkers was still in the parlor listening to
the radio. Ringo leapt into the room and curled up in
a laundry basket that was set next to a paraffin stove. I
figured I'd at least listen to some tunes and talk aviation
with the pilot.

"Be my guest, bud," said Yonkers, pointing to the
rocking chair across from him.

"You're new around here, aren't you?"

"Just got through eight months training in Canada,
only to get here and learn that they're about to send me
home again, ya know?"

I did know, as a matter of fact. Now that America
was in the war, and fighting on two fronts—against Japan
in the Pacific and the Jerries in Europe—the country
needed their pilots back. Churchill didn't like the idea
of giving up the three Eagle Squadrons, not after all the
trouble the British went to train them. But he couldn't be
too sorry about the deal. Most of them would be returning wearing U.S. Army Air Forces uniforms, escorting
B-17s while they bombed Berlin to smithereens. And

the truth was, the pilots wanted to go home. Because of a cockamamie Neutrality Act, they lost their American citizenship when they joined up with the Canadians. Before America jumped into the war, if they went home to visit their mothers they would've faced two years in the slammer. The minute bombs started dropping on Pearl Harbor, those Eagle Squadron pilots were on the train to London to talk the American Ambassador into letting them back into the fold. For one thing, the U.S. Army Air Forces paid a fella twice as much as the RAF. For another thing, they'd be fed hamburgers and hot-dogs, peanut butter and jelly on Wonder bread. They'd never see a kidney slobbered with Marmite again.

Problem was, for my brother it meant he had to get hitched before the deal went through. Otherwise Daphne would be stuck in London, maybe start up with a viscount or something. Once Jack married her, she would be a war bride and an American citizen, to boot. She'd sail away from England with him, leaving me behind.

Jimmy Dorsey started playing a jazz number on the radio and I became homesick.

"I'm a little worried about the transfer," I told Yonkers.

"Oh, yeah? Why's that?"

" 'Cause it's gonna mean I'm stuck here in England, while my brother and his bride are billeted on Pearl Harbor, sunning themselves on a Hawaiian beach."

"Have to stay with your folks, huh? That's understandable."

"My folks are on Long Island. My ma is missing

me like there's no tomorrow. She can't sleep at night for worry. And she's got an ulcer now and can't eat anything but saltine crackers and milk. But there's no way to get across the ocean, not with the war full blast. Not unless you're lucky enough to get on a troop carrier. I'm a civilian if you haven't noticed."

"Why don't ya just come back with us?" Yonkers asked. "We'll sneak you on the ship, piece a cake." He had a good idea there—one, funny enough, I'd never considered.

"Gee, thanks," I said. "I'd appreciate that."

"Piece a cake, I'm telling you, piece a cake." He reached into his shirt pocket and pulled out a pack of cigarettes. He banged the pack against this knuckles, then held it out to me saying, "I won't tell. Go ahead."

"Not on your life," I said. "Might as well call those things coffin nails."

"Original. Like I haven't heard that one before," said Yonkers, reaching into his back trouser pocket for a lighter. "Well, suit yourself." The blue bud of a flame lit the wick, lighting up his face red and orange. The radio switched to a new tune just then, Vera Lynn singing "We'll Meet Again." I couldn't help but notice the engraving on the side of Yonker's brass lighter: an eagle with outreached wings, grasping something in its talons. I leaned a little closer, so that I could be sure of what I was seeing. The eagle should've been grasping arrows and an olive branch, like an Alaskan eagle. But Yonker's eagle was holding onto a wreath with a swastika in the center. I knew the symbol: a *Parteiadler*—emblem of the

Nazi party.

"That's some lighter you got," I said, looking around the room for a weapon.

Yonkers took a long drag from his cigarette, pointing his mouth to the ceiling and blowing three smoke rings before speaking. "Took it off a Luftwaffe pilot whose Messerschmitt I downed with an expertly aimed three-second squirt, ya know?" He stared at me without blinking, every muscle in his body flexed.

I took a good look at my situation: We were all alone in the house. He was at least six-foot tall and 185 pounds. His shirt size was something like 17-17½ inch neck and 35-36 inch length. Once my brother came home, we'd take him out together. For now, it was best to play it cool.

"Messerschmitt, *ja*?" I said, with a perfect Deutschland accent. I'd learned the lingo during my preparations to rescue my brother. I never made it to Germany, but it was coming in handy now. "*Beeindruckend*," I added. "Impressive."

Yonkers' eyes went blank, pretending he didn't understand a word I'd said.

I rose from the rocker. "Well then, *Gute Nacht*. It's past my bedtime."

The news broadcast came on just then and Yonkers got up to retuned the radio, stopping on Marlene Dietrich singing "You Do Something To Me." He began grinning like Rommel in a black and white taken the day the Wehrmacht rolled into Paris.

I backed out of the room and out the front door.

Then I spun around like a top and ran down the cobblestone driveway like an Olympic gold medalist in the 100-meter dash.

CHAPTER TEN

IN MY MAD ESCAPE from Yonkers, I didn't pay attention to which direction I'd bolted. Stopping to gulp air and get my bearings, I realized I was someplace I never was before. Cows mooed in a pasture next to the road. The moon wasn't up yet and I didn't have a flashlight. I'd taken my jacket off in the overheated parlor, and was wearing nothing but a flannel shirt topping an undershirt. A white cloud blocked my vision whenever I let air out of my lungs. I picked up the pace, hoping to keep warm.

Then I fell to the ground and banged my fists against the asphalt: I'd stuck Ringo with a Nazi. Squadron Leader Kennard would never recommend me for the RAF.

After a long hike, I found myself near the South-end-on-Sea pier. Before the war it was the English version of Coney Island. "Sun and fun," Daphne moaned, back when she told me about it. "All gone because of Hitler." She had a point: in front of my face was a naval base, taking up the pier and most of the town. They'd renamed it HMS Leigh, thinking that the original name—Peter Pan's Playground—didn't work for a military installation. I wanted a look at the fleet. Problem was, they'd never let me past the gatekeeper without an escort, and a fella could get shot trying to sneak in. Come to think of it, I wouldn't even be let back into RAF Rochford without Jack being there, or someone else who could sign me in.

I sat on the curb hugging my shaking body, rubbing my arms and stamping my feet to get the circulation going. A thick fog was rolling in off the English Channel. Overhead I heard a bomber plane flying back from a mission. Sounded like one engine was out. I squinted, trying to figure out if the bomber was American or British. Even through the fog I seen flames coming from one of the engines. I yelled into the pea soup, "Good luck, boys," giving them the thumbs up, too. I just hoped the navigator could find the runway with such low visibility, and I prayed his instruments were in working order after battling anti-aircraft guns all the way from Berlin. A group of sailors got out of a taxicab, looking up at the sky, too, shaking their heads. One of the sailors raised his arm and pointed in the direction of the nearest runway, as if that might help.

I jumped into the back seat of the taxicab.

"Where will it be, lad?" asked the driver, looking at me by way of his rearview mirror. He was wearing a tweed cap, just like mine, only his was holding down a head of curly gray hair.

"The WAAF mess, sir."

"More than one, you'll have to be a wee more specific than that."

"The white building with the shrubs in front, two

stories, circular driveway."

"That narrows it down to four possibilities. Can you do better?"

He put the car back in park as he waited. I had to employ all my powers of observation to conjure up a picture of the building. To bring it into sharp focus, I pressed my forehead. Then I snapped my fingers: "The one with the letter S worked into the iron gate."

"Why didn't you say so in the first place? The old Sheffield place. Know it well." He wound up the meter, moved the gearshift to drive, and slid away from the curb. "Have to take it slow, being that I can't use the headlights. But don't you worry none—it won't cost you a cent more. There's the waiting charge and the moving charge and it don't matter if you're moving fast or slow."

"Oh, I trust you," I said, not that a New Yorker trusted a cabbie.

"You're not from around here, are you, lad?"

"Laclede Ave, East Hempstead, Long Island, New York, U.S.A. I'm visiting my brother who's with the Eagle Squadron. Why do you ask?"

"Just curious. Get all kinds these days. Used to be locals and holidaymakers come down from London, mostly day-trippers. Now it can be anyone: Yanks, Poles, Czechs, Frenchies, you name it. I've had them all in that seat you're in. Had one from Trinidad once. I had to ask where that was. He was an Indian too, even though the island turns out to be in the Caribbean."

"Apache Indian?"

"India Indian."

"And Germans?"

He rubbed his chin and squinted his left eye. Everyone has his own method for deep thinking. "Now that you mention it, yes, I have. There's been one or two tell me how they fled tyranny. Come over to help us get rid of the blighter. And then there's the girl married a Southend boy right before the Great War. Although, after all these years we consider her one of us."

We were pulling into the driveway of Geraldine's mess when I asked, "And this German lady who married the English boy. You wouldn't know her name by any chance, would you?"

"As a matter of fact, name's Sheffield." As we rolled past the gate, he pointed to the ironwork letter. "This place is hers. Till it was requisitioned for war use, that is."

The taxi came to a sharp stop, kicking up gravel. The cabbie pulled down the meter handle, stopping the clock. "You know," he said, "this meter here was invented by a German—Baron von Thurn und Taxis was his name." He pointed to the fare. Getting out of the taxi, I reached into my pocket and found the right change. Lord Sopwith paid me for running errands. I even had enough for a tip. The cabbie deserved a tip since he'd given me one. He pulled away, honking the horn and waving goodbye.

Warning bells told me there was a German spy living on the property. Light peeked from the sides of a blacked-out bedroom window. A light was on downstairs in a room at the back of the house. Wedging myself between two shrubs, I spied between a chink in the curtain, spotting Blanche bent over a desk. Her eyeglasses perched on the end of her nose. Her lips were pouted and her nose wiggling. A palm was placed on the desk and she was using her fingers to count. It was like she was taking a whack at a trigonometry equation but forgot her times table. I'd seen my sister Mary with the same look while trying to do simple addition.

Spinning around, I noticed a small stone cottage, set back from the house in a patch of woods. Smoke came from the chimney. Faint and flickering light escaped from a downstairs window. It was a wonder the Home Guard didn't come down on the lot of them for violating the blackout laws. Pressing my nose against the windowpane, I seen a lady sitting in a wingback chair facing a stone fireplace. A sheepskin rug draped over her legs. She wore men's gray felt slippers and a man's bathrobe, too big for her bird-like frame. A book laid on her lap. By the way she turned the pages, I knew she was a speed-reader. Her hair was twisted up in a tight bun. For a split-second, firelight refracted off a diamond ring. It must've weighed two carats, at least.

Fräu Sheffield. The German.

She was riveted to the book. Probably *Mein Kampf,* that nasty book by Adolf Hitler. Being a bookworm myself, I knew the book would distract her long enough for me to have a look around. A rose trellis, leaned up against the wall, served my purposes. By the time I reached the upstairs window, my right hand was torn up by thorns. Pulling up the window sash and shoving aside a blackout curtain, I entered the room and turned on a reading lamp that sat on a night table next to a canopy bed. And so I wouldn't leave a trail of blood behind me, I wrapped my hand in a stocking I found laying on the floor.

The night table was piled with books, every one of them English. I read the spines: Wilkie Collins, Josephine Tey, and Agatha Christie—detective novels. My ma read books like that. Her favorite was *The Woman in White*. It made perfect sense for a German spy to study English detectives. I slipped a paperback into my back pocket, thinking I'd do the same myself. The night table on the far side of the bed was empty, with not so much as a reading lamp on it. I wondered what happened to Mr. Sheffield.

I found his photograph on the mantelpiece: a handsome man with a handlebar mustache, wearing the uniform of a cavalry officer of the Great War, jodhpurs and all. A bayonet stuck from a sheaf strapped to his waist. Must've been strange, having to fight against his in-laws. There was also a wedding photograph, the sort taken in a studio—Woolworths was my guess. The couple stood leaning against a fake Roman column. The bride was decked out in a long lace number, trimmed in pearls. The train was wrapped around her legs. For sure, that dress set her father back a truckload of Deutschmarks.

Returning to the night table, I opened the top drawer. There in plain sight was all the evidence I needed. Hefting the pistol, I eyed the markings. *Jäger-Pistole* was engraved on the barrel. Cocking the gun, I saw it had one bullet left in the chamber. Before I had a chance to think what to do, Fräu Sheffield was standing on the landing, looking right at me.

She let out a bloodcurdling scream. I swung to face her, aiming the pistol right at her foot by mistake. She screamed again, and I dropped the gun in fright. It went off, putting a hole in the carpet. Fräu Sheffield kicked the gun under the bed so's it was out of reach.

"*Wer bist du, wirklich?*" I asked.

"Who are you to question me?" she said, wagging her finger in my face.

I heard stomping on the stairs. Any second and I'd be outnumbered. Turning, I jumped back to the window, thinking to make my escape. But as my wounded hand reached for the rose trellis, another hand grabbed my back trouser pocket, pulling me onto the bedroom carpet.

I was done for.

"Oh, no you don't," said Daphne.

Geraldine, Blanche, Beetle, and Alice were all there too. Alice had her arm around Fräu Sheffield, who was wiping tears from her eyes.

"He gave me such a fright," she said. "He really did."

"Nothing to worry about, Lady Sheffield. He's harmless—usually," said Daphne in my defense. She turned and gave me the evil eye.

"You're a little thief," said Alice, almost spitting. "Caught in the act again."

"Did I miss the first act?" asked Geraldine.

Fräu Sheffield grabbed me by the arm. She reached

down into my trouser pocket, retrieving the paperback. Shaking her head, she said, "*The Man in the Queue*. And I wasn't half through reading it."

"Thomas," said Daphne, sighing. "There's a well-stocked library at Warfield Hall."

When you're caught red handed, there's only one course to take. I took it. "I apologize, Fräu Sheffield, with all my heart and soul. I'm addicted to reading, you see. Have mercy on me, a sinner. I'm begging you." I got on one knee like I was proposing to the woman. Daphne swiped my head before pulling me to my feet.

"He's my fiancés little brother," she said. "Perhaps we might work out a deal."

"What sort of deal?" said Fräu Sheffield.

"Might I suggest chores in exchange for jail time?" said Daphne. I started to answer back but Daphne gave me a look that said, *Don't you dare open your trap*.

"Well, I could use help with the garden," said Fräu Sheffield. She spoke with a perfect upper crust British accent, but she didn't fool me. My finely tuned hearing could detect German undertones—when she said *garden*, she hit the G too hard. Like when she said, "The *ga*—ardener has been called up, and I do so want to trim back the shrubs and rose bushes." She stopped to think up more chores. "And pick up leaves and dead *ga*—rass," she said.

As much as I hated chores, all and all, I couldn't've asked for a better turnout. I'd have one eye on the shears and the other on Fräu Sheffield. I said: "Please, ma'am. I love yard work—and, and—I was hoping to find out how the book ended. I stupidly left my copy back in Southampton."

"Then tomorrow after church you'll start work," said Fräu Sheffield. "And because I'm such a good sport, you may borrow the paperback in the meantime."

CHAPTER ELEVEN

Back in the main house, we sat around the kitchen table dunking digestive biscuits in tea. A digestive biscuit is a fancy way to say vanilla cookie. Alice said she had a splitting headache and went up to bed without one.

"Please let me sleep on your couch," I begged.

"Don't tell me the Nazis have taken over Jack's mess," said Daphne. "Don't even start." She was wearing a frilly bathrobe, borrowed no doubt.

"Ghosts," I said. "The place is haunted."

"Really?" asked Blanche, eyes wide-open. "How very exciting."

"You're making this up," said Daphne, on to me. There was practically no one in the world who knew me better. It was getting harder and harder to fool her. If I even veered toward a little white lie, a slight exaggeration or elaboration, she caught it. I winked—to let her know I knew she knew I was making this story up. But she looked at her engagement ring just then and yawned with her eyes closed tight.

"It's the ghost of a dead pilot," I said.

I could hear the mantle clock ticking, it was that

quiet. I'd hit too close to home. One of Jack's friends had been killed in action a month before. The base had already lost 16 men and the year wasn't even out. "Pilots of the Boar War," I said, before they got weepy.

I'd heard something about Churchill fighting African boars when he was a wet behind the ears soldier. The Boar War was one of them wars we never learned about in America, same as how English kids didn't study the Mexican-American War or the Civil War. I tried to change the subject: "Back in New York we got a brand of cold cuts named Boar's Head—the label's got an ugly-as-get-out pig on it."

Someone started laughing and everyone joined in.

"It's the *Boer* War. Not the *Boar* War," said Geraldine. "Boars are wild pigs, of a sort. Boers were Dutch Afrikaners."

"Was the ghost awfully handsome?" asked Blanche. "Dutch or English?"

"The Boer War?" asked Daphne, raising an eyebrow. "And he came all the way to England from South Africa to haunt the Eagle Squadron officer's mess? Fascinating."

"It's quite possible that he was Dutch and wanted revenge," said Blanche, shaking a bit. "Was he very tall? Dutchmen often are."

"My grandfather fought in the Boer War," said Daphne. "It began in 1880 and ended in 1902. And if I'm not mistaken, there wasn't a single airplane used in that war. Really, Thomas, you'll have to do better than that."

I laughed extra hard, like it was a joke all along.

But I needed to find another excuse for sleeping over or they'd kick me out. "It's too quiet over at the officer's mess, what with most of the pilots out. Besides," I said, "you know how it is—those pilots take off their flight boots and boy, oh boy." I squeezed my nostrils. "Get's so a fella can't sleep. But it smells just fine here. Like a bouquet of pansies."

That buttered them up good and had them pulling extra blankets out of the linen closet and putting clean sheets on the couch in the main parlor. Geraldine fluffed up a pillow and threw it at me, along with a kiss. Daphne tucked me in and turned the light off as she left the room.

"Any word from Jack?" I called after her.

"Nothing," she said, biting her lower lip. "I'm sure he'll turn up in the morning."

I tried to think what could be holding my brother up. It didn't make sense. Jack loved to fly. He wouldn't waste time getting back. On top of that, he knew that Daphne and me were waiting for him at the base, and he was crazy about the both of us. *If only I can get my hands on a set of car keys*, I thought. I might head up to Garsington while it was still too dark for a cop to spot me behind the wheel. Getting off the couch, I pulled back the blackout curtain and took a look at the driveway. My wish was answered instantly. Just then, a military jeep came driving up the circular driveway, stopping in front of the door.

A man in an RAF issue jumpsuit was in the driver's seat. On his sleeve was the insignia of a sergeant. He opened the passenger door for a WAAF. Even after he helped her out of the car, he kept hold of her hand. He spun the WAAF around, so that her back was against the tailgate, kissing her in a way that had me squirming.

They drifted to the front door, his mouth chewing on her ear the whole time. The lovebirds stopped inches from the window I was standing behind. That's when I seen it was Wilson, the aviation mechanic assigned to Jack's squadron. His jumpsuit was covered in grease, meaning he was a fitter. They're the ones who work on the engines. A rigger, on the other hand, patches a bullet-ridden plane.

A key turned in the lock and I jumped behind the couch.

"I can't let you in, Henry," said the WAAF.

"Just for a minute, Dot," said Wilson. "Give a chap a drink, would you?"

"All right, darling, but we'll have to be quiet. Take your boots off." She was whispering, but I heard every word.

Wilson sat on the couch, not noticing that it was made up like a bed. He was putting grease all over the clean sheets. The room was still dark, no one had turned on a light. I heard the clinking of crystal glasses.

Dot sat on the couch next to Wilson and began a sniffly kind of cry. "I can't bear it much longer," she said.

"Then you needn't," said Wilson.

"All this sneaking around behind people's backs—having to look people right in the eye and tell bald lies. I'm telling you, Henry, it's doing me in. It can't go on. I swear, I'll have a breakdown."

"Then we finish this business once and for all, Dot. You know that I'm ready at the drop of a hat. I'm only waiting until you are absolutely certain. Because once the deed is done, there will be no turning back. And I can't have you regretting the decision later—blaming me. Growing to hate me in the process."

Dot sucked in air and then blew it out like a hurricane. After that, they were so quiet I worried they'd nodded off. But before long, there was the sound of ice being swished around an empty glass. Liquored up, Wilson had a temper.

"What does it matter if your family disowns you?"

"Henry, please."

"You say they'll no longer welcome you and that you'll be the scourge of polite society. Well, good riddance to the lot of them is what I say."

"I'll have to leave the country," said Dot, whimpering.

"There's always Australia. We can get ourselves a nice little ranch. A few herd of cattle." He shifted his weight and the couch springs creaked.

"Tasmania shan't be far enough," said Dot with a sigh. "And could you see me as a cowgirl?"

I'd only gotten a glimpse of Dot, and that in the dark. But I'd been through her drawers and, in my opinion, she wasn't cut out to be a cowgirl. Maybe a socialite, like Lady Sop. Or a cigarette girl in a fancy nightclub. She might get a job at one of them chichi Bond Street stores, selling cuff links to royalty. But they weren't asking for my opinion, so I kept my mouth shut.

"Whatever comes, it will be worth it all," said Wilson. "I can promise you that. And I don't think we have a choice."

I wanted to interrupt and suggest they go to India. In India they had princesses living in swank buildings like the Taj Mahal. I'd seen a Kodachrome View-Master slide of the place. Dot would fit in great there. They probably wore silk underwear, too.

"I need a little time, Henry," she said. "I know that I've been a complete coward up until now, and I hope you can forgive me. I ought to be braver. You know how I feel, you know the passion I—" They were moving around on the couch, rearranging themselves in what I suspected was a horizontal position.

"Stop, darling," said Dot, jumping from the couch so that the springs whined. "I'm sorry, but you'll have to go now."

"I get it," said Wilson, his fuse getting shorter by the second. "Stop, go, stop, go, STOP!" He changed moods and laughed it off. It reminded me of Dr. Jekyll and Mr. Hyde. They walked back to the front door, me peeking over the couch. Dot kissed Henry Wilson one last time before he left, then locked the door behind him. She came back into the parlor, poured herself another drink and sat back on the couch. That's when she had the breakdown she was so worried about earlier. Meanwhile, I was stuck sleeping on the hardwood floor.

Besides that, Henry had driven off with the jeep.

By and by, Dot rose from the couch and went upstairs. I was wide-awake and thinking hard about her and Wilson. Didn't somebody say she was dating one of the Millionaire pilots from Squadron 601? What was she doing getting all smoochy with a fitter? Two-timing, was my guess. Now that the squadron was stationed in Malta, she figured she could get away with it.

She and Wilson had something they were hiding, even from Dot's family. When it came out, they were going to have to leg it to Tasmania, go undercover as ranchers. It was on account of being sleepy that it took me so long to put it together: *What if they're German spies?* I thought. I remembered the letter I'd taken from Dot's underwear drawer, crumpled in my front pocket. But I couldn't take the chance of getting caught red-handed with it. At any minute one of the WAAFs might come downstairs for a glass of water or a midnight snack. Whenever my sister Mary claimed to be on a weight-reduction diet, she'd make raids on the kitchen when everyone was asleep. "The evidence is hanging on your waist," I'd say, when she blamed me for the missing pies.

I found a flashlight hanging from a nail in the kitchen. They call it a torch in England, like it would burn you or something. A narrow door led to a basement. I'd be able to read the letter in peace down there. No one had been down them stairs in a long while. I walked smack into a wall of spiderwebs soon as I opened the door. Looking around the kitchen, I spotted a broom, which I used to blaze a path. The door slammed behind me, but not loud enough to wake anybody. The steps were made of stones and turned my feet to ice. The flashlight beam fell on junk furniture: broken chairs, a sofa without cushions, a table with three legs, a grandfather clock without hands. A giant chest sat in the corner, a pile of old moldy quilts on top of it.

I needed to take a look inside the chest, before anything. The old padlock was so rusty it fell to pieces the second I laid hands on it. Inside the chest were worm-eaten ledger books, green with mold. Each book was engraved with a year. From what I could tell, they all dated back to the time of Queen Victoria. She was the one who took the Koh-Noor diamond from India. There could be a clue leading to another diamond in the ledgers. But it turned out that they were for a hotel called the Inn at Branch Fork. All sorts of people had registered to stay back between 1824 and 1912.

I turned my mind back to Dot's letter. It was one of them letters that turn into an envelope when you fold and paste the sides shut. The paper was thin and blue, printed with a faint cartoon of an airplane. Written on the front was ARMED FORCES AIR LETTER and than Air Mail. The stamp was the current King George, of course. The postmark was Egypt, not Malta. I was getting more excited by the minute. Another handstamp showed that the letter had passed through a censor, with the censor's personalized number written under. If anyone let a German coded letter through by mistake, the right head would roll. The handwriting was in blue fountain ink. Some of the letters were rubbed off—like maybe it got caught in a sandstorm.

The opening, which should've said *Dear Dot*, instead said *To my own Nefertiti*. No one but a budding Egyptologist would have gotten the reference. Holy mackerel, did this fella know how to write a love letter! Nefertiti was the wife of Ramses II, famous for her swan-neck. Dot had a long neck too, come to think of it. I tried to remember where I'd seen a picture of Nefertiti, in a magazine probably. I racked my brain for the details: might have been *National Geographic*, on the side table at the dentist in East Hempstead, right before I had ten cavities filled—not an experience I was likely to forget. In the magazine article they showed a statue of Nefertiti. And under the photo was a caption saying where that statue was located. Suddenly it came to me:

Berlin!

I scan through line after line of mushy love-talk, until my eye caught the name of the letter writer. *Chas.* Which stood for Charles. This Chas fella sure was keen on Dot, that much was clear. He couldn't wait to get hitched, wished they'd done it before he'd gone off to XXXXXXXX. (A black censor's mark covered the word.)

I scanned down to where the letter picked up. He'd written something cryptic about a tomb he and his friends were exploring, excited about a line of hieroglyphs they were hoping to decode. Then right there on the page were the symbols—amazing that it got past the censor—because chances were, it was a Nazi message.

A falcon, an eye, and waves of water.

I knew that a falcon was part of the Nazi party symbol. Didn't I just see that very symbol on Yonkers' lighter? The eye could mean, *Keep an eye out*, and the water symbol might be letting a Nazi secret agent, disguised as a WAAF, know that the Germans were coming by sea.

The naval base! I swallowed hard.

The letter was mailed just before the Germans attacked Southend. From what my brother told me, two Messerschmitts showed up in broad daylight, dropping bombs and doing serious damage to the downtown shopping strip. Jack and his friends chased them away, but not in time to save the jewelry store. Why I didn't think of this earlier is anyone's guess, but now I had an interesting thought: *Maybe they were aiming for the jewelry shop all along!*

I heard on the radio that the Germans were running out of money. They were making airplane petrol out of potatoes, that's how hard up they were. What better way to fund the Nazi war machine than bomb British jewelry shops, and then have secret agents ready to run in and grab the loot? I remembered the dozy of a diamond ring on Fräu Sheffield's finger. It could be that her and Dot were in cahoots, just waiting for an opportunity to sneak the diamonds out of the country. In the morning, I decided, I'd go scout out the wreckage, see if I could find clues. If not, maybe find leftover jewelry—a little trinket the Nazis overlooked.

I crept up the cellar stairs and back to the sofa. I was dead tired, so I stuffed some tissue into my ears. That way the ladies wouldn't wake me when they all got up for church in the morning. All but Alice, that is.

CHAPTER TWELVE

MI5 Headquarters,
Wormwood Scrubs, East London

THERE IS A KNOCK on the door, three quick taps. "Good morning, sir," says Agent Ellis. "Thought I'd pop around and bring you up to date on the latest citizen report."

"What now?" says Brigadier A.W.A. Harker, Deputy Director General of MI5, adding a "harrumph."

"We've gotten a report from a woman out in Dover, sir." Ellis opens a manila folder and flips two pages, finding the one he wants. "Yes, here it is. A Mrs. Charles Sanders, widow, age 62, seamstress. Says that she's an insomniac. Only thing for it is to take a stroll in the middle of the night." He glances over the rim of his reading glasses, not surprised to see a look of impatience on Harker's face. He buries his head in the folder. "Yes, well—Mrs. Charles Sanders claims to have seen a fishing boat returning to the pier at all sorts of odd hours, during the curfew...always with the lights shut off in the cabin."

Harker slaps his desk.

Even from his vantage point at the door, Ellis sees

that the man's left eye is twitching.

"That again?" says Harker. "Does she not realize how difficult it is for fishermen ever since this bloody war began? I know there's no excuse for breaking the curfew, but, that said. As any sport-fisherman will tell you, the best catch is had in the hours before sunrise. How are we to keep food on our tables, I ask you?" Harker waves a hand dismissively. "Impound the boat, if you must."

"Sir, I was thinking to go down to Dover and have a word with the fisherman." Ellis thinks about the mounting stack of similar reports on his desk. It makes him feel dizzy. He hasn't been out of London in weeks, sleeping at his desk most nights. "I could catch the 10:15 and be back in no time."

Harker knocks his knuckle against the desktop, thinking to bring the conversation to a close. "Waste of valuable time, Ellis."

"But what if...Remember that chap went by the name of Walter Simon? The Abwehr landed him on the Dingle Peninsula…"

"In Ireland, for pity's sake! A rank amateur, if you ask me. Seen burying his AFU transmitter on the beach, then asking locals when the next train was due to arrive…when the bloody train hadn't run on that line for 14-months! Decided he'd warm himself up at a local pub before commencing his mission. The chap was picked up drunk as a skunk, identified by the sand in his shoes."

Ellis hesitates, reluctant to contradict his superior. "But perhaps they've learned from their mistakes, sir. I know we have."

Harker leans back in his office chair. "You're referring to Operation Shavetail, unfortunate business that." He lets his voice trail off, but then raises it almost to a shout. "I refuse to give credit to this, this busybody widow who has nothing better to do than make trouble for honest fishermen! If you want my opinion, the government ought to put a stop to those ludicrous posters giving everyone the impression that there are German spies listening behind every hedgerow, behind every rose bush. How many false citizen reports have we had to date, Ellis?"

"About 15,000 this month alone, sir." He brings up an image of the mounting stacks on his desk and signs.

"Waste of time, Ellis. Waste of valuable time. No need for bored widows to be snooping around fishing piers. Chaps at Bletchley Park are breaking coded messages at lightening speed, ever since the invention of the, the, that contraption called the—" He snaps his finger.

"—the Bombe machine, sir."

"It was on the tip of my tongue. Well, ever since the Bombe machine we're cracking messages so fast we know an enemy agent is coming before he does. Close the door as you go."

As the door shuts, Hacker is heard laughing to himself.

Why, he thinks, *they don't even have time to nip into the pub.*

CHAPTER THIRTEEN

"But I'm Catholic!" I moaned when Daphne shook me awake and told me to get ready for church. "I can't go to an Anglican Church. My ma would have a conniption!"

"Well, aren't you a lucky boy then. Blanche has volunteered to take you to her church," said Daphne. "Roman Catholic. They've got confession booths, candles, holy water, and whatever else you'll be needing. You can write your mum and tell her what a saint you are for going without an argument."

I opened one eye and looked at the ladies, all dressed up in their Sunday best. There was Blanche holding her rosary beads in one hand and a missal in the other. Even Daphne was going to church. I knew there was a synagogue in Southend, but they met on Saturday. She'd made up for it Friday night, by lighting a candle before we ate our Wartime Vegetable Pie. She'd even recited a prayer in the ancient Jewish language, which she was teaching me.

"Gee," I said. "Can't a fella get a break?"

"You'll have fun," said Blanche. "Today is the fête. Everyone brings a pie and we have a contest after church. We lay wages on who can eat the most pie. The steeple bell needs refurbished, you see. It's got a crack. And what a good time to fix it, now that church bells are permitted to ring again. If we don't raise enough, we'll have to have a jumble sale next month. So everyone is going full-on at pie baking."

Catholics knew all the tricks. If it wasn't pie contests, it was Bingo. I jumped from the couch like a shot. "You can carry my offering, it's in the kitchen," said Blanche. "And if I turn a blind eye and a big chunk goes missing, no one will be the wiser." I ran into the kitchen and spotted a chocolate cream pie, covered in globs of whipped cream. The cream was probably fake, but so what? I was feeling grateful to God just then. I reached my finger into the cream. It was the real deal. Blanche must've used a year's worth of ration coupons to get it.

We walked all the way into town, me nibbling on the pie the whole way. The Anglican Church was right down the block from the Catholics, so we walked together. Dot dragged her feet and we kept waiting for her to catch up. When we got near the church, I heard a dog bark. It was Ringo, attached to a leash. And holding the leash was my brother, Jack.

"We thought we'd surprise you!" said Daphne, pinching my arm. "He rung up this morning and said he was back!"

"Hey, kiddo," said my brother, fluffing my hair. He didn't seem to have a bruise on him, unless you counted the dark circles under his eyes. "Sorry about the Crown Jewels and all. Crying shame."

"Missing out on the hamburger and fries," I said, "that's the heartbreaking part."

"Ma always said your stomach was a bottomless pit. Figured you'd show for the pie eating contest. I see you've gotten a head start on the rest of the faithful." Jack gave Daphne a peck on the cheek, probably worried that a nun was in the area—waiting and watching. Then he handed me the leash. "No wonder Ma doesn't let you have a pet. Sel's goldfish was belly-up this morning and starting to bloat. I had the honors of flushing it down the toilet. He's gonna miss that fish. He was awful attached, even gave it a name."

My brother pretended to sock my arm. I felt bad about the fish. I'd failed in my duties. "Are you hurt?" I asked.

Jack took his cap off and leaned down, pointing to the top of his head. There was a gash at least three inches long—a big bloody scab with hair stuck in it. Daphne gave a gasp and got wobbly on her feet. "I thought you told Geraldine that you weren't hurt?" she asked.

"This didn't happen when I bailed out," said Jack. "It happened when I was in a pub afterwards. I was just having a bite to eat before heading back to the base when some nutcase must've mistaken me for someone else. Clubbed me over the head. Knocked me out cold."

"Did you see who it was?" I asked.

There were no witnesses, he said. "Nope. When the girl came with my pint, there I was laid out on the floor, blood gushing from my skull. She figured me for dead. And I might have been, too, because the guy'd used the blunt edge of an old rifle they had hanging on the wall above where I'd been sitting. A decoration—thank God the gun wasn't loaded."

"Pubs are dangerous places, aren't they?" I said.

"You betcha," said Jack, patting my shoulder. "All those drunks under one roof. If you take my advice, Tommy, you'll stay clear of them." He rubbed his head. "I might take my own advice, in fact."

Daphne said, "Oh, Jack. Shouldn't you be in hospital! You might have a concussion like Sel."

"You're out of luck, babe." He grabbed her to him. "I'm fit for duty. Not even able to go to Mass. I barely have time to lay my eyes on you, hand over Ringo to the babysitter here, and be off again. These are desperate times."

I looked down at the ground and kicked a stone. "Rotten Nazis," I said. "Keepin' a kid from his brother."

"With any luck, I'll be back for an early dinner, maybe some leftover pie."

"There won't be any, not if I can help it," I said.

"Rhubarb," he said.

I thought he meant pie. "I'll try and snag a piece for you."

Jack laughed. I realized he meant he was going up on a mission to find and destroy German military positions across the Channel in occupied Europe. For some reason they called these missions *Rhubarbs*. I threw my arms around him, not knowing if I'd ever see him again.

"What about your Spitfire?" said Daphne. "Surely it was wrecked."

Jack kissed her on the lips and smiled. There were plenty of Spitfires sitting around now that so many pilots were laid up with injuries. A jeep drove up, Wilson in the driver's seat. Before I could alert my brother, he jumped in and they were speeding off toward the airfield.

"You!" I said to Ringo. "I can't seem to shake you."

The church bells started thudding on account of the crack. The bells stopped ringing while there was a chance of an invasion, saving them for warning bells instead. So it was a good sign that they were ringing again—or thudding, that is. Blanche took my arm and escorted me into the church. We were splashing holy water on our faces when a priest spotted Ringo, wagged his finger and pointed to the door.

"Sorry, Blanche. They won't let us in," I said.

"Not that easy," she whispered, grabbing the leash. "Wait here whilst I tie her up outside." When she came back, she put a hand on my shoulder and walked me to a pew. She did a genuflect and then slid in. I followed behind, bowing my body from the waist. The church was overheated and I yawned. Blue-haired parishioners turned around and shot me dirty looks. *Judge not!* I wanted to yell out, quoting Jesus. How many of them had been hiding behind couches half the night? I stuck my tongue out. After that, my eyelids defied gravity. I shook my head trying to wake myself up. It didn't work. Soon I was dreaming that I was a gunner on a B-17 Flying Fortress.

I woke up when something hit my right toe. As

I leaned down to see what it was, I saw Blanche was kneeling on a cushion, her eyes shut, reciting the Nicene Creed along with everyone else. The priest stood in a carved wooden perch, leading everyone in ancient Latin, his eyes closed too. This was my chance for escape.

Ringo had snuck back into the church and was sleeping on the cushion meant for my knees. On top of my foot was Blanche's missal, her prayer book. The cover was open to a page for family history: birth, death, and marriage dates. I reached down and took the book in my hands, scanning the handwritten list of Blanche's family members. The priest said, "*Qui cum Patre et Filio simul adoratur et conglorificatur.*" Just a few more lines before everyone opened their eyes, and my shot at freedom was over.

*Blanche Ann Wickersham, born on April 25, 1916.
Married on January 4, 1938.
To Siegfried Hutzel.*

German.

Looking over at Blanche, I zoomed in on her wedding ring finger. It was steepled upwards with the other nine, ringless. With a light touch, I placed the prayer book next to Blanche and slid to the end of the pew, pulling on Ringo's leash. A nun stood guard at the front door. When she got a look at the dog, she ordered us both outside. In the direction I needed to go.

Blanche, I thought. She hadn't been on my list of suspects. Seemed so innocent, for one thing. Virginal, almost. This was spy craft: pretending to moon over

Millionaire pilots and ghosts of the Boer War. It was probably Siegfried who recruited her for the Abwehr: the German spy department.

A traitor to her country. And to the Holy Catholic Church. And yet, I knew what love could do to a dame. It screwed up their heads, made them do crazy things and whatnot. I'd spent enough time with Daphne to see the results.

Just as I was pondering this, the leash was pulled from my hands. Ringo went flying down a side path that led to a creepy old cemetery—the kind they've got all over Europe. She made straight for a tombstone, squatting down and peeing right above where the deceased's head would be.

John Sheffield, CBE was engraved on the stone. *Dearly beloved husband of Rivka. 1882-1939.* Then a clue to a Bible verse: Numbers 6. Somewhere in the Old Testament, I knew that much. It might be a code, put on the tombstone right before the war got going. There'd been plenty of German spies in England then, scouting out the best place for a future invasion. I looked up at the church: gothic with gargoyles. So Lord Sheffield was a Catholic, too. And his wife's name—I'd never heard of a dame called that before. Rivka. *Must be a German name*, I thought. I took a look at the tombstone next to Lord Sheffield's. It was a brand new stone. It said *Reginald, 1921-1942. In service to God and King.* At the base of the stone was a bunch of flowers: fresh, like they'd just been put there.

"My son," came a voice behind me. "We lost him

less than two weeks ago."

I spun around and saw Fräu Sheffield standing not four feet behind me. She was patting the corner of her eye with a lace handkerchief. "Are you enjoying the book?" she asked.

"Did he die in the war?" I pointed to the tombstone. She started talking, but it was almost like she wasn't talking to me. So I didn't interrupt.

"He should have been at Bletchley Park. That's where he was working. But he was found in his flat in London. The coroner ruled that he died by ingestion of some toxin or another. Mercifully, it was ruled an *accidental death*. I was afraid at first that they'd say it was suici... My, I can't bear to say the word. There was a note, you see. Written to me by his own hand."

"Murdered," I said. "Who would do such a thing?"

"The Nazis, naturally," she said.

Time to get thinking, I thought. She might be telling me this to throw me off the trail—the one that led straight to her door. "Why would they target your son?" I asked, paying careful attention to what she did with her hands, seeing if I could catch her in a lie. Hand twitches are always dead giveaways.

She reached for the top of her blouse, unclasping a couple of mother-of-pearl buttons, reaching for a gold chain. *Here it is*, I thought, *the secret symbol.* I stepped closer to see the small medallion that hung from the chain. She bent down. We were eyeball to eyeball, and everyone knows that liars have trouble doing that.

"Now do you understand?" she said.

I did.

CHAPTER FOURTEEN

"You remind me a little of my son Reggie at your age," said Lady Sheffield, as I bit down on a jam filled bun. She'd offered to take me to the bun shop across the street from the Catholic Church; it was the only place in town opened, probably owned by atheists. "Reggie was precocious, like you. Always getting into mischief, but oh so brilliant. He rarely was caught." She took a sip from her teacup.

"My German teacher was Mr. Fisch," I said, "who lives down the street from us in New York. He told me all about how Hitler was treating the Jewish people. Most Americans don't know," I said. "Then I seen for myself when I was in Paris. They tried to take Daphne's aunt who is Jewish, but my brother saved her."

"My late husband was a student at the University in Bonn," said Lady Sheffield. "He was reading theology at the seminary there. This was before the last war. My family always struggled financially and my father supplemented his income by tutoring some the seminarians in Hebrew and Aramaic. My father was a cantor—the one who sings the prayers at the synagogue. I came home one day to find James Sheffield sitting in my father's study. He was reading from *Tehillim*—the 145th Psalm. I stood outside the door listening as he said, *ChaNûn w'rachûm y'hwäh erekh' aPayim ug däl-chäsed*, in English accented Hebrew. He read beautifully, like the poet I later came to know he was. *The Lord is gracious, and full of compassion; slow to anger, and of great mercy.* It had always been my favorite scripture."

"And then you fell madly in love and got married," I said, wanting to get through this part fast.

Lady Sheffield began touching a yellow flower, stuck in a pickle jar and meant to spruce up the table. She stretched over her teacup and saucer, so her nose was right up against the petals, taking a big whiff. "I converted to the Catholic Church to marry him— although I still wear my Magen David pendant." She let her hand rest on her throat. "My parents tore their clothing, signifying that I was dead to them. Year after year, I've written to Germany, my letters always coming back unopened and with the address crossed out. Always in my father's handwriting: *Return to Sender. Addressee unknown.* Then in 1938 the letters ceased to be returned. I suspected that either the letters hadn't arrived to Germany or they'd arrived and been intercepted. Or worse—perhaps something unthinkable had happened to my father."

I took a big gulp of air. I knew what she was getting at.

"Then the day came that MI5 paid me a visit, wanting to know why I had tried to mail letters to Germany." She laughed for the first time in our conversation. "Like you, they suspected me of being a German spy."

"I—I," I stammered. She waved her hand, meaning all was forgiven.

"I told them my whole story, just as I've now told you. It must be that you remind me of my son. I could always speak with Reggie. But since he died, everything has been bottled up." She took a deep breath and then opened her handbag and crushed her handkerchief into it. "Well, later, when I heard that the RAF needed places to billet WAAFs, I volunteered the manor house. I wanted to do everything in my power to stop Hitler. Everything sped along nicely with the RAF, especially when I mentioned that I had already been vetted by British Intelligence. Do you think they would have let a German live in the groundkeeper's cottage without a thorough background check? I'm happy to do my part. So, you see, my dear boy, I am not the one whom you seek."

"That shortens my list of suspects," I said, believing every word she said. German spies don't go around wearing a Star of David tucked under their blouses. Forgetting the date on his tombstone, I asked her what happened to her husband, if he was killed in the last war with Germany.

"Goodness gracious no," she said. "He came home to me after the Armistice and we had a wonderful marriage until his heart gave out." The pistol, she told me, was a souvenir of her husband's from the war. "When another war with Germany seemed eminent, he instructed me to keep it beside my bed. So that in the event of an invasion I might fight back. In 1939 that scenario was a real possibility."

"If the Germans invade England and I'm still here, I promise to come and fight alongside you, Lady Sheffield."

"You are a darling boy, even if you do have sticky fingers."

"I'm five pages into *The Man in the Queue*." It was the truth.

"Keep it then," she said, patting my hand. "I can order another from the bookseller."

I knew then that Lady Sheffield would work with me to uncover a German agent. Information came pouring out of my mouth, all my suspicions about this and that person.

"You have such a vivid imagination. Just like Reggie," she said. She paused, thinking. "You can cross Alice off your list. She and Reggie were in love."

"Alice?" I said, surprised. She didn't seem the lovey-dovey type to me. But it seemed I was wrong there. Turned out that Reggie met Alice on a visit home, and the two fell for each other right away—one of them whirlwind wartime romances: introduced on Friday, engaged by Monday. Reggie even gave Alice a diamond engagement ring, a Sheffield family heirloom.

"The dear thing returned it to me when Reggie died. True, they'd only been together a week… Still, she didn't have to return the ring—it was hers by rights. But it had been mine before her engagement and she felt it was proper that I should have it back." She held her ring finger out to me, showing me the rock. I had to sit on my hands.

"Dot is my chief suspect," I said. "She says she's going with one of the Millionaire pilots, but I know for a fact that she's in cahoots with Henry Wilson, a mechanic. I saw them kissing with my own eyes."

"Oh, my," she said. "That happens all the time, my dear. A boy goes away and a girl gets bored and takes up with someone else. It doesn't mean that she has anything but unfaithfulness to hide. Dot seems like a blue blooded English girl if ever there were one. Come to think of it, I believe her father is in the House of Lords."

"They're up to something, I'm telling you."

Just then, people came pouring out of the church. It reminded me about the pie eating contest. I wasn't about to miss it. When I explained my need to run, Lady Sheffield said, "Didn't those three buns fill you up?"

"Plenty of room left," I said, wiping my mouth. I excused myself, patting my stomach while sucking it in. "And thanks for the intelligence."

"You have chores," she reminded me. "But they can wait, I suppose. Now that we're friends." She winked.

Lady Sheffield was A-Okay. I promised to come back to the house after the contest and help her pull weeds.

"It's as though you won the battle, but lost the war," said Daphne, looking at the ribbon pinned to my chest. Her hand was on my back, my head hovering above the toilet bowl. Vomit dribbled from the corner of my mouth.

Who'd of thought there could be anything left in my stomach?

But there was.

If I had it to do over again, I would still of ate the pies. Afterwards, a nun said she was proud of me, forgetting that pride and gluttony are two of the seven deadly sins. Not only did I get the blue ribbon but a one-pound note, too. On top of that, the priest promised that when the bells were fixed, he'd let me be the first one to ring them.

Daphne put her wrist against my sweaty forehead. "You're not going to say the Nazis poisoned the five pies you ate, are you? Six, I mean." She remembered the chocolate cream I'd wolfed down on the way to church.

"Look," I said. "I'm in no mood for your wisecracks. If you can find some Pepto-Bismol I'd be mighty grateful." Even though it was an American concoction, they sold the pink medicine in England. I'd already spotted the bottle in the bathroom medicine cabinet, but I didn't let on.

Within an hour I was fit as a fiddle, pulling dead dandelions out of the lawn. Lady Sheffield sat in a chaise with a paperback mystery in her hand, shouting instructions to me.

"Not my lavender!" she said when I reached for a clump of weeds. Five minutes later she yelled out when I reached to pull up a scraggly bush with shriveled brown seedpods. The leaves smelt like parsnips. "Not that either, dear," she said. "I'll deal with that myself. Now go wash your hands with soap and water, and then join me for tea."

That was my cue to put down the trowel. When I saw the plate of little cakes, my stomach began protesting. "Tea, please," I said. "And no sugar." I couldn't believe my own lips.

"Hands first, dear," she said, pointing to the dirt under my fingernails. "Give them a good scrub, would you? There's a nailbrush next to the bar of soap at the kitchen sink." I obeyed and entered her cottage, finding everything right where she said it'd be. When I joined her back outside, she inspected my hands and then shooed me into the chair next to her. I noticed she set two places next to a fancy-pants tea service set, made of .925 pure silver.

"I made ginger tea for you," she said. "It settles the stomach. My mother used to know all the folk remedies. There's so much healing in simple herbs." Lady Sheffield sighed. I tried to look sympathetic, which wasn't hard. When she poured my tea, little slices of ginger floated to the top of the gold-rimmed teacup. "My Reggie was such a good child," she said. "Brilliant in school. Why, the teachers couldn't keep up with him. He'd always be asking 'why this?' and 'why that?' So inquisitive. Drove my husband and me crazy." She laughed, half-hearted. "What I wouldn't do for some of his questions now."

She told me that, with war on the horizon, Reggie got in touch with an acquaintance of his father's—a man in intelligence during the Great War. At the time, Reggie was in his final year of an advanced degree in mathematics at Cambridge University. "He was invited to visit an old monstrosity of a house outside of London, where his professor was setting up a secret department."

"Hush-hush," I said.

"Between you and me and the four walls, I suspect it was established to decipher German wireless messages."

We were sitting in the garden, I pointed out. There were no walls.

"I spoke German to Reggie when he was a child. And Yiddish. I wanted him to have a head start on language. They say a mind that is good at languages is also good at maths—so, maybe it helped."

"I haven't found that to be true, Lady S., but go on."

"The war hadn't begun yet, but everyone knew that, sooner or later, push would come to shove. I suppose I shouldn't tell you this."

"I'll keep my trap shut. I already got classified information in this head." I tapped my skull. "And I'll never give it up. Not even if they pull my fingernails out, one by one."

Her body shivered. True, it was a bit chilly. "Please don't be so graphic," she said, then poured more tea into our cups. My stomach was feeling better, thanks to her ma's recipe. She kept talking: "I was so relieved. I mean—Reggie would have a safe desk job. I'd been worried that he'd be sent overseas. Of course, even then, we knew Hitler's intention toward the Jewish people. I'd read *Mein Kampf*."

I told Lady Sheffield that I'd read *Mein Kampf*, too; that it kept me up nights; that my German instructor,

Mr. Fisch, gave it to me in preparation for my trip to Europe—the one where I rescued my brother. I told her that it was because of that book I was extra vigilant in protecting Daphne. That it was one of the reasons I worked nonstop to stop Nazis, when most kids were shooting dice and playing with Pick-up sticks.

I was about to confess to spying on her while she was reading by the fireplace the night before. Agatha Christie, probably. Me thinking she was studying that awful *Mein Kampf*. But before I could, she looked up at the sky, lost in her thoughts, and said, "I should have known that whatever they were up to at Bletchley Park would draw the attention of the Germans, and that Reggie's life would be at risk—even if he was safely on this side of the Channel. Hitler's hand reaches very far."

I asked her how she could be sure it was them who killed Reggie.

"It was the note—what they termed 'the suicide note.' Although it was no such thing."

I asked if she still had it. She rose from the chaise and I followed her into the house, up the stairs and into her bedroom. She opened the drawer with the German pistol. I'd missed the note in my search—my eyes had bugged out soon as I seen the gun.

"I'll go downstairs," she said, "and leave you to read it."

When she left the room, I sat on the bed, my hand trembling and the note shaking back and forth. The note would hold the key to the whole mystery.

Dearest Mother, it said. *I shan't return home as planned. Perhaps not for a good long while—my heart is too heavy to write more. Mother, you were right about one thing—*

There the note ended. Without so much as a too-dle-oo or a signature. I reread it a few times over, not sure why the note made Lady Sheffield jump to the conclusion that the Nazis murdered her son. After putting the letter back in the drawer, I made my way downstairs. Lady Sheffield had hot cocoa ready—or something approximating chocolate. "Carob," she explained, grown in her own garden. It was better than any chocolate substitute I'd tried yet. Maybe I'd take some back to Mrs. Balson, the cook at Warfield Hall.

"What's the one thing?" I asked her, after taking a sip. The drink was so hot, my tongue stung.

"The what?"

"The one thing you were right about? Reggie wrote: *Mother, you were right about one thing.*"

"I only wish I knew," she said. "I was the sort of mother who was always giving advice. What he should wear, how he should have his hair cut… He might have been referring to a million things. I assumed he meant that I was right about Hitler. I'd seen this coming back in 1932, when a friend in Germany sent us a copy of that vile man's book—may his name be blotted out forever. That was long before anyone else in this country began taking the threat seriously."

I had a sudden thought: maybe she'd warned Reggie off Alice. I didn't like the woman one bit. And since I liked Lady Sheffield so much, it stood to reason that she didn't like Alice either. But I was wrong there—she'd given Alice the thumbs up from the beginning. Alice and her became pals even before Reggie showed up.

"Alice was perfect for Reggie," she said. "They had so much in common."

"Like what?" I asked.

"For one thing, they both loved to travel. *Wanderlust* is what you call it. Why, from the time Reggie was old enough to read, he gravitated to adventure novels and the memoirs of the great explorers: Richard Burton, Livingstone, and the like. Alice was the same. They were planning a round-the-world honeymoon once the war was over and it was safe to travel again. Reggie had a trust fund, you see. I was afraid he'd spend it gallivanting around the planet with Alice and have nothing left to support a family." She made one of those laughs that aren't funny. "And they both loved puzzles and mechanical things. Reggie was always building radios, and train sets, and—" She stopped to sniffle. "Most girls haven't the least interest, but Alice isn't like most girls."

I'd say.

When I finished my cocoa, my stomach began rebelling again and I asked to be excused. By then it was almost suppertime. Even though I was in no shape for food, I wondered if Daphne and me would be meeting Jack for supper.

Lady Sheffield was brokenhearted to see me go. "You may tell the warden that your sentence had been suspended," she said as I left. "Although I'd always welcome a visit."

I pulled up a few extra weeds on my way back to the main house, that's how sorry I felt for the lady.

CHAPTER FIFTEEN

"THERE YOU ARE," said Daphne, when I entered the back door and stepped into the kitchen at the main house. She was rinsing out teacups. "Geraldine will get us back into the base, and we can check and see if Jack has yet to return."

"Mount your saddles!" said Geraldine, bouncing down the stairs, back in uniform.

Alice was at the table, dressed like she'd been to church, even though I knew she'd played hooky. She was reading a newspaper and ignoring me as usual. Suddenly I realized that it might be the murder of her boyfriend that made her so grumpy. So I said, "Nice to see you Alice." She looked up and nodded her head.

We rolled down the driveway, me with the bicycle all to myself. That is, unless you counted Ringo, who was rolled up in the front basket. Daphne was sidesaddle on Geraldine's bike rack, clutching Geraldine's heavy military issued black leather briefcase.

We were almost to the base and nearing the front gate, when Daphne fell off the bicycle in one great thud. I was right behind—only my lightening-fast reflexes prevented me from running over her. I jumped off of my saddle and got on my knees next to her. Ringo began yelping and running around us in circles. Daphne's face was blue, and her eyes rolled around in her head. Beads of sweat dripped from her skin, even though the temperature was cold as an ice-cream pop. She gasped for air. When I took her hand, it trembled like a drunk gone off the wagon.

"I'll fetch a doctor," yelled Geraldine. "Tommy, you mind her."

"Daphne!" I said, "Say something!"

"I can't move my limbs," she said with a slurred, gasping voice. She stared straight up to the sky and whispered, "By all means marry," breathlessly. Then she conked out.

I slapped her face, like I seen in a movie once. All that did was make a red mark on her cheek. I grabbed her wrist and felt for a pulse. There was none. I prayed to Jesus, Joseph, and Mary—Saint Simon of Cyrene might not be high enough up the ladder. With no one there to see, I let myself tear up. My stomach began tumbling again, from the worry.

Thump. Thump. Her pulse was as slow as the chugging of a choo-choo train leaving the station. An ambulance raced in our direction, ringing its bells. Daphne's hand was in mine. It felt cold and clammy and still. Which worried me more than the tremor had. The ambulance stopped short and the back door swung open. Jack jumped out, along with two nurses. Geraldine came running along on foot, with Squadron Leader Kennard right behind her.

The nurses placed a mask on Daphne's face. Attached to the hose was an oxygen tank, the kind fitted into Spitfires. Jack lifted her onto the stretcher and helped carry the stretcher into the ambulance. No one spoke. My brother slammed the doors shut and jumped up onto the back bumper. The ambulance sped off toward the base hospital. The three of us trailed behind in the dusty tracks it made. Geraldine put her arm around my shoulder.

Squadron Leader Kennard said, "Food poisoning again."

I was no doctor, but Daphne didn't have the same symptoms as the others. They'd all vomited. She'd turned blue and passed out. Come to think of it, she didn't complain about her stomach, not once.

Squadron Leader Kennard signed me onto the base and we headed straight for the hospital. Jack sat on a bench outside the operating room. He was still wearing his flight uniform: parachute harness, helmet, and Mae West flotation vest. I sat next to him. Kennard took a seat on the other side of Jack. They both looked done in. At first, Jack didn't notice us. He was leaning over with his hands pressed to his eyes. Geraldine stood right in front of us. She reached into her briefcase and pulled out a small silver flask, handing it to Jack.

"She'll pull through," she said, without much gusto. Anyone who'd seen Daphne laying there on the road would expect to see her laid out in a coffin next.

"I don't get it," I said. "She was fine one minute, and then the next—"

"Did she say anything before she passed out?" asked my brother.

" 'By all means marry.' That's what she said."

"That's my girl," said my brother Jack, his eyes watering up.

"Why, I *do* believe she was quoting—" began Kennard, who was cut off when the doctor came out from the operating room.

"We're running tests," the doctor said. "The good news is that we have her breathing again. I'll say though, it was touch and go for a moment. She's on a respirator. We've gotten everything out of her stomach. Fortunately, we acted in good time. She'll stay with us overnight and we'll monitor her progress carefully."

"She said she couldn't move her limbs," I said.

"Is that so?" said the doctor. His face had the look of wheels turning. "Well, there's one piece of a puzzle, information that may be of use in making a diagnoses. You'll excuse me?" He raced off down the long corridor. The taps on his heels made clickety-clack sounds on the floor. We were all watching him go—like he was our last hope in the world. The doctor screeched to a halt, so that his shoes slid on the waxed floor. I was afraid he'd fall. He made a note on a clipboard and walked on, even faster.

The operating room door swung open and two medics wheeled Daphne past us. There were all sorts of tubes coming from her mouth and nose, and more tubes stuck in her arm and attached to bags of clear fluids. She was dressed in a green muumuu, and her eyes were shut.

Jack jumped to his feet, wringing his hands—I did the same thing; it was always that way when I was with my brother; if you didn't know any better, you'd think we were playing Simon Says. When we started following behind the stretcher, one of the medics told us to go to the waiting room. We found our way there, not saying a word.

"I'm starving," I said finally, not thinking. Jack looked over at me, as though to say, *How could you think of food at a time like this?*

"Actually," he said, "come to think of it, I'm famished myself. Haven't eaten so much as a crumb all day." He took my hand in his and squeezed hard. He didn't mean no harm, but it felt like he'd crush my fingers. "I don't want to leave her though," he said.

"See here," said Kennard, standing up quickly. "I'll take the motorbike into the village and bring us back supper. We can't trust the base fare, obviously. How does fish and chips sound to everyone? And perhaps a beer?"

"Make that two, sir," said Jack.

"Make that a soda pop for me," I said. "Sir…please."

"I have to report for duty, I'm afraid," said Geraldine. "I'll check back soon as I have a break."

"Jolly good," said Kennard, clapping his hands and trying hard to cheer us up. "Back in a jiffy then."

"A fella couldn't ask for a better commander," said Jack, once Kennard was gone. Then he moaned, "Oh, Daphne! Daphne!" Anyone could tell he was in agony. "When I get my hands on that base chef—"

I said, "When I get my hands on that chef!"

But I knew Daphne hadn't touched the base food. We'd been put off the stuff the second Geraldine vomited up her Marmite breakfast the morning we arrived.

Figuring I'd take Jack's mind off of our current problems, I said, "Get any Nazis today?" Jack always liked to talk about dogfights.

"We went on a Rhubarb over the Netherlands," he said. "Just Kennard and me. Gee whiz, that man knows how to fly a kite. I learn a lot going out with him. We were strafing minesweepers near Flushing. Peppered the heck out of several before we ran out of ammo and had to turn back. I wouldn't be at all surprised if a couple of those boats are at the bottom of the sea right now, the crew swimming toward Amsterdam."

"See any enemy aircraft out there?" I asked. I loved to hear about aerial combat. Some of Jack's adventures made the hair stand up on my head. More than usual, that is.

"Boy oh boy, did we!" said Jack, smiling. "Had a whole squadron on our tails all the way back to England. Caught a few bullets in my aileron—no worse than that. Shame of it is, we had no ammo left to take them on—not one bullet, unless you counted the ones in our service revolvers." He patted his holster. "But I wasn't about to let them get close enough for me to use it. Once again, our Spits got us out of a nasty scrape. Boy, that baby can boogie when she has to." He smiled but then his face dropped, thinking about Daphne, and that he might never dance the boogie-woogie with her again. Just when they were becoming expert jitterbuggers, too.

They'd recently entered their first contest, winning third prize: two tickets to a London play. The winners got orchestra seats and backstage passes. Second place got mezzanine and a coupon for the bar. Daphne and Jack were in the rafters getting nosebleeds. It was me who taught Daphne her first move: the rock-step.

"Say," said Jack. "Let's ask the nurse if we can sit in the room with Daphne."

The answer was a big fat no. "No visitors," said the nurse. "Not until the doctor allows."

We stepped outside and Jack bummed a cigarette off an airman who was going into the hospital carrying a bunch of flowers. I wondered if he was visiting a sick person, or dating one of the nurses. My money was on the nurse. Jack had quit cigarettes, all because Daphne didn't like the smell on his breath or the taste on his lips when they kissed. "I shouldn't," he said, striking the match. "But it calms my nerves." His hand shook as he touched the match to the end of the cigarette. "Gee, I don't get this rattled in a dogfight."

That made me think of something I'd been meaning to ask him. "How'd your Spitfire go down, anyway? Geraldine told us you said something like, 'The Germans didn't get me.'"

Jack took the cigarette from his mouth after one drag, threw it on to the pavement and pulverized the thing with the toe of his flight boot. "Aw—I don't want to break my promise to Daphne," he said, choked up. He reached into his pocket and took out a pack of chewing gum, offering me a piece. Once we both had the gum chewed up soft in our mouths, the conversation flowed again.

"Funny thing is, I wasn't shot down by the Messerschmitt chasing me. I'd bet my life on it. I had just gained altitude and was about to flip the Spit over, so as I could come up on his tail, when the engine began misfiring. I saw the speedometer needle jolt. Then: chug, chug. I thought, *What bad timing!* I remembered Wilson telling me that he'd just changed all the spark plugs. Heck, I saw him doing it with my own eyes.

"Then the Spit began losing speed and I heard a small explosion—from *inside* the engine. By then, I was out of firing range of enemy aircraft." Jack chewed his gum with his mouth open. I did the same. "Before I knew what had happened, the engine was in flames. Kennard came alongside of me and saw the fire. He radioed, ordering me to gain enough altitude for a bailout. The Spit had just enough life left in her to take one last climb. I took Daphne's photo from the instrument panel, kissed the throttle goodbye and jumped. I was sure sorry to see her fly off without me."

"What could'a gone wrong?" I asked.

Jack took off his leather flight helmet and scratched his head. I scratched my head too. Obviously, he had no idea: "As soon as I got back to the base, I went to have a talk with Wilson. He showed me the log where he'd recorded the maintenance. Sure enough, he'd replaced the plugs the day before and had gone over everything with a fine-tooth comb. He's good at his job—darn good, even if it's one he doesn't want."

"Why's that?" I asked.

"He wants to be a pilot is why. Heck, he *is* a pilot. Had more hours in before the war than any of the Americans in the squadron. Between you and me, most of us cooked our flight logs before we headed up to Canada to enlist. Some of us had barely soloed. But Wilson—now, he'd logged over a hundred hours in solo flight. Some of that on Hurricanes! But the RAF was short of expert mechanics and Wilson had been working for Hawker Aviation as a maintenance mechanic. He knew a Hurricane left and right, inside and out. They needed Wilson to train up others to be aviation mechanics. Had him training lorry drivers and London cabbies. Meanwhile, us wet behind the ear Yank kids are going up to Canada and jumping into flight school."

"Does seem like a rotten deal," I said.

"That's just it. Now that we have the Spits, Wilson wants his shot and who can blame him? I don't know what I'd do if I had to watch us taking off everyday and having to hear our glory stories at the end of every op. The whole time being stuck on the ground with a wrench in my hand, knowing that I was just as qualified—no, better qualified—than anyone. Like you said, it ain't fair. A lot of the other fellas feel the same. We think he should have a shot at flying."

Jack stopped talking long enough to blow a huge bubble. When it popped, there was gum plastered all over his face. I gave a hoot, scaring a nurse who was walking into the building. Jack, with gum still stuck to his cheek, opened the door. The nurse giggled, batting her eyelashes. "Why, thank you, Lieutenant. How thoughtful." Jack was having none of it and turned his attention to me.

"Let's go bug the head nurse into letting us see Daphne," he said. "And if she has the nerve to turn us down again—"

"We'll sneak in," I said, finishing his thought.

"Thatta boy. Thinking just like a Mooney, you are."

I chewed my gum and tried to make a bubble the way Jack had, but it was a no go. I'd have to practice.

CHAPTER SIXTEEN

A CURTAIN BLOCKED our view of the nurse's station, where a few minutes before we'd been ordered to leave the hospital. Our backs were pressed to the wall.

"That's the best thing about being an officer," my brother said, "I don't have to take orders from that nurse, no siree. I outrank her."

"Then why are we hiding behind this door?" I whispered. Jack didn't answer my question. He just shrugged.

It was time to create a diversion, one of my specialities. It was as simple as going outside, finding an unlocked window leading into an unoccupied room, and start moaning and groaning. Then I leapt out the window, sprinted back into the front entrance and motioned for my brother to join me in the dash past the nurse's station. Before you could say *Stop!*, we were looking at Daphne. All sorts of monitors were connected to her. One showed her heartbeat, zigzag lines, all the same size, a pulse of 95 beats a minute. We were happy to see that.

"Thank God her ticker's working," I said. "But as for the rest of her—"

Daphne was always neat as a pin, but now her hair

was a rat's nest and her skin pasty white. Without lipstick on, she looked anemic.

Jack, a brave man in most circumstances, was a train wreck. He steadied himself by gripping the metal bed frame, covering his embarrassment by grabbing a clipboard hanging from the bedpost. I ducked under his arm so that I could read the doctor's notes and hold him up at the same time.

"Suspected poisoning!" I said, a little too loudly.

"And do you notice that it doesn't say *food* poisoning?" said Jack. He dropped the clipboard and it slammed against the bed frame. Just has he took Daphne's hand in his, the duty nurse came running into the room squawking like a goose and threatening to call the MPs. Those are the dreaded military police—the English equivalent of the Gestapo. We knew it was time to leave.

We were escorted back to the waiting room, the nurse threatening us with a hypodermic needle. The waiting room smelled like a fish and chip shop. Squadron Leader Kennard waited with two greasy bags, beer bottles sticking from his trouser pockets. When he saw me, he turned around. And there, peeking from his back pocket, was a bottle of Strike Cola.

"You're okay, sir," said Jack. I seconded the motion.

"My pleasure," said Kennard, as I removed the soda bottle, opening the top by hitting it against a metal chair. Jack took the two beer bottles and opened the caps against each other. The nurse came rushing at us, waving her arms wildly, all hell's bells. Like one man, we made a dash out the front entrance, where we could sit on the steps and eat our supper in peace.

"Poisoning," said Jack to Squadron Leader Kennard. "Who would poison Daphne?"

"Isn't it obvious?" I said. They both stared at me, each with a chip in his hand. "A Nazi agent. Maybe the same Nazi who killed Lady Sheffield's son Reginald. I bet he died of poisoning, too. Maybe the same Nazi who threw me into the Frigidaire yesterday, and the same one who poisoned the mess food, and the same one who tripped Sel and the other pilots."

"You don't say?" said Kennard, snickering. "Any suspects?"

"Yonkers, for one," I said. "Ever notice his lighter?"

My voice was drowned out by the sound of an air-raid siren. Jack and Kennard stuffed fish and chips into their mouths, not knowing when their next meal might come. I'd already finished mine.

"Tommy, get into the shelter," said Jack, pointing to an Anderson shelter just outside the building. It looked like a dog kennel. I didn't mind putting Ringo in there but not myself. Already there were too many people cramming into it. "Now!" he yelled, giving me the heave-ho. Before I could explain about Yonkers and the lighter, Kennard hopped onto a motorbike and was kicking the starter with the rubber heel of his flight boot. Jack put his flight helmet back onto his head and jumped on the back. Bomber engines grinded overhead, ready to make mincemeat of us.

"Daphne!" said Jack, getting off the motorbike. "Sir, I'll follow you."

"Don't be daft, Mooney! They have orderlies and an evacuation procedure. You'll be a better help to her up there." He pointed to the sky. Jack hesitated. Kennard said, "That's an order, Pilot!" We heard the first of several explosions, too close for comfort. "Get on, this moment!" said Kennard. Jack had to obey.

As they rode off toward the airfield, I yelled, "Don't worry Jack! I'll take care of her!" But I don't think he heard me over the ruckus.

A German bomber flew so low the hospital windows rattled. I took three stairs at a time and then ran down the long corridor headed to Daphne's room. The corridor seemed twice the length as it had been. A bomb hit the far side of the building, not close enough to kill me, but near enough that asbestos tiles dropped from the ceiling onto my head. My ears started ringing and then went quiet, same as what happens when you drive down a Adirondack mountain pass. When I got to Daphne's room, she was still laid out in the bed. Lucky for me, the bed was on wheels. I began rolling it to the door. The problem was they'd attached her to machines and tanks and I was scared. If I pulled the wrong plug, that would be the end of her.

I started bawling, with no one around to see me. I didn't want to let Daphne or my brother down. But the truth was, I didn't have first aid training beyond the basics needed to earn a Boy Scout badge. I could make a splint, staunch bleeding by pressing down on the wound and raising the limb above the heart. I could wrap an ACE bandage around an arm until it looked like a mummy. But Daphne's situation was way more specialized than anything I'd faced in Cub Scouts.

"Help!" I yelled at the top of my lungs.

Two medics came into the room, along with the duty nurse. I stood there while they unhooked Daphne and then wheeled her—along with the oxygen tank—out the door. They'd turned the bed into a stretcher by folding the legs under. In that way, they carried Daphne down a flight of stairs and into a basement shelter. I followed close behind. Already there were other patients down there, all wearing matching green muumuus.

A pilot from Jack's squadron saw me right away. He turned around and bent over so that his muumuu opened at the back. Then he wiggled his hairy backside at me. That took the tears right out of my eyes. The basement walls shook when another bomb fell somewhere close. I stopped laughing and grabbed hold of Daphne's hand. In all the confusion, I'd grabbed her big toe. It did the trick though, or maybe it was the sound of the bomb detonating. In any case, she came to.

"Jack?" she said, looking at me. I was the spitting image of my brother.

"Calm yourself, Daphne," I said, taking her hand this time. It was a very British thing to say. She shut her eyes and didn't respond, even when I shook her and shouted in her ear. I didn't mean to shout, it was just that the Germans were making a real mess of the hospital above us and it was the only way to be heard. "Daphne! Wake up!"

A nurse came over and took Daphne's hand from

me, feeling for a pulse. Then she wrapped a blood pressure monitor around Daphne's arm and pumped the rubber ball, looking at the needle as it moved around a small dial. "She'll be fine," said the nurse.

"Really? You're not just saying that to cheer me up?"

"I'd say your friend has as much chance of surviving this night as any of us. That's my considered opinion, for what it's worth."

Another bomb hit. Dust and dirt fell from the low ceiling, onto our heads. Two rats scurried out from under a cabinet. A few of the nurses saw them and began wailing like banshees. They were more terrified of the rats than of the Germans, if you ask me. People started coughing because of all the dust.

Then things settled down a bit. Before long, we heard an all-clear siren. A man shouted down: "Everyone tip-top down there?"

The head nurse swung her flashlight around the space, taking an account. That was when I realized the lights had gone out: a blackout—I loved blackouts. The nurse cupped her hands around her mouth, making a megaphone. "All present and accounted for, sir!"

"Remain where you are," said the man, who I figured was with the Home Guard. "Must assess the damage first, make sure things are safe up here."

"There are rats!" cried one of the nurses. "Let us up!"

"Now, now," said the head nurse. "No need to go off the rails. They don't like you any more than you like them. Please get control of yourself, sister."

Sister? I didn't know the nurses were nuns. That explained a lot of things.

Some of the nurses stood on wooden crates, not realizing that a rat can climb a ten-story apartment building if it wants. I took a seat on the floor, hoping a rat would jump out. Being from New York, I wasn't the least afraid of them. More rats in New York than people, and some of them bigger than cats.

"When will this war end?" said one of the nurses standing on the crate. "It's one thing after another. I'm fed up to here." She made a motion against her neck.

"Get a hold of yourself," repeated the head nurse, slapping the younger one across the face when she began wailing again.

"Clear to come up," said the Home Guard man, who came down the stairs carrying a lantern. "One at a time, and no rushing, mind you. We've cleared a path to the exit. Single file, if you would."

All the English folks stepped in line, *queuing up* as they say, in as orderly a line as was possible in the cramped basement. The American pilot cut in front, but the nurse made sure Daphne's stretcher went up first. She ordered the pilot to take one end of the stretcher, even with his plaster cast leg.

What a mess. Part of the roof had caved in and there was rubble everywhere you looked. We were instructed to watch our steps, the Home Guard pointing out obstacles in our path. A fireman pointed a hose through a broken window and gave us a good soaking.

"The hospital experienced a near miss. A direct hit on one of the outbuildings," said the Home Guard man, waving his fist in the air. "They're not supposed to drop bombs on a hospital. It's against the rules. Hague Convention and all."

"But how can they tell a hospital from any other building?" I asked, not that I wanted to defend the Luftwaffe.

"Why, it's got a big red cross painted on the roof, laddy."

"But it's nighttime, sir. And besides, Nazis don't follow the rules."

"You got it right there," said a nurse, stepping over a fallen beam.

We made it out to the front where two ambulances waited. "We're taking your friend to the public hospital," said the head nurse, looking at me. "You'll inform your brother, Lieutenant Mooney?"

I asked if I could come along, but she refused. When the ambulance pulled away, I had a sudden realization that something was missing.

Ringo!

CHAPTER SEVENTEEN

I COULDN'T REMEMBER the last time I seen Ringo, the squadron mascot. I knotted my eyebrows, hoping that would jog my memory. When that didn't work, I rubbed at the bridge of my nose like Lord Sopwith. That worked: I seen her yelping and running around in circles, right after Daphne passed out. *Hours ago.* Did she follow us back to the base? I didn't think so.

I had to find her before Squadron Leader Kennard returned and asked after her. My whole body stiffened like a sphinx. Ringo would end up like the goldfish, floating on the top of the fishbowl, belly up, her body slimy and beginning to stink. I walked in the direction of the front gate, hoping that maybe the guard had seen her. Or that maybe I'd see a trail of pee, the way slugs leave trails of slime behind them.

"Seen a stray mutt?" I asked the duty soldier, who was listening to a news broadcast on a radio in a dented car parked next to the gate. He jumped when he seen me and turned the volume to a whisper. I figured radio listening was against regulations: dereliction of duty, they call it.

"Shush," he said when he realized he had nothing

to worry about. He tuned the dial, so that the reception was clearer. A newscaster was telling the country about the attack on the base. We were famous. I hoped that my ma back in New York got the signal, but maybe it was better if she didn't. It would worry her sick, thinking that she'd get a telegram bringing bad news. She'd think I was fine, holed up at the Warfield Hall with the Sop-withs. But she'd worry about Jack, stop eating, light extra candles at Saint Brendan's until she got news that he'd survived the attack. The newscaster had one of them low pitched voices of people who smoked ten packs a day:

"No casualties have been reported thus far, in a raid on Southend-on-Sea naval and RAF bases this evening. A military hospital received heavy damage however, an-other dastardly act by the German aggressors. And this just in: We are happy to report that a counterattack by the RAF has resulted in a downed Dornier bomber. It is believed that all of its crew has been captured—having bailed from the fiery furnace of what was once one of Hitler's deadliest weapons, now consigned to the scrap pile. All and all, a good night for Britain."

"A good night for Britain?" said the soldier, shak-ing his head. "Is 'e joking? This ain't my idea of a good night. Duckin' ten-ton bombs full of TNT? Wha'd you say about a dog?"

"Have you seen a small dog. A short hair mutt? Probably left a trail of pee?"

"Can't say as I 'ave, mate."

I walked out the front gate and then turned around: "Say, you'll remember me if I come back into the base, won't you? I mean, I've been signed in already. But now I have to search for the dog. It belongs to the squadron leader. She's the mascot." I explained how a mascot brought luck to the squadron, that the original word meant *lucky charm* in Latin, or maybe that was Greek. I showed him my one-leaf clover, glued to a card, three clumps of glue where the missing leaves had been. "We need that dog," I said, telling him that if I didn't find Ringo, worse things might happen to the base.

"Search and rescue, are you? They must be short 'anded tonight." He laughed. "Sure. I'll remember you. But I can't say what 'appens when I go off duty in—" He looked at his wristwatch. "—six hours and twenty minutes from now."

I walked down the dark road, stopping were Daphne fell. Leaning against a chain-link fence was the bicycle I'd been riding. In New York, that bike would've been stolen by now. That made me remember my Schwinn Camelback, the bicycle I'd left at the Brooklyn Harbor months before when I ran away from home to search for my brother. The English bike was a clunker and no match for the Schwinn. Besides, it was a girl's bike—the kind with a lowered top bar so you could get on wearing a skirt, which I had no intention of doing. It was embarrassing riding a bicycle like that. Still, I was in no position to complain. I was glad it was still there and that I wouldn't have to hoof it. I was getting dog-tired by then, because I'd gotten no sleep the night before—what with the lovebirds on my couch and church being at an ungodly hour, as usual.

I yelled out Ringo's name and waited for the sound of happy dog panting. But I was disappointed: the only thing I heard was an owl hoot. The dog was threatening to take my sister Mary's place as the thorn in my flesh, the bane of my existence. Why, Mary hadn't pestered me much since I left New York. Just one snide comment written on the back of a letter from my ma. *Take your time getting home*, she'd scribbled. My ma crossed it out, but Mary's words stayed legible, barely. Her penmanship was dismal.

I pedaled down the road, screaming Ringo's name until my throat was sore and my voice sounded like a BBC newscaster. Coming around a tight bend, I avoided a head-on collision with a car.

"Watch yourself, you pillock!" yelled the driver, with his closed fist threatening me. Tough guy.

"Stuff it!" I yelled back.

His headlights were masked, which was the problem—not the fact that I'd been riding in the middle of the road pretending to be an airplane. Soon I made it back to Jack's mess. All the lights were out, or at least the blackout curtains made it seem that way. I was hoping Ringo found her way home like a pigeon. Dogs do that sometimes. I once read in the paper about a Labrador who went on a cross-country trip with his family. They kept him in the teardrop travel trailer they'd hitched to the back of a Chevy. But some idiot left a window open and he jumped out. This happened somewhere between Reno, Nevada and Frisco, California. So the dog was good and lost and likely to die of either thirst or starvation. The family gave up and drove back to New Jersey, crying the whole way. But then a few months later, they woke to find the dog sleeping next to the milk crate. His paws were blistered and he had a permanent limp after that. Skin sagged from his skeleton. Chewed off fur. Cuts and abrasions and one missing eye. Seemed he'd fought every stray cat along Route 66.

The front door to Jack's mess was locked. I walked around the whole building calling out for Ringo. Then I heard a growl coming from inside the kitchen. I tried to peer in, but without a flashlight it was impossible. When I called Ringo's name again, she barked. I had to find some way in, fatten the dog up with pie or something before Kennard suspected anything. Circling back around to the front, I tried windows but they'd been locked. Arched windows, leading into the dining room, were blocked by shrubs. I had to wedge underneath, getting scratched by branches and pointed Christmas-type holly leaves.

As I stood up between the shrub and a stucco wall, a shot of pain went up my foot—agony all the way to my head. A shard of glass had pierced the sole of my sneaker near my big toe. Reaching down, I pulled the glass from the shoe and removed my sneaker to get a look at the damage. Blood gushed all over my white sock, black in the moonlight. The window glass had been smashed near the latch. *One of the fellas forgot his key,* is what went through my mind. Like a fool, I was.

I brushed broken glass from the window sill with a big leaf, then leapfrogged into the house. Ringo came charging up to me, licking my bloody toes. It would be no one's fault but my own if she started chewing on my foot like it was a sirloin steak: dogs are carnivores. I thought, *I'd better go into the kitchen and find the stash of dog food.* Honest to God, that's all that was on my mind.

I wiggled the kitchen light switch, but the power was out. Stumbling toward a sideboard, I felt around like a blind man until I found a candlestick and a box of matches next to it. I struck the match just as a hand clasped over my mouth.

"*Ruhig,*" whispered a voice in my ear.

All I could see, before the match burnt out, was the edge of a black cuff. An embroidered band ran full circle around it. Woven in silver thread was the ominous name: Jagdgeschwader Mölders.

It was the name of Germany's top ace, who shot down at least a hundred RAF planes. His name was worn as a badge of honor by Luftwaffe pilots wanting to be like him. Just the way kids back home swung bats with the names of their favorite World Series champions carved in the wood. My eyes were adjusting to the darkness, helped by a beam of moonlight coming into the window above a porcelain sink. The crystal face of an IWC German Luftwaffe pilot's wristwatch gleaned near my right eye. If I won this battle, I was keeping the watch.

"Yonkers—I know it's you," I said.

"*Ruhig,*" he whispered again, telling me to shut up. Yonkers dragged me to a chair, tying me up using dishrags. I wasn't happy about how things were shaping up.

Ringo started jumping up at Yonkers, growling fiercely and trying to take bites from his leg. Yonkers cussed in German and kicked the dog in the stomach. Ringo let out a moan that sounded like a death knell.

"You won't get away with—" I said as a sponge was shoved into my mouth. The last thing I saw, before a wet dishrag was tied across my eyes, was Ringo being grabbed by the scruff of her little neck and flung across the room, colliding with a garbage bin. I was pretty sure Yonkers had murdered the dog. The room was dead silent again. I felt awfully bad for Ringo. She'd been the squadron mascot, after all. At least I wouldn't be blamed when Squadron Leader Kennard lowered her limp body, crammed in a shoebox, into a shallow grave.

My ears were the only part of my head still unobstructed. I listened and heard the sound of creaking linoleum, as Yonkers walked in the direction of the icebox. I heard the sucking rubber of the door opening, milk bottles being moved around. Then the sound of chewing. *My God, how could he think of food at a time like this*, I thought.

"*Besser*," he sighed. Better. He burped.

Where are your manners? I wanted to say, but the gag prevented me.

He was opening and closing cabinets, throwing things onto the floor then gathering them up. Into a sack? I couldn't be sure. *He's making a run for it*, I realized, knowing I was on to him—that I'd been one bloody step away from blowing the whistle. I squirmed around in the chair, in a wasted effort at loosening my bonds.

Yonkers knew how to tie a knot. He'd probably been in the Hitler Youth or whatever they had over there in the Fatherland.

My heart started racing when I heard a motorbike driving down the road leading to the house. I prayed it wouldn't pass by and that maybe it was my brother and Kennard returning from their mission. I prayed in Latin, too. The engine noise grew louder, the sound of a BSA backfiring. Yonkers heard it too. He stood still, all ears. Tires rolled on the gravel driveway. Yonkers made a run for it then. His heavy flight boots stomped down the hall corridor and into the dining room where I'd left the window open, giving him easy access to the backyard and forest behind.

I wiggled with all my might, trying to scream. But my cry was muffled by the dish sponge stuck between my teeth. It tasted like rotten potatoes.

The front door opened. There was a beat before my brother said, "I'll check the fuse box, sir."

"Whiskey and soda?" said Squadron Leader Kennard, all casual. "We've earned a stiff drink tonight—a little celebration is in order, I should think."

"Won't say no to that," said Jack.

Enough with the drinking! I thought. *Think food!*

I heard Kennard yell, "Could do with a sandwich. You in?" Just as I'd wished.

Through the edge of the skewed blindfold, I knew Jack had managed to get the electricity working again.

"What in the world?" Kennard said, standing in the doorway and taking in a view of the kitchen. "Ringo!" he cried, not even noticing me. "Oh, dear, dear girl."

What about dear, dear, Tommy—tied up and the life seeping out of the gash in his foot?

"Tommy?" I heard my brother say. "What the heck?"

The blindfold came off of my eyes and the sponge from out of my mouth. "He's getting away!" I shouted.

"Who?" said Kennard. Ringo was cradled in his arms.

"Yonkers!" I shouted. "Untie my hands, Jack."

Behind Kennard, a black shadow moved down the dark hallway. Light from a bare lightbulb hanging from the ceiling fell onto the shadow's face, which was now right behind the squadron leader—within striking distance.

"Him!" I shouted when I seen it was Yonkers.

"What's going on in here?" he said. He stepped around Kennard and stood in the center of the room. "Jeez Louise, what a mess, kid."

By then my hands and feet were free and I lunged at him, trying to knock him to the ground. But he was like an ancient oak tree, the kind with names carved into the trunk. He reached down and grabbed me by the scruff of my neck, lifting me from the ground like I was a piece of fluff on a bird's underside.

"Whatta 'ya in all in a huff about, anyways?" he said. "And with me helping you to get home to yer mom."

He put me down, planting his two legs a couple feet apart and crossing his arms over his chest—daring me to take another shot. My eyes were about level with his wrist and I seen he was wearing an RAF issued Omega watch; my brother had one just like it. Yonkers was in an RAF flight uniform: a fleece-lined leather jacket flung over his shoulders. I was close enough to feel the cold coming off the leather.

"What's gotten into your head, Tommy?" said Jack.

"I think I owe Yonkers here an apology," I said. Then looking up to Yonkers: "I thought you were a Nazi. It was the lighter—your Nazi Zippo."

Jack slouched in the chair, pulling off his helmet and raking his fingers through his long bangs. "Yonkers?" he said. "Is that your nickname for Pete? Pete O'Reilly? Whose folks are fresh off the boat immigrants like Ma and Da?"

"Fresh off the boat, ya know?" said Yonkers, grinning wide. "County Cork." He loosened his posture.

"And for crying out loud, Tommy. We've all got lighters just the same," said Jack, reaching into his pocket and showing me his. It was exactly like Yonkers' only more dented. Squadron Leader Kennard reached into his back pocket, removing another one. The three of them flicked the lighters until they flamed. The room smelled like lighter fluid. Jack patted his front pocket, an old habit.

"Souvenirs," he said. "I got mine in France."

"Then I hate to tell you this, but a genuine Nazi just made a break for the woods. He was in uniform. Luftwaffe. He was *sprechening* the Deutch." I raised an eyebrow toward the back door.

"You're not pulling our legs, are you?" asked Jack. " 'Cause if you are—"

"Do you honesty think I tied myself to the chair?" I was acting indignant, which was what the situation called for. "He had a Jagdgeschwader Mölders cuff-band," I said, drawing a line across my left wrist. It was that detail, I think, convinced them. Even I couldn't make something like that up.

"Jumping Jehoshaphat," said Jack, hitting his forehead. "From the Dornier crew, no doubt."

"No," said Kennard. "A Jagdgeschwader Mölders insignia is on the uniform of Luftwaffe squadron 51. That means the FW-190 you shot at went down."

"Congratulations, Jack," said Yonkers, patting my brother's back. "What does that make it, seven?"

"You think it was Werner Mölders himself who tied me up?" I asked, wide-eyed.

"Nothing doing," said Jack. "Mölders bought it when a Heinkel He 111 bomber he was a passenger on went down in a thunderstorm last year. They say one of the engines failed. When your number is up, your number is up." Jack was as happy as a camper with a bag of marshmallows and a stick. "Still—a FW-109 *and* a Dornier in one night. Not too shabby."

"It *is* a good night for Britain," I said, quoting the BBC newscaster.

"And Ireland," said Yonkers, smiling at me. "Don't forget the old country, ya know?"

Kennard handed me the broken body of Ringo. I could feel her tiny dog heart beating against my arm. Believe it or not, it made my own heart leap. The three men went storming out the door leading to the backyard. I wanted to go after them, but my foot hurt like all get-out. Ringo howled.

"Okay pooch," I said. "Let's get you and me to the nuns."

As I headed for the front door, I heard the kitchen door open and then slam shut. Jack called out for me. "I lost my head there for a second," he said. "Let the other fellas go chasing after Nazis, I've got my girl to look after. And you, Tommy-boy. What'd you do to that foot?"

I told him all about the direct hit on the hospital and he turned white as a sheet.

"She's safe. I made sure of it," I said. "Not to brag or anything, but you might say I saved her bacon tonight." My brother hugged me to him and then took a step back and saluted. Then he made me put my arm around him as I limped to the motorbike.

I mounted first and took the laundry basket holding Ringo. Jack shot straight through the gears and within seconds my hair was whipped off my face. We rocketed down the country road toward the base, flying over potholes and taking corners so fast the foot-pedal scraped the gravel a couple of times. I figured I'd get Ringo patched up, have my foot looked at, and then report the loose Luftwaffe pilot to the MPs.

Maybe now someone would take me seriously.

CHAPTER EIGHTEEN

MI5 Headquarters,
Wormwood Scrubs, East London

THERE IS A KNOCK on the door, three quick taps.

"Good evening, sir," says Ellis. "Working late again, I see. Thought I'd pop around before pushing off—bring you up to date on the latest citizen report."

"What now?" says Brigadier A.W.A. Harker, Deputy Director General of MI5.

"It came in the evening post." Ellis holds up a letter. "Shall I read it to you, sir?"

"Paraphrase, would you?" says Harker. "I was just about to head home myself."

"It's from a woman in Cornwell. At least, I think it's a woman by the look of the handwriting. The name is Frances, which I suppose settles the question. I mean Frances, ending in E.S. Rather than Francis ending in I.S.—which would have indicated a letter sent by a male citizen." Ellis holds the envelope to his nose, as if there might be a whiff of perfume to prove his point. "She reports that several bicycles have gone missing during the last month. The police, it seems, are satisfied that it's the work of juveniles—pranksters, sir. I've already had a word with them. Frances McAllister, she believes otherwise. She is convinced that Nazi agents are making their way from their drop points by bicycle."

Hacker wipes his brow with a handkerchief and then refolds it into a tidy square before returning it to his pocket. "Who do they think we are—Miss Marple? Amateur sleuths? Send off the boilerplate response thanking Mrs. McAllister for her vigilance."

Ellis shuffles the letter to the bottom of a short stack. "I suppose you'd like me to do the same with the others, sir?"

Hacker coughs into his hand, the sort of cough that signals the end of a conference. Ellis doesn't seem to get the hint. "You'll be pleased to know, sir, that we've solved the mystery of the suspicious foreigners, overheard speaking German in a pub over in Chelsea. If you recall, it was a barmaid who made the report. I decided to take the initiative on that one. Did the surveillance myself. I wouldn't mention it but for the bar tab. I have it here along with a reimbursement form number 3674. If you could just initial it, sir." Ellis steps forward and lays a form on Hacker's desk.

Hacker glances at the receipt, paperclipped to the form. He says, "£10.5! Are you mad?"

"It was a long few nights until the suspects returned, sir."

"Did you at least round up a ring of Nazi spies, Ellis?"

"No, sir. It appears that the suspects were pilots of

the RAF, wearing civvies. From Czech Fighter Squadron 310, to be exact."

Hacker waves a hand toward the door. "Close it when you leave, Ellis," he says.

CHAPTER NINETEEN

WHEN WE PULLED UP to the hospital, Jack said, "Holy tomato." Only he said it like an Englishman—*toe-mat-oh*—no "ay" in sight. I could see why our ma wanted him transferred back to the States.

I heard stories about London during the Blitz: houses knocked to the ground, people trapped under piles of crumbled bricks, folks searching through rubble hoping to find their pets—and treasures, let's not forget about treasure: ladies crying over their broken pottery and burnt up music boxes, clawing through debris looking for their cameo pins and diamond tiaras. Men crying over shattered radio sets, with no way to hear the cricket matches except to go to a pub. 18-karat wristwatches and emerald-studded tie pins deep under the ruins of what once was their castle.

Seemed like heaven for a treasure hunter, if you stuck to the upper crust neighborhoods like Mayfair, where my guardians for the duration—the Sopwiths—once had a townhouse. In that neighborhood, a fella could find jewels once belonging to Maharajas, candelabras lit by Marie Antoinette, chairs sat on by Mr. Chippendale himself. And don't forget about strongboxes filled with pound sterling notes and rare stamps. Almost made you hope for another good attack on London. Not that I wanted anyone killed, of course not. Good heavens, no.

But then Lord Sopwith had to go and squash my enthusiasm by telling me that the Home Guard had the power to arrest treasure hunters. *Looters*, he called them. In fact, a couple of looters got plugged by an irate home-owner, driven to violence at the sight of them looters making off with the monogramed family silver.

The base hospital looked like how I imagined London during the Blitz. Everyone had been evacuated. Army tents were being set up on the lawn. Nurses rummaged through the rubble, salvaging anything of value before a big rainstorm came along and turned the Band-Aids to pulp. We spotted the head nurse in one of the tents, sorting through boxes of medicine and bandages—the same nurse who'd chased us out of the hospital earlier. Jack asked her where they'd taken Daphne. Then he raced out of the tent, leaving me behind. "Make him stay here," he yelled back, ordering the nurse to be my jailer. The roar of the motorbike grew faint before I even thought to protest.

The nurse looked down at me. She was over six-feet tall and wore white stockings and matching wood-heeled clogs that could wound anyone who got in their way. "What a night," she said, taking me into her confidence. "While we've succeeded in evacuating the patients to a nearby hospital, we must be prepared to receive new patients—should one of our RAF or naval crew return from duty wounded. It *does* happen, my dear."

"Burns, right?" This was my greatest fear. I knew my ma lost plenty of sleep after she read about the American flyer, Billy Fiske was his name. His hands were too burnt to slide the canopy open and jump out. This was the stuff of nightmares.

The nurse waved her hand around the tent. "This reminds me of the Great War. I was a field nurse in Northern France, very near to the front. The Somme— oh, it gives me the willies to think about it."

"A lot of blood and guts, huh?"

"We operated from a tent not unlike this one. I was only recently out of training—merely a girl. Well, let's pray we shan't have to operate in here. That was ghastly. We had to amputate men's legs with only a kerosene lamp for illumination. And once when we ran out of anesthesia…oh my, I shouldn't be telling a boy this… but—" She paused.

"The screams," I said. "It must've been terrible for you." My voice was shaky, and my stomach was doing the jitterbug again, but I wanted the gory details and she was willing to give them.

"Some nights there would be a pile of limbs stacked outside the tent door, no one available to take them to the incinerator." She put my wounded foot in her lap and peeled back the bloody sock. "Perhaps some of those legs and arms might have stayed attached to a body, if we'd had a proper facility. Makes me shiver just thinking about it." She made her whole body wiggle; she had some extra poundage and it reminded me of a bowl of jelly. "God forbid it should come to that again."

"Are you a nun?" I asked, getting ready to run. I'd had my fair share of run-ins with Sister Bridget at Saint Brendan's Catholic School back in New York. The thought of her still made the hair stand up on my head.

"No, no. What ever gave you that idea?"

"You said, 'let's pray,' for one thing. And 'God forbid.' And earlier I heard you call one of the other nurses *sister*."

"I suppose that term is left over from the days when all nurses were nuns—in the Middle-Ages. But not me, luv. I'm widowed with three grown children, and a grandchild on the way. I'm a Methodist, and we haven't got nuns. Between you and me, I'm on the lookout for husband number two. Now, that brother of yours is right handso—"

I had to stop her. "Jack's twenty-two-years-old, for crying out loud! He's about to get hitched to Daphne. Remember her—your patient?"

"Oh, well. So be it." She dabbed her lips with a handkerchief: one of the ways ladies cover their embarrassment. Since they were short of patients at the moment, I asked if she was willing to look at Ringo.

"I'm a dog lover, bring him in," she said. But as I limped out of the tent to retrieve Ringo from the basket, she cried out, "Come back and let me see to your foot first. *Boys before dogs,* that's my motto."

"Oh, I'll hold," I said, continuing on my way. Ringo was in critical condition.

The nurse took me by the shoulders, turned me around and led me back into the tent. "Prop your foot up on this chair, and I'll fetch your dog. He doesn't bite, does he?" Opening the tent flap, she cried out, "The pitiful little puppy!" She'd been a nasty piece of work earlier in the day, when all we wanted to do was visit Daphne, but now she was bending-over-backwards nice. That's what a near death experience does to people. It wasn't the first time I'd seen it happen.

I sat in the chair, raising my foot so it rested on a cot, glad to be off of it. The nurse returned carrying Ringo and wagging an unlacquered fingernail at me. "You oughtn't to have brought a dog into hospital, you know. Had you obeyed the rules and tied her up outside, she wouldn't have been hurt in the bombing."

"That dog was tortured by a real live Nazi," I said.

"Get out!" She put a hand to her heart.

"He bailed from his fighter plane and is loose on the base, probably torturing women and children as we speak."

"No! How dreadful." She was terrified, shooting a look around the tent and thinking the Luftwaffe pilot would jump out and murder us. "This is exactly like France!" she said. "We shan't be safe in our beds tonight."

I forced her to fix up Ringo first: I was *that* brave. Or maybe it was that I knew what was coming, and wanted to put it off. While we talked, she injected Ringo with a sedative, then reset a broken leg, putting a couple of stitches to a cut above Ringo's pointy nose. Ringo laid out on her back with her tongue hanging out, with a splinted leg shooting straight up in the air.

"Are you aware of the fact that your dog has fleas?"

asked the nurse. "I'm afraid there's nothing I can do for it—I've never had a patient with fleas before tonight. Worms, yes, but never fleas."

"I had worms just last week. The cook where I'm staying said they probably came with the lettuce."

"We've all had them, luv, and that's the truth. Although some are too proud to admit it in polite company."

"That's not us, though!" I said.

The nurse laughed her head off. I did too...until she uncapped a bottle of alcohol, poured it over my foot, threaded a needle, and began stitching.

Once I recovered from the shock of the operation, the nurse introduced herself. "I'm Sister Hopkins. Lieutenant Hopkins, that is. Only senior officers may call me Hopkins. You may call me Auntie, if you like."

"Why would I do that? You're not my aunt."

"Now you rest back on this cot I've just made up and take a wee rest. I can't release you until your charming brother returns." She fluffed a pillow and placed it behind my head, then found a blanket and threw it over me, tucking in the ends just like my ma would've done.

I was so tired by then, I dropped right off. The next time I opened my eyes, Sister Hopkins was gone. In her place was a younger version, a carbon copy of the actress Carole Lombard. She was asleep in a chair with a magazine on her lap, and paying no attention to me. Ringo slept in the laundry basket next to my cot. Someone had put a pillow under the dog. When my bed creaked,

Ringo opened her drippy eyes and yawned. I knew then she'd live and that I'd get the credit for it.

But I had no intention of being cooped up in the tent all night—not while everyone else hunted for a Nazi. My bandaged foot screamed as I jammed it into the bloodstained sneaker. My ma sent those sneakers to me in a package addressed to Jack, so I wasn't about to leave one behind. Boys in England wore stiff leather lace-ups, the kind kids in America were forced to wear to Sunday Mass. I leaned over and whispered in Ringo's ear, "Stay here, girl." She gave a pathetic whine, but was so bandaged up she had to obey. To be on the safe side, I put her collar back on and knotted the leash to the cot frame.

All I had to do was duck under the tent flap and hobble away.

My luck was holding: standing out on the grass was one of Jack's pilot friends, a fella named Ciesielski. He'd once been an airmail pilot based in Warsaw, but when he seen which way the wind was blowing he let it take him to England. That was the same day the Germans invaded his country, a day before they confiscated the airmail planes. Now there were plenty other Polish pilots in the Royal Air Force, fellas who'd first gone to France. They ended up forming their own squadrons—two bomber squadrons and two fighter squadrons—but Ciesielski decided to stick it out with the Brits.

Right then he was flirting with a nurse.

"You recovered from food poisoning?" I asked, because the day before I'd seen him throwing up into a flowerpot.

"Stuff yourself with hay," he said, strangely, with an accent that made him sound like Bella Lugosi in *Dracula*. It didn't seem to be scaring the nurse off. She ran her fingertips over her neck like she was wanting to be bit.

"You remember me, right? Jack Mooney's brother? We ran into you in London once, at Piccadilly Square, to be exact. Then Jack and you and me went for bangers together, only you called it *kielbasa*. So I was wondering if you could help me out with a ride? As you can see, I can't walk very far." I pointed to my bandaged foot.

"Little lamb," said the nurse, kissing my cheek.

Ciesielski gave me the evil eye. "As you Americans say—scram kid."

"The thing is, sir, there's a Luftwaffe pilot who's getting away as we stand here doing fat nothing."

"*Vat?!*" he yelled. Anger flashed in his eyes. He was remembering his vow to liberate Poland. He bowed to the nurse, "You will please excuse me, my angel."

"You have a car?" I asked.

"I have a Spitfire!" he said, scanning the sky.

I explained that the Luftwaffe pilot was on foot. Ciesielski jutted out his lower jaw, moving it left to right and back again—his way of coming up with an idea. Then his eyes settled on a Morris Minor parked across the street and left unattended with the windows rolled down.

"You can't nick a car!" said the nurse. "In England it's against the law."

"We will borrow the car, then," said Ciesielski. "—

under the circumstances." He was my kind of guy. He jumped into the driver's seat and I slid in next to him. Ciesielski reached down under the steering wheel, pulling down a few wires. Within a minute he had the engine going.

"I hope this car does not belong to a wing commander," he said.

"It's called commandeering," I told him.

"This word I never hear," he said, as we pulled away.

The nurse must've been keen on him. She ran after the car, waving her arms and shouting, "Wait for me! Wait for me!" Ciesielski brought the car to a screeching halt and she jumped into the back seat.

"You think I'd miss all the fun, did you?" she said, winking at him.

I directed us back to Jack's mess, figuring we start from the last place the Luftwaffe pilot was seen. Ciesielski had to keep the headlights off because no one had masked them and it was against the blackout rules to turn them on. He drove ten miles an hour saying he was worried about hitting a cow, which was a possibility seeing that most of them were the black angus variety.

"Keep your eyes peeled," I said. "He's wearing a black uniform, perfect camouflage for a blackout."

"This is thrilling!" said the nurse, shaking all over. "I've never chased a real Nazi before. What will we do if we find him?"

"We shoot him," said Ciesielski with a growl. "Just as they do to my people."

"We will do no such thing," said the nurse.

"Then we strangle him."

"Why, Andrzej, that's barbaric! You're in England now. We must find him a job as a farmhand. I hear that that's what we're doing with prisoners."

"You Englishers," said Ciesielski, spitting out the window. "You have no notion of whom you deal with. So naïve—like little children."

"That's what I say," I said. But I'd had enough bloodshed for one night. "How about we tie him up good and bring him to the MPs?"

Ciesielski answered by patting his service revolver.

We drove at a snail's pace down a road wide enough for one car. Dried out cornstalks lined both sides, with not so much as an inch of shoulder. The stalks blocked our view every time we took a bend. Luckily, my night vision surpassed a panther's. As we came around a hairpin turn I caught sight of a fleece-topped flight boot as it disappeared into the cornstalks. "Holy Toledo! There he is!" I shouted. "Stop the car."

Ciesielski had seen him too. He leaped out the door and into a wall of corn.

"Mercy me!" cried the nurse, cowering in the backseat.

I flew after Ciesielski, ignoring the pain that shot up my foot. Before long, I was lost in a sea of corn. I stood still, hoping to catch a sound. But it was dead quiet. Then I heard rustling stalks. Someone shouted, *Helfen!* It meant *help* in German.

The crack of gunshot rang out just then and I froze in place, everything but my shaking knees. Close by,

I heard someone moan, *yug*. I couldn't tell if it was a German or Polish *yug*. The stalks rustled again: someone running in my direction. Any second he would crash smack into me. I braced myself for impact.

Next thing I knew, I was flat out on the ground with the nurse bent over me, slapping my face. "Are you all right?" she said, her voice all choked up.

I sat up, more embarrassed than anything. "Who got shot?" I asked.

"*Ruhig*," said a voice I was already acquainted with.

"We must do as he says," said the nurse.

"Ciesielski?" I whispered, as she helped me to my feet. The nurse didn't answer. Instead, she grabbed my hand and squeezed. It wasn't a good sign. Plus, her face was wet from crying.

"Let me attend to my friend. Please, I'm begging you," she said to the Luftwaffe pilot. As my eyes adjusted to the darkness, I could see he was holding a revolver. German pilots were issued a gun for just such an event.

"I don't think he speaks English," I whispered. I searched my brain for the right German words. I'd gotten a bit rusty with no one to practice with. But once a week, I cracked open the German dictionary in the Sopwith's library at Warfield Hall. So my vocabulary was around about 1800 words. A-F, mostly. Slowly, I translated her request. "*Bitte*," I said. "*Freund*." I tried something else and then another thing. Either he didn't understand or he was ignoring me. He waved the gun in a downward spiral, signaling for us to turn around. The nurse—whose name I still didn't know—began gulping cries. We both knew what was about to happen: cold-blooded murder, you call it. I began praying under my breath. I'm not what you'd call the religious type but I had nothing to lose. I tried to remember my sins, asking for forgiveness. *Forgive me for detesting my sister Mary*, I said under my breath. *Forgive me for causing the death of the goldfish.* It's true what they say—your whole life passes before your eyes: I seen myself as a baby, being tickled under the chin by my ma; I pictured my da tossing me a softball; Mary stabbing me with a pin; Jack waving goodbye as he left for Canada and flight training; me sitting in a confession booth and lying through my teeth. When I felt the muzzle press into my back, I said, "Hail Mary, full of grace!" out loud. Then I waited for the bullet to pierce my heart.

"Take pity on us, I beg you." The nurse's voice cracked.

"*Bewegen!*" said the German. It meant *move*.

I let the air out of my lungs. "He's not going to kill us," I whispered. "At least not yet. But I'd say we were hostages. Or prisoners of war, more like."

"*Bewegen!*" he said again, poking me in the kidneys.

We walked back to the road, with the Luftwaffe pilot behind us. He directed us to the Morris Minor, which stood idling. Vapors come from the exhaust pipe and hit the cold air making a sort of smoke signal. He made the nurse take the driver's seat, with me next to her and him in the backseat.

"*Wie heissen Sie?*" I asked, wanting to know his name. I turned my head slightly, so I could see him in the rearview mirror. It was a shock seeing his face: like a rabbit caught in the headlights—about to pee in his pants, I'd of said. His upper lip was covered in peach-fuzz, a lame attempt at growing a mustache. He had acne, too—red patchy scabs all over his pimply face, whiteheads begging to be popped. He couldn't've been much older than me.

"Fritz," he said, to my surprise. He tried to act tough by pointing the gun at the nurse's head. She whimpered.

"Better do as he says," I said, terrified myself. Even if he was just a kid, he did have a gun and nothing was more dangerous than a kid with a gun. My guess was it had a full chamber, minus the bullet in Ciesielski. The nurse's hand shook as she shifted the car into first gear. I wanted to calm her so she wouldn't do anything silly.

"What's your name?" I whispered out of the side of my mouth.

"Beatrix," she said.

"*Bewegen!*" he said, like a tough guy.

Beatrix put her foot to the pedal and we rolled down the road. Fritz ducked behind the seat, out of sight. I got the gist of what he was saying, even though his voice was muffled by an afghan: if we called out for help, we were dead meat.

"*Welche Richtung?*" I said, which meant "which way?" I'd learned the phrase back when I thought I'd need it to find my brother's Spitfire. As it turned out, I didn't need it until now.

"London," came the answer, in perfect English.

CHAPTER TWENTY

As we headed toward the teaming metropolis, Fritz removed his coat, throwing it from the open window and into a ditch. He took the Iron Cross medallion from his neck and stuffed it into his black wool trouser pocket. He was wearing only a blue shirt and under that a wool jersey. Somewhere along the way, he'd ditched his flight suit, helmet, and leather overcoat. Probably burned his documents, too. Standard procedure for downed pilots—the first thing they did after landing in enemy territory.

For all we knew, his name wasn't Fritz.

The crocheted afghan that was draped over the back seat was now wrapped around his shoulders. If you didn't know no better, you'd think he was just a plain ol' English boy out for a ride with his pals. Nothing but his black trousers gave away his political persuasion: they were the kind that balloon at the thigh. Then again, Lord Sopwith had a pair like them for horseback riding and fox hunting. But he wore them with a red coat, a coat he kept insisting was pink.

I drew a few items from my pockets, waiting for the moment when Fritz would duck back behind the seat.

One by one, I tossed them out the window. My hope was to plant a trail—like bread crumbs leading to a mouse-trap. Problem was, only my brother would recognize the items as belonging to me: a marble, a card with one clo-ver leaf, a pack of chewing gum, and a snapshot of my ma and da standing in front of our barn in East Hemp-stead, N.Y. Lastly, the *piece de resistance*, as the French say: a postcard of the Empire State Building with a note on the back from my ma, saying how much she wished Jack and me were along for the elevator ride. It was ad-dressed to the Sopwith manor house in Hampshire. The stamp showed Lady Liberty holding up her torch. Soon as they saw the stamp, the American Ambassador would get involved. He'd notify the president, who'd mention me in one of his fireside radio chats. They'd send out the Marines. I hoped so anyway.

We came to a T in the road. The Home Guard had removed the road sign, thinking to confuse the Nazis in the event of an invasion. Only the Home Guard didn't count on Beatrix being at the wheel of a car with a Luger pointed at her head.

It was a two hour drive to London. Fritz let us stop when I complained about my bladder. I didn't really have to go, but I was hoping to make a break. But he kept the gun at Beatrix's head the whole time. He motioned for Beatrix to put her hands over her eyes while he unbut-toned his balloon trousers to relieved himself. We were back in the car before I could think up a plan B.

Beatrix drove with both hands clutched to the steering wheel, her knuckles protruding out of her skin from the pressure she was applying. She was leaned forward so her head was almost over the steering wheel, practically on top of the dashboard. I couldn't tell if she was trying to see better in the dark or trying to distance her head from Fritz's gun.

Lightening-fast, she reached over and turned the headlights on. I knew what she was thinking: that hopefully we'd get pulled over for breaking the blackout. Problem was, we were still in a rural farm area—maybe once we got closer to London. If the Home Guard saw us fly by with the headlights blaring, they'd be on us like the Feds chasing Bonnie and Clyde.

We came to civilization, passing through villages with everyone still tucked into their beds thinking they were safe from the Nazis. Since Fritz didn't speak much English, I was pretty certain this was his first visit to England. That meant he wouldn't know his way around. As we came into London, I looked over at Beatrix, trying to speak to her telepathically. I could tell she had a plan up her sleeve. Then she whispered, "There will be night guards at the British Museum."

Making a break there was a brilliant idea. I knew those corridors like the back of my hand, especially in the Egyptian wing. I would lose Fritz somewhere on the second floor, where me and Beatrix could hide out in the coffin holding the mummy of Horneditef.

The car sputtered to a stop right in front of the entrance gates.

"The British Museum," I said in German. "So vast a clever fella could get lost in there." I hoped Fritz would take the bait.

"*Heraus*," he said, telling us to get out of the car.

Fritz stepped behind us, keeping the gun at our backs and hidden under the afghan. He began panicking when a police car turned onto our road. Beatrix was about to shout out when Fritz put the gun to her head again. Then he made us squeeze through a gap in the iron fence. We walked along the edge of bushes and into the courtyard, to the limestone stairs that led to the front doors. The building was modeled after the Parthenon in Athens, Greece: the very building Lord Elgin took the marble frieze that, in peacetime, was displayed in the museum. Most of the treasures had been moved during the Blitz.

Fritz told me to open the door. It was one of them huge numbers that would take a weight lifter to budge. He jabbed the gun into my right kidney, and I did as I was told. Just like I thought, the door was locked. He pointed the gun to another door, this one much smaller and next to a statue of a lion. Someone must've just oiled the door, because it moved without a single squeak when I applied pressure to the brass handle. Inside the door sat a security guard, on a wooden chair and sound asleep. His snoring drowned out Fritz as he ordered us to move along the corridor.

I purposely bumped into a trash bin. The guard stopped snoring for just a beat, then went back to dreaming. With this kind of security, anyone could break into the museum. I made note of the time on a clock above the guard's chair. Maybe he had the same shift every night. I needed to come up with a wedding gift and a Grecian vase might be just the thing.

We entered into the Great Court. I swerved left, taking us into the Egyptian sculpture hall. We paused next an empty glass case, once containing the Rosetta Stone: the ancient tablet that unlocked the key to Egyptian Hieroglyphics. A French soldier discovered it when Napoleon ordered him to gather rocks for a fortress. Then the British took Egypt and they shipped Napoleon to Elba, the Rosetta stone to England. I'd been dying to see that stone. I snarled at Fritz. It was his fault the treasures had been moved, him and his Luftwaffe buddies.

He stopped to listen for sounds.

The empty case gave me an idea. The case might be empty but the alarm system might still be turned on. All I had to do was touch the case and we'd know.

Bells went off all over the building.

"Run, Beatrix!" I shouted.

I grabbed her hand and we ducked behind a second-rate statue of a podunk pharaoh; his nose, ears, and one eye were missing. I was thinking of pushing the pharaoh over and crushing Fritz, but even with Beatrix helping the statue wouldn't budge. By now, Fritz was twirling around, both hands clutching the gun and swinging it left and right looking for his target—like a kid in a carnival aiming for ducks, hoping to win a Kewpie-doll for his sweetheart. Only, we were the ducks in this case.

Hearing the bells, Sleeping Beauty came rushing

into the room, wielding a nightstick. Fritz took aim and shot him in the foot. The guard cried out as Fritz raced into ancient Greece.

"Follow him!" I shouted to the guard. Beatrix clutched the pharaoh's toe for dear life, not willing to let go. The guard sat on his duff, examining his own toe and yelling at us for trespassing.

If I didn't want Fritz to escape, I had no other option than to go after him myself. The galleries were dark and I had no flashlight. I took off my sneakers, so they wouldn't squeak on the marble floors and alert Fritz to my presence. I could picture the headline on the morning edition of *The Guardian*. Lord Sopwith would learn of my demise while he ate his breakfast toast with homemade marmalade. *Brave American Boy Killed In Deadly Duel With Escaped Nazi*, the headline would read.

It felt like a cherry pit was stuck in my throat when I gulped. I tried to translate in my head the words, "Come out with your hands up. We have the joint surrounded." My German was lacking, though. Instead I said, *Die Engländer sind wunderbar, Fritz.* (The English are wonderful, Fritz.) It was true. Unlike Germans, they didn't throw their prisoners into death camps, they made them hoe potatoes instead.

But Fritz wouldn't surrender, no matter how lovey-dovey the English were. I stood stone-cold still—like a statue of Ramses—hoping to hear a footstep. For all I knew, Fritz had already found an exit. Then I felt the cold steel of the Luger against my left temple. Fritz wanted a hostage and I was it.

I turned my head and saw he had his flight boots clutched under his armpit. He'd snuck up behind me in his military issue socks.

"You will take me to a back exit, and no tricks this time," he said in my ear, articulating the German words so there would be no misunderstanding. At least Beatrix had gotten away. I hoped at my memorial service she'd give a nice little homily commending me for bravery.

Like I said, I knew the museum like the back of my hand. I'd searched every corner for treasure, hoping a curator had dropped something in the mad rush to save everything from German bombs. There was a rumor treasures were being kept in the basement. I'd already tried every door and staircase hoping to find my way to the Mother Lode.

I led Fritz into a small café that, during opening hours, served tea and Victoria sponge cake to pooped out museum goers. "If you're hungry, this is the place to grab a bite to eat," I said, realizing that somewhere during his escape, Fritz had lost the picnic lunch he packed back in the kitchen at Jack's mess. If I acted fast, I could find something to bop him over the head with— if only I could distract him long enough.

"Huh?" He didn't understand me.

"Wienerschnitzel," I said, hoping he'd get my drift. I heard his stomach growl. I egged him on by saying, "Strudel."

He stopped long enough to take in a view of the room. Fortunately, a bit of moonlight came through a window and landed on a crumpet. Fritz jumped toward it and stuffed the whole thing into his mouth, offering none to me.

I looked around the café for a weapon—a cake knife or even a butter knife would have served my purposes. The busboys had done too good a job cleaning up. All I could think to use in my defense was a stool, but some genius had bolted it to the floor. Fritz saw me try and budge it and pointed the gun back at my nose.

His next move was to throw something at me. I felt a prick as it landed in my hand. It looked like my last meal on earth would be a watercress sandwich, held together with a toothpick. Then he waved the gun again, making me open an exit door that led us back outside.

CHAPTER TWENTY-ONE

WE CIRCLED AROUND UNTIL the Morris Minor came into view. Parked next to it was a police car and two bobbies chitchatting. Fritz shoved me in the opposite direction, until we were out of sight. Then he reached into one of his flight boots and removed a slip of paper that was wedged under a removable insole. He stuffed it into his pocket and then made me help him get the boots back on. All the while, he held the gun to my head. *The nerve*, I thought. I'd tied my sneaker shoelaces together and slung them around my neck. I asked Fritz for permission to put them on again. I think he let me only because a boy walking around London in his socks would draw attention.

He took the slip of paper and held it up for me to read. It was an address in London, written in blue fountain ink, smudged by what looked like a tear.

"You will take me here," he said, pointing to the address. I had never heard of the street. The address of a safe house for German spies, I figured. I was now in possession of information the Nazis wouldn't want leaked to British Intelligence. This wasn't boding well for my future health and well-being.

"You have the address memorized?" he asked, speaking in German. He made me repeat the address. Then he swallowed the note.

Fritz was keeping me hostage because he needed someone to guide him to the address. He wasn't onto the fact that I was a foreigner myself, that I always got lost in London. Fritz would've been better off taking a London cabbie hostage. But I wasn't about to tell him.

Under the address there had been a scribbled note: *Between Hyde Park and Grosvenor Square.* My luck was in: the American Embassy happened to be on Grosvenor Square, and it would be opening up before long. I looked around to get my bearing. Fritz reached into his pocket, removing a compass.

"Will this help?" he said, handing it to me.

(To save ink, from this point on, I will stop mentioning that me and Fritz communicated in German. My translation of our conversations might lead you to believe my German was high school level. Don't be fooled. I had the basics of the language, taught to me by Mr. Fisch, who lived in the Tudor down the street from my house on Long Island. At the time of our lessons, I was focused on trying to find my brother who was missing in action in German-occupied Europe. So I'd focused on phrases like: *Have you seen the Gestapo around here?* And: *Have you seen a downed Spitfire?* Useless phrases in the situation I now found myself in.)

"Indubitably," I said, taking the compass. "I have a penchant for compasses."

We headed toward Oxford Street, a direction I

knew would take us to Hyde Park. When I seen the Tottenham Court Tube station, I suggested we take the train—thinking there might be a policeman down in the station. "It's a long walk," I said.

Raising the cuff on my jeans, I explained that my foot had stitches in it. But his sympathy for my plight ended with the watercress sandwich. He poked me in the ribs with the gun and we kept walking.

The sky was beginning to lighten and the city was waking up. We passed a few merchants who were opening the gates to their shops and a fruit vender who was stacking oranges. A truck drove alongside us and a boy stood at the back with the roll-up door open, throwing bundles of newspapers to the street. I wondered if me and Fritz were on the front page. Lord willing, they had my picture plastered below the masthead and someone would recognize me and call Scotland Yard. For the time being, no one took notice of us. Even though Fritz still had the crocheted afghan draped over his shoulders, which looked a little ridiculous if you asked me.

We stopped in front of a travel agent because Fritz had to relieve himself. In the window was a poster that read: DON'T MIND HITLER, TAKE YOUR HOLIDAY! BOOK HERE. Next to the travel poster was an advert for Imperial Airlines. It showed a cartoon of a stewardess with wings on her shoes. The headline said: "EVERYONE FLIES NOWADAYS!" I looked over to Fritz who was buttoning his pants. *Sure,* I thought, *only some people fly Messerschmitts.*

We came to Oxford Circus. Ringling Bros. and

Barnum & Bailey it wasn't. Maybe back in medieval times they had a Big Top tent up in the place, but now it was just a busy traffic intersection with lots of stores. I'd been to Oxford Circus before, with my brother Jack. We ate fish and chips from a booth that was now shuttered closed. Too bad, because the cook might've remembered me.

There were lots of billboards posted on top of buildings. I spotted one for the movie *Eagle Squadron,* starring Robert Stack, whose character I suspected was based on my brother Jack. Most of the fellas in the squadron didn't like the flick, because it made it seem like they'd saved England single-handedly, and that embarrassed them with the British pilots. Even worse, the movie showed an Eagle Squadron pilot flying a bomber plane. I pointed to the billboard hoping Fritz might be interested. All he did was grunt.

"I bet there are Messerschmitts in that movie," I said. "The billboard says, *You dare not miss this!*" I hoped a dare would work.

"*Ja wohl. Messerschmitt!*" he said all excited, but than poked me again when I hesitated. We kept walking.

"Look! It also stars Diana Barrymore!" I made a curvy motion with my hands meaning *bombshell.* But he'd never heard of Diana Barrymore. Hollywood films were banned in German-occupied Europe—by order of Joseph Goebbels, the Nazi Propaganda Minister. "Marlene Dietrich!" I tried. It was the wrong thing to say.

"Traitor," said Fritz. What he wanted was a Goebbels endorsed Nazi propaganda flick directed by Leni

Riefenstahl, the fräulein who'd filmed the 1936 Berlin Olympics. Good luck finding a film like that in London. *I'm sure they show them at the Nazi safe house*, I thought and shuddered. "Do you think I'm an idiot?" he said. "I know who wins in your British propaganda movies."

I stepped out into the street, forgetting traffic went in the opposite direction of America. A taxicab swerved to avoid hitting us. I turned like a top, thinking I might push Fritz into the taxi's path, but it had already gone its way.

We came to Grosvenor Square, which some people were calling "Little America," because of the American Embassy and all the hubbub caused by the American Armed Forces streaming into England. If I had any hope of escaping, this was going to be the place. We passed an American woman dressed in an army uniform. I winked. She winked back and passed on, giggling.

We were almost to the far side of the park when I spotted Ambassador John G. Winant himself, walking toward us on his way to the embassy. I recognized him from the cover of *Time* magazine. He was wearing a camel hair coat, with a black homburg on his head. His owl-eye spectacles were same as Roosevelt's. The ambassador was carrying a small aluminum suitcase that contained state secrets. No kidding: it was chained to his wrist. I glanced past him and saw we were about to leave the square. John G. was my last hope.

"Help!" I shouted. "I'm a hostage of the Nazis!"

Ambassador Winant heard my cry. Our eyes met across a bench.

Fritz laughed like a loon and patted me on the back. He whispered, "Do that again and I will shoot both this man and you."

Did I want the United States Ambassador's blood on my hands? In a time of war? And more to the point, did I want a bullet lodged in my own skull? I looked into the ambassador's eyes and shrugged my shoulders, like it was all a big lark. He had no idea what that cost me. My consolation was knowing that when he put two and two together, he'd recommend me for a posthumous Medal of Honor. It was the least he could do.

"Not funny, young man," said the ambassador, as he strolled on by. I wanted to start blubbering.

CHAPTER TWENTY-TWO

THE SIGN READ *CULROSS STREET*, just like on the note in Fritz's stomach. It was a two-story house—what the British call a mews house, because it's where they kept cows at one time. We were right near Hyde Park—the Central Park of London—where they'd once grazed cattle. Mews houses were simpler than the fancy mansions they stand next to. This one had two garage doors at the ground level, both painted green. There wasn't a Nazi swastika flag flying from the roof, like you find in Paris. Fritz looked into the glass windows on the garage door. I took a peek myself. Inside was an open topped Crossley, a British car. And piles of cardboard boxes.

He shoved me to a door and made me ring the buzzer. No one answered. Maybe they were still sleeping. Fritz leaned over, pressed the muzzle of his Luger to the buzzer and held it there. I heard a window sash slide open above us. Both me and Fritz looked up.

An old woman with curlers in her hair was leaning out of the window so she could get a good look at us. She was wrapped in a pink chenille robe. Nazis will stoop to any level to disguise themselves. Fritz took a step backwards, so the secret agent could see him clearly.

"Peter!" she shouted. "Oh, my Lord!" She slammed the window shut. I could've sworn she spoke like the queen.

I looked at Fritz, "Peter, you rotten liar." Just to annoy him, I was going to keep calling him Fritz.

The latch was slid open and there she stood, not even five-feet tall. I bet she was strong though, her arms were as thick as a prizefighter's. "Come in!" she whispered, "Quickly now." She shut the door behind us, put a key in the lock, turned it, and then placed it back in her robe pocket. She grabbed Fritz, smooching him all over his pimply face.

Very odd behavior for a secret agent, I thought.

Fritz hugged the lady to him, rested his head on her shoulder. "*Omi,*" he said. "My plane was shot down. It was *furchtbar*. It caught on fire and I baled out. I had nowhere else to hide. Mutter gave me your address. She put it in my boot, just in case."

I couldn't believe what I was hearing. The lady was Fritz's grandma.

"And whom might you be?" she asked me.

"I'm the hostage."

"Dearie me!" she said. "Whatever are we to do?"

"Let me go, that's what."

"*Nein, Omi!*" said Fritz.

The lady was rattled, that's for sure. She was jerking her head back and forth, her mouth opened wide enough to catch a fly.

"Aiding and abetting a Nazi is punishable by death," I said, not sure if my facts were straight, but laying it on thick anyway. "Beheading in the Tower of London."

She put her hands around her neck.

Fritz began speaking to her in rapid-fire German, explaining that if they let me go I'd run for the police.

He had that right.

"It's not the police I'm worried about," she said to me, in English. "I don't know if you are aware, but recently a mob of angry Englishmen lynched a downed German airman. You must believe me when I tell you that I'm *not* a Nazi sympathizer." She shook her head. "Why, my other two grandsons are serving in the Royal Navy as we speak. It's just that—" here she started crying—"Peter is my grandson, too. My stupid, misled, foolish grandson, yet my grandson none the less. I won't have him face an angry lynch mob. Please, stay a moment and we will try and sort out a plan for his surrender. That wicked man has divided my family and wreaked havoc on the world."

I knew she meant Hitler.

Fritz stood there looking baffled, not getting much of what his grandma said. I had to say, she had me confused too. I'd read stories about the Ku Klux Klan lynching innocent people in Alabama. One photograph gave me the willies, nightmares for months. But Fritz wasn't innocent, I told myself. *He's a Nazi, right?* I took a good look at him: freckles dotted his nose and cheeks. But it was the fuzz above his lip that got to me. And that stupid afghan.

"How old is he anyway?" I asked.

"He's just turned seventeen," said his grandmother.

"His father is a general in the Luftwaffe and taught him to fly when he was still in knee breeches. Hermann Göring is a madman—he'd let toddlers fly bombers if they could. Please, I'm begging you. Peter is just a child."

My eyes were bugging out. "Hermann Göring is his father?"

"No, no," she said. "You misunderstood me. Peter's father is only a *Flieger-Generalingenieur,* not the *Reichsmarschall.*"

Seventeen wasn't a child in my book. Heck, twelve wasn't. Still—Fritz had probably been brainwashed in the Hitler Youth. He wasn't even drinking age. In America, he'd still be in high school. And I didn't want anyone hanging from the end of a rope. But on the other hand, I wasn't going to help him get back in a Messerschmitt. Or a FW-190, for that matter.

We were still standing in the foyer. Fritz was gripping my wrist the whole time, so I couldn't escape. The grandma was begging me to come upstairs and have a *cuppa.* "Tell Peter to leave the Luger downstairs," I said. My plan was to bolt down when I got the chance and snatch it.

She began pleading with her grandson to do as I wanted. He started to lay the gun on the welcome mat. But he changed his mind and stuck it in his holster, instead. At least it wasn't aiming for my body. He made me lead the way up the narrow and steep staircase that opened into a warm and cozy parlor. A fire crackled in the grate. The place smelled like fresh baked bread. The grandma headed straight to the fireplace mantel and took a framed photograph in her hands, bringing it to me.

"This is Peter here." She pointed to a small boy standing next to his mother. He was cute, I had to say: curly blonde hair and a pug nose. She was good at getting the sympathy vote.

Fritz looked exhausted. He yawned and his eyes rolled around in the sockets. I'd missed another night of sleep, myself. Suddenly, I felt my knees buckling. Fritz took a seat in an upholstered recliner. He leaned back, making the footrest pop up and the back lay down. The minute he was horizontal, he conked out. I wasn't feeling sorry for him exactly, but he'd had a rough night—flying all the way from Germany, a dogfight with one of the RAF's top ace pilots, bailing out of a fiery plane, then an all night escape across England. I was falling asleep just thinking about it.

"I'll put the kettle on and we'll have a cuppa," whispered Fritz's grandma, pointing me to the kitchen.

"No thank you, ma'am," I said, mostly because I hated tea. "Get me some rope." When she backed away with her hand on her heart, I said, "I'm warning you lady. If you don't do as I say, I'm ratting on you to Winston Churchill. You know what they do to collaborators?" I jumped toward the mantel place and grabbed a poker. No way I wanted to clobber an old lady with curlers in her hair. But look—this was war, not the Boy Scouts.

She pointed toward a wooden box sitting next to the recliner. When I opened the lid I saw dozens of balls of yarn in a rainbow of colors.

"It's the best I can do," she said, "honest to God."

It would serve Fritz right for tying me up with dish-rags. First I removed the Luger from his holster, checking to see the safety was on. I was planning to wedge it in my waistband and didn't want it to go off by mistake. I knotted the end of a ball of red wool to the armrest and ran circles around the chair, repeating the move with each ball of yarn in the box, making sure his arms and legs were pinned down good. Before long he looked like one of my sister Mary's knitting projects. Fritz didn't even move a pinky finger the whole time.

"Shall we have that cuppa? I *do* so need it." Fritz's grandma was as British as Marmite yeast paste.

We went into the kitchen. A small paraffin heater was warming the room nicely. There were loaves of homemade bread cooling on a rack on an oak table in the center of the room. I preferred Wonder Bread, but I wasn't complaining. The grandma slobbered marmalade all over a big slab and handed it to me.

"Would you like for me to fry up some bacon and eggs?" she asked. "One of my grandsons is a vegetarian and he gives me his meat rations."

I should've been making a run for it just then. Only I felt like Robinson Crusoe stuck on a deserted island with nothing but bugs to eat, then along comes a ship.

Before I knew it, a nice breakfast was laid out in front of me. In no time flat I was licking egg yolk from the plate. I knew it wasn't proper table manners—my ma wouldn't like it—only I had no idea when my next meal would be. I put away a whole loaf of bread and most of the jar of orange ginger marmalade. Meanwhile, Fritz's grandma went on a yarn:

"My husband worked for the Foreign Service, and we were assigned to Berlin. This was before the Great War, mind you. Gerard was thrilled—Gerard was my husband, my late husband. Relations with Germany were in a precarious state at the time, simply dreadful, with that Kaiser Wilhelm flashing his sword left and right."

"Was he really?"

"Just a figure of speech," she said. "For an ambitious man in the Foreign Service, it was a chance to shine. And we loved Berlin—such old world charm. We went to oodles of social gatherings. It was all part of the job, you see. Our daughter was at the age when young girls beginning courting. We couldn't refuse her when she wanted to go to parties. If we had known what was coming around the bend, we would have shipped her home. But fools that we were, we watched as she threw herself at a handsome young pilot of the German Luftwaffe. Hans is his name. He came from such a good family—practically royalty—and we were all taken in by his good looks and pitch-perfect manners. Why, he'd bow deeply whenever he saw me. Made me feel like the queen. But he was a snake in the grass. Before we knew it, our Carolyn was in the family way."

She stopped short for some reason. "What kind of snake?" I asked.

"Just another figure of speech—all right, a boa constrictor, that's what he was. *Is.* They were married just as we were ordered to return home. Then the war, the Great War—that dreadful bloodbath. It all started as a family squabble, if you want my opinion."

I asked her to elaborate. I'd always loved military history. That's when I found out the kaiser was the grandson of Queen Victoria, if you can believe it. And the queen's husband was German and so was her mother. According to Fritz's grandmother, the first war with Germany started because the kaiser was jealous of King Edward, his cousin, and decided he wanted control of the North Sea, where the Royal Navy had supremacy ever since Lord Nelson crushed the French back in 18-something. It sounded like two spoiled kids playing with tin soldiers. And yet millions of people died. I'd once met a Frenchman up on top of the Eiffel Tower, whose lungs were damaged by mustard gas in the Battle of Ypres. He wasn't happy about the Nazi flag hanging from the steel beams all these years later.

"My son-in-law, Hans, became an ace and a hero in Germany during that war. Carolyn fell pregnant again with our second grandchild while the war was still raging."

"Fritz?"

"No. They named him Wilhelm, after the kaiser." She paused for a minute to stack dirty plates in the sink. "We weren't even able to meet our grandsons until after the Armistice. Peter arrived after the war." She counted on her fingers, then said, "1926. I went over for his birth. That might account for the sweet spot I have for the lad."

She looked toward the parlor. I'd had my eye and ear on Fritz the whole time. We could hear his snores. The grandma continued with her tale of woe.

"By then our two nations were friends again, the kaiser dethroned. Everyone hoped that Germany would become a parliamentary democracy, like Britain or your America. No one knew then that Adolf Hitler was waiting in the wings: a monster a million times worse than the kaiser."

"So you knew Fritz—I mean Peter—was flying for the Luftwaffe?"

"I feared as much. He'd always been keen on airplanes. There was a mobile hanging over his crib, little Red Baron biplanes twirling around in circles. I prayed this war would be over before he was old enough to join up. Obviously, my prayers went unanswered."

I asked who she'd prayed to, and she gave a vague answer. I suggested she try Saint Simon of Cyrene next time. Then I got back on track. "Where's your telephone?" I asked. While she'd been telling her story, I'd decided to call the base and talk to Jack. He'd know just how to get us out of this mess.

"I haven't one, I'm afraid," she said.

Just in case she was holding out on me, I scoped the place. No telephone.

"There's a telephone box at the corner," she said. "What is your strategy?"

She agreed that calling the RAF was a good move. She said, "We British have a policy of never firing upon an enemy airman while one is parachuting from his plane, nor once he's on the ground. It's part of the RAF code of honor. I'm less certain of the police or Home Guard, though. Everyone's touchy since the Blitz. Why, if I saw a Nazi in London I might be persuaded to act rashly myself." She took a deep breath and started tearing up. "Now my imbecilic grandson—he's a different story. All I want to do is give him a good thrashing and send him to bed without supper."

"He was shot down escorting a bombing raid on a naval and RAF base. They dropped bombs on a hospital."

"Oh, good gracious. I can't bear it. My own flesh and blood!"

"And he tortured a puppy."

I wasn't sure what to do. If I went to the pay phone myself, she might help Fritz escape. If I sent her to make the call, she might claim that she called when she didn't. I rubbed my forehead, stimulating my brain.

"Now, listen up," I said. "You call my brother. I'll write down the information for the operator. If *he's* not there, ask for Squadron Leader Kennard. And if he's not there, talk to a WAAF named Geraldine Noble. And just so's I know you're not pulling a fast one, ask them for the name of the squadron mascot. Got that?"

"Squadron mascot—Squadron Leader Kennard— WAAF named Geraldine Noble," she said.

"And ask for the squadron leader's first name." I wasn't taking chances.

"Very well, if you insist. But you must see I want this more than you, child. For starters, I'd like nothing better than to deprive the Luftwaffe of a pilot. And do you imagine for a second I want my Peter killed in a daredevil battle with the RAF? The best thing is for that boy to sit out the war in a prisoner camp, and if I can do anything towards that goal I shall do so forthwith." She shoved a pencil and a pad of paper toward me and I wrote down Jack's name and airfield.

"And tell my brother to get here as fast as he can. Tell him to fly his Spitfire and land in Hyde Park if he has to."

"It might not be safe to land a Spitfire in the park. People are often found strolling there."

"He'll figure something out," I said.

She wanted to take the curlers out of her hair and make up her face before she left. I patted the Luger and told her to get moving. At any minute, Fritz might rise all chirpy and I was in no shape to whoop a seventeen-year-old.

"Oh, my!" she said, wrapping a scarf around her head, biting her lips to get color into them, and putting a mackintosh over her nightgown. Then she placed a pocketbook over her wrist, first checking to see she had enough change for the phone. Leaning out the window, I watched as she walked to the end of the block. A red phone booth stood on the corner. She opened the door and stepped in.

A picture of the king hung from a hook above the recliner where Fritz was passed out. I wished I had a camera right then. The photo would've been perfect for a *Life* magazine article featuring yours truly. Dribble from the corner of Fritz's mouth wet his blue Luftwaffe shirt. I looked up close and saw sleepers near his tear ducts: those little globs of dried gunk you have to wash off in the morning.

I headed straight for the bookshelves, since books tell you a lot about a person. No surprise here. Not a swashbuckler in sight. On a sideboard I found leaded-crystal decanters. I uncorked one: it smelled like gooseberry wine. Another bottle contained whiskey. Fritz's grandma was a drinker. Other than that, the only thing interesting was a collection of little ceramic figurines, most of them of children playing instruments: flutes and banjos, violins and drums. The figurines were made in Germany and the children wore lederhosen. They looked so sweet. Who would believe they would grow up to be storm troopers?

I put a log on the fire and stifled a yawn. Then I took a seat on the couch. It was one of them Victorian numbers with springs in the cushions that stuck you in the rear end. I managed to get comfortable by sitting on a needlepoint pillow. The huge breakfast was taxing my digestive system. I glanced over to Fritz and knew he was out for the count. My eyelids slid over the balls.

I dreamed I was flying a red biplane. But there were strings attached to the wing struts. Baby Fritz was cooing in a crib below, wrapped up in a multicolored crocheted afghan. Only the baby had blonde fuzz above his lip, which turned into a little black mustache. Then the afghan turned black, with a big red swastika stitched into the weave. The baby's eyes popped opened and they were red like the devil's. The baby raised its hand in a *Heil Hitler* salute.

I woke with a start, my eyes falling on the empty recliner. Pieces of yarn littered the floor. And the Luger was gone from my waistband.

From my position on the couch, I could see Fritz and his grandma seated at the kitchen table. Fritz was stuffing his face. Grandma was shoveling food onto his plate.

Like an alley cat hunted by a dog, I slinked down the stairs. The door was locked and there was no way to open it without a key. The sound of flight boots made the floor above creak. Fritz stood on the landing, pointing the Luger at my head. I felt like the biggest nitwit in the world.

"Up you come," he said. He shoved me into the kitchen. Taking a roll of tape, he fastened my hands behind my back, made me sit in a wooden chair, taping my hands to the rails and my ankles to the chair legs. His grandmother looked like a wreck. The curlers had come out of her hair, but it was sticking up all over the place with bobby pins pointing in all sorts of directions. Perspiration beaded her upper lip. Until then I hadn't noticed her mustache. She wiped her brow with a hankie and then blew her nose. She begged Fritz not to harm me.

"He's just a child, Peter," she said, using the same line that had worked with me.

I wasn't sure where we stood. Had she phoned Jack? Or had she made a call to some Nazi group. Maybe the

British Union of Fascists, lead by Oswald Mosley.

While Fritz's back was turned, she mouthed something. I couldn't understand what she was trying to tell me, but her attempt to communicate gave me a glimmer of hope. For one thing, if Fritz knew she'd called my brother he'd have high-tailed it out of there. He wouldn't be wasting time taping me to a chair. A wall clock said it was half past ten. I'd been asleep for more than an hour.

"Fritz," I said, "good job with the tape." I didn't want to do anything to make him run, just in case my brother was flying toward London at 400 miles an hour. Best to keep him distracted.

"Shall we listen to the radio?" said his grandma. I was starting to think she was on my side after all. The radio was a clever idea because it would drown out the sound of Jack busting down the front door.

"Please," I said. "Let's have some boogie-woogie."

"Let's do!" said Grandma, like she was dying to jitterbug.

"You may use the radio, Omi. Only please bring me a map of England," said Fritz. Omi, by the way, was a German nickname for your mother's mother.

"You'll find an atlas in the sitting room, on the bookshelf," she said. "I have to use the loo, little mouse." She called him *Mäuschen*, which referred to a member of the rodent family. She got up and stomped in the direction of the bathroom, which was just through a small pantry. Fritz, meanwhile, had walked into the parlor. The grandma slipped off her shoes, did an about face, and shuffled to my chair.

She whispered in my ear, "Ringo and Hugh. I spoke with Warrant Officer Noble." I knew she'd reached the base and help was on the way. She shuffled back to the bathroom and flushed the toilet just as Fritz returned carrying a fat world atlas.

"I have an itch on my head," I said. "Would you help a guy out, Fritz?"

"My name is not Fritz. Please desist in calling me such."

"Oh really? What exactly is your name?"

"Peter Albert Loehlein," said his grandma.

"Omi. Please do not give information to the enemy."

"Aren't you supposed to give us your name, rank and serial number?" I said. I'd seen the procedure in plenty of pictures. Only it usually wasn't the fella strapped to the chair doing the interrogating.

"And to what purpose will it serve to disclose my rank and serial number?" said Fritz. "I have no intention of remaining in your country."

"This isn't my country, bub." He found that interesting. "My name is Thomas Robert Mooney the II. And I don't have a rank or serial number. I'm twelve-years-old. In America, where I'm from, they don't let you join up till you can grow a beard."

While we'd been talking Grandma went into the parlor to turn on the radio. The Two Leslies were singing, "We're Gonna Hang Out The Washing On The Siegfried Line" It was a catchy song. I tried tapping my foot. I yelled, "Turn it up, would you?" Then turning to

Fritz, I said, "Ya gotta love this tune."

"You will translate the words to German," he said.

I told Fritz it was a love song about a girl named Sue who meets a fella on an airplane and falls head over heels. The song was really about the Allies getting to Germany and whooping the Nazis. I sang along.

"Lovely tune," said Grandma, coming back to the kitchen. "And I can't wait for the day!" I opened my eyes wide, so she'd know to clam up. She pretended to cough and said she had to use the loo again.

"You English drink too much tea, Omi."

I had to agree with him there.

CHAPTER TWENTY-THREE

FRITZ OPENED THE ATLAS, found the page for England and moved his finger over the south coast, leaving a grease smudge on Dover—the shortest point across the Channel. I'd crossed over from Dover in a speedboat. Fritz was either planning to swim or steal a boat. Both options were possible. There was the chance he'd be eaten by a shark or torpedoed. But on the flip side, he might make back to France. And within a day be back to London in a fighter plane.

"I'll need a change of clothing, Omi," he said. "Something warm. Perhaps a raincoat. Do you have any of Grandfather's?"

Grandma shot me a pathetic look. She was in a jam, not wanting me to tell people she'd collaborated. We both knew Fritz was going to go through her drawers and closets no matter how she answered. I nodded my head, giving her permission.

"You're much taller than your grandfather," she said. "And much broader in the shoulders. I don't think his clothes will be a proper fit."

I had to hand it to her. She was trying.

"And shoes, Omi. I can't wear these boots. Maybe

you have a pair of Grandfather's waterproof gardening boots?"

"Wellies, you mean. Oh, my," said Grandma. "I'd been so meaning to sort through Gerard's things and donate them to charity. Stupid, sentimental me. I hadn't the heart."

Soon Fritz was standing before us looking like a man going out to catch trout. He wore a tweed jacket and vest over forest green wool pants. He had on a school tie. On his lapel was a little pin from the Masonic lodge. On his head was a tweed cap, and on his feet were rubber knee-high boots. He'd completed the disguise with a fishing pole and tackle box. Into the tackle box he stuffed a loaf of bread, a pickle jar, can of beans, two apples, and the decanter of gooseberry wine. No one would see him coming.

I could see the wheels were spinning in his head. He knew the second we walked out that door, I'd sic the Home Guard on him. "Have a nice trip, Fritz," I said. I wanted to get his mind on the obvious.

"You are coming with me," he said. "And you also, Omi. We will take the car."

"But I can't drive, little mouse. That old motor car hasn't been taken out since your grandfather passed. Why, the tires are flat and it's out of petrol. I haven't any petrol coupons, besides."

"We will find a petrol station," said Fritz, waving his Luger.

It looked like I'd be doing the driving, since Fritz would want to keep both hands free for the trigger.

"Let me get into warmer clothes," said Grandma. She was still wearing a nightgown, so it was a reasonable request. "And I ought to find something suitable for the boy. We can't have him freezing to death, Peter."

He motioned her into the bedroom and took a seat opposite me. I knew Grandma had something up her sleeve. I hoped it was a pistol. A few minutes passed before she appeared again, bundled up and carrying a suitcase. She'd found a wool overcoat for me, and a hat, scarf, and glove combo I was sure she'd knit herself. Fritz cut me loose with his grandma's pinking shears. He handed her the world atlas.

He said, *Ruhig*. I was back to square one.

The grandma led us back to the staircase, descending to the front door. Fritz had the gun in his jacket pocket; his finger was on the trigger. He made me carry the fishing gear. I didn't even like fish. Back home, Ma forced me to eat flounder every Friday.

"Let me lock up, little mouse." Grandma found a ring of keys in her coat pocket and took two off, handing them to Fritz. "This one will open the garage door. If I'm not mistaken, the larger key is for the car."

Fritz walked me over to the garage door. His back was to his grandma. He threw me a key. I was going to play the part of his lackey, obviously. Bending down to reach the keyhole, I caught a glimpse of the grandma. Even viewed upside down, I was able to see her snatch a piece of paper from her pocketbook. She tossed it into the foyer and pretend to lock up. British Intelligence was going to have to hire this lady.

The garage door opened on its rusty hinges, revealing the Crossley open top sedan. My guess was it was a 1920 model. Fritz kicked the front tire. "Goodness gracious," said Grandma, "I forgot that your cousin Harry borrowed the motor car last week."

"How is Harry?" asked Fritz.

"He's in the army, little mouse." I knew she was lying to Fritz. Earlier she'd told me that both her English grandsons were in the Royal Navy.

Fritz poked me with the Luger. "Can you drive a motor car?" he asked.

"At your service," I said.

He motioned me into the driver's seat. Grandma got in on the passenger side. Fritz headed toward the back seat. But instead of sliding in, he fussed with the rag-top. I preferred the wind whipping through my hair, my face in full view to passersby, but Fritz wanted the top up. He pulled it over our heads and fastened the clamps near the front windshield. Then he jumped into the driver's seat, pushing me to the center with his rear end.

What a dirty, crummy trick, I thought.

My feet were up on the middle bump, my knees hitting my chin and the stick shift too close to my private parts. Fritz moved the Luger from his right pocket to the left, so I couldn't get at it. The engine turned over and the Crossley started right up. There was a full tank of gas, to boot. Since I was squashed up against the grandma, I said, "Suppose it's time we were introduced."

"My name is Mrs. Harriet Wigglesworth. Pleased

to make your acquaintance." She reached out a bent hand.

"Was Harry named after you?"

"You're clever to have made the connection." We'd slipped into English.

Fritz shouted, "*Sprechen Sie Deutsch!*"

"*Freut mich* to meet ya, *Fräu Vigglesworth*," I said, shaking her hand.

Fritz parked the car in the street and went to close up the garage. This would have been my chance, if only he hadn't taken the car key with him. I looked down the block: empty as a church on Monday. If I made a move, he'd shoot me in the back and speed away in the Crossley. I'd be laying there with my brains splattered on the pavement and no one to give me the last rites.

Once Fritz was back in the car, he said, "Omi, you will be my navigator, yes?"

"Fighter pilot's don't have navigators," I said under my breath.

"We will be driving to Dover," he said, "to those pretty white cliffs I have flown so often over. Please find it on the map, Omi, and plot a direct course—one that will avoid checkpoints."

"Peter, I know the way to Dover," she said. "You might have left the atlas on the bookshelf."

He shifted the car through three gears and took the corner without making a stop, like he was flying a Messerschmitt. A red double-decker bus swerved and blew its horn when Fritz cut in front of it. After making a right turn, we headed south along Hyde Park. The whole time, my eye swung left and right and up and down, hoping to catch a glimpse of my brother—our only hope of rescue.

We were halfway down the block when a two-tone maroon and black car drove toward us. The driver was wearing an RAF uniform and in the passenger seat was a woman. I could only see the sleeve of her blue uniform. My heart raced like a horse at Belmont, and I reached for the horn. Fritz blocked me with his elbow. My head swung around like a ventriloquist dummy, so I could get a good look as the car passed us headed toward Culross Street. I let out a moan. The airman had a nose a half-inch longer than Jack's and was twice his age.

In the rearview mirror, I watched as the car turned onto Mrs. Wigglesworth's street.

CHAPTER TWENTY-FOUR

MI5 Headquarters,
Wormwood Scrubs, East London

Brigadier A.W.A. Harker, Deputy Director General of MI5, hears the rat-a-tat-tat of heels coming along the corridor. By now he can recognize the footsteps of Miss Havilland, his secretary.

"Come in, Miss Havilland," he says, without even looking up.

"Sir, there is a Miss Whitehead on the line. She works under Lizzy Nel at 10 Downing Street."

This is the living end! thinks Harker. That the call has not come from the prime minister himself, nor from the prime minister's secretary, Elizabeth Nel, but, rather, from the *secretary's* secretary! So, this is what they think of him after twenty-seven years service in British Intelligence? It was bad enough that they'd demoted him after a brief stint as Acting Director General.

"And what does this Miss Whatever-Her-Name-Is want?" asks Harker.

"Miss Whitehead, sir. It seems that 10 Downing Street is being harassed by a woman from Dover, sir... a

Mrs. Charles Sanders, who complains of not having had satisfaction after multiple reports made through proper channels."

"Meaning us."

"Yes, sir, meaning us. Something about a ring of German spies working from a fishing boat. She's made multiple reports, sir. And now she is showing up at the doorstep of 10 Downing, sir, making a nuisance of herself. Bothering the guards. Shouting out for the prime minister to come to the door. 10 Downing says that it *must* stop. Mr. Churchill, it seems, can't think straight with all of the commotion."

Harker slumps in his chair. "Ask Ellis to come see me, there's a good girl."

CHAPTER TWENTY-FIVE

WE HAD ONE THING going for us: driving in Monday morning traffic kept us at a snail's pace. I was happy to see that Fritz was frustrated. He was, after all, used to going a little faster. "Just like traffic in Berlin," he said, "Although our people are better skilled motorists." We stopped behind a meat truck; a ham was painted on the rear doors. Fritz laid on the horn, straining his neck out the window and trying to see what the hold up was. We rolled forward and he said, "I am sorry, Omi, that my visit has to be cut short. Soon we will mount the invasion and I will return for a longer stay. Then I will be happy to have a tour of this fine city, with my dearly beloved grandmother on my arm. I will bring my dress uniform for the occasion. It is so grand, Omi. You will be so very proud."

Mrs. Wigglesworth let out a gasp.

We glided past a policeman, directing traffic. I yelled out, "Help!"

Fritz stuck the Luger between my fourth and fifth rib and saluting the policeman.

The policeman blew his whistle and yelled, "Move along!" Fritz put the pedal to the floor. Now we were driving through another park, which dumped us smack in front of the place the king lived.

"That's Buckingham Palace," said Mrs. Wigglesworth, pointing out the entrance gates. It was the first thing she'd said since leaving her street. Maybe she hoped her grandson would stop to take pictures? Everyone knew the place was swarming with guards. And they had rifles, too.

Fritz's eyes bugged out. "Oh! This is where your führer resides!"

"Only we don't call him the führer, Peter. He's our sovereign king."

"King, kaiser, führer, what's the difference?" said Fritz. "In any case, you will soon have the führer living here in your palace." He looked like a cat at a bowl of cream.

In front of the gate were two soldiers, decked out like nutcrackers, with these ridiculous fur hats that stuck three feet above their heads. They stood like marble statues. Fritz leaned out the car window and laughed. The soldiers didn't bat an eyelash.

He looked at his compass. I wish I'd tossed it in a bush when I had the chance. It was clasped in Fritz's sweaty palm. He did an illegal U-turn and headed down what they call The Mall, a wide avenue lined by trees. "I like this," he said. "This avenue is reminiscent of the Champs-Élysées in Paris. I had the honor of flying in formation with my squadron over the Arc de Triomphe as Field Marshal Rommel rode triumphantly into the city."

"You were fourteen in June 1940," said Mrs. Wigglesworth. "Therefore, you must have been sitting on your father's lap." His face turned beet red. "Is that what they taught you in the Hitler Youth, Peter? How to fib and boast?"

We cut through St. James Park and soon we were passing Big Ben. I looked over at Mrs. Wigglesworth and whispered, "Don't point out the landmarks." I didn't want him leading a bomber squadron to the Parliament buildings.

I tried to see the time on Big Ben, but it had gotten foggy and the clock was a blur. I looked at Fritz's wristwatch instead: both hands pointed to twelve. The big clock started ringing as we crossed the Thames River.

"Is this the famous London Bridge?" asked Fritz.

"Yes, little mouse. It is indeed." She was lying, of course.

"Wunderbar!" said Fritz.

We were passing near the Imperial War Museum, closed since the Blitz. Some of the collection was now being used in the war effort. Even the museum's trench raiding clubs, dating back to King Arthur, were used by the Home Guard.

Fritz made a wrong turn. We were lost in a maze of narrow streets. "Omi, you promised to navigate," he said.

"What use is this atlas, Peter? We ought to have taken your grandfather's *Bacon's Gem Map of London and Suburbs.* Perhaps we return home and fetch it."

"Verdammt!" yelled Fritz, a cussword. Using his Luger, he popped open the glove box. Sitting on top of

a stack of maps was the yellow foldout *Bacon's Gem Map of London and Suburbs.*

"What do you know?" said Mrs. Wigglesworth. "Harry must have put it there."

"Good old Harry," I said. "What would we do without him?"

"You be the navigator," Fritz said, handing me the map.

He kept ogling the damage made by German bombs. As we passed a city block blown to smithereens, he said *Wunderbar* one too many times. His grandmother began hyperventilating, reached over me and slapped Fritz in the face. "You are a naughty boy, Peter," she said. "A naughty, spoiled rotten boy who needs a good walloping. I have a mind to write you out of my will."

"Feel free to write me in instead," I said.

"I might just do that."

"Do you think I need your English pounds?" said Fritz. "They will be worthless once England is joined to the Reich. Then heroes of the Luftwaffe will have bank vaults full of Reichsmarks. Ha!"

While they had their family spat, I tried to come up with a plan. *The map*, I thought. It was one of them foldout kinds that are impossible to read while driving, the kind that have caused untold accidents. I began unfolding it, stretching the map out until it blocked Fritz's line of vision.

"*Dummkopf!*" he said. It meant *blockhead.*

"Navigating, just like you asked," I said, as the car slammed into the back of a taxicab. The cabbie got out of the taxi to assess the damage. A crowd of concerned citizens formed around us. Mrs. Wigglesworth jumped from the passenger side, holding tight to my hand. Fritz grabbed my elbow. I felt like a wishbone.

"I will not hesitate to kill the boy," he said to his grandma in a low growl.

"Goodness, Peter. You must be barking mad!"

"Omi, I must do my duty."

An observer pointed at Fritz and said, "Saw it all with me *hown* two eyes, Constable. And it was clearly *'is* fault."

Mrs. Wigglesworth was holding on to nothing but my pinky finger. Fritz reached across me and shut the passenger door, leaving her standing in the street. A policeman made his way through the crowd of rubberneckers, getting ready to make notes in his little pad. Fritz yanked me from the car, dragging me toward a staircase that led down to a Tube station.

The last thing I heard was the policeman lecturing Mrs. Wigglesworth. "Madam," he said, "it is against the law to allow youngsters to operate a moving vehicle."

That's, unfortunately, the last I seen of her.

CHAPTER TWENTY-SIX

A TRAIN STOOD AT THE PLATFORM, a bell rang. Fritz forced me to jump the turnstile, then threw me into the car. He motioned for me to take a seat away from the doors. The Luger was jammed into my appendix. There was a couple smooching and two old ladies sharing a newspaper. Otherwise the car was empty. The bell went off again and the doors began to close. An RAF airman leapt from the platform and took a seat across from us at the opposite window.

Thank God, I thought. And then it came to me: I'd seen that profile before. I began racking my brain, with my eye on the airman's nose as he reached into his pocket and pulled out a giant handkerchief. I leaned away when he sneezed.

Fritz said, "*Gesundheit.*"

The airman said, "Thank you."

I started whistling "Yankee Doodle Dandy," which helps me think better. Even third-generation Irish-Americans say "Gesundheit" when someone sneezes. And it didn't mean they were Nazis. I heard Daphne's voice in my head say, *Thomas, you're letting your imagination run wild.* Boy, did I miss Daphne just then.

The airman eyed us like a shopkeeper who suspects you of shoplifting. Perspiration beaded Fritz's fuzzy upper lip, like he knew he'd just made a gargantuan blunder.

"*Danke schön*," I said, hoping that would tip the airman off.

He reached inside his coat pocket and removed something. It turned out to be a pack of chewing gum. Leaning across the aisle, he offered to share it with us. Fritz refused with a shake of the head, keeping his lips shut tight. I snatched up two sticks. The tackle basket with the food was left back in the car.

"Nippy out," said the airman. "Dreadful fog coming in. Glad I'm not flying tonight."

Fritz poked me. I wasn't sure if he wanted me to shut up or say something. "At least the fog will keep the Germans away," I said.

"Harrumph," said Fritz. I was figuring out that he could understand a bit of English. Made sense being that his mother was born and bred in London. She must've sung English lullabies to him when he was a baby.

"Where are you headed?" asked the airman.

"Dover!" I blurted out.

"I'm headed that direction myself. Back to the grind." He laughed and patted his navigator wings. The train came to a stop and he stood, steadying himself by holding onto the back of our seat. He motioned us to the door, "Well, this is our stop then—Charring Cross Station."

I knew Fritz understood, because he lifted me from

the seat by my elbow using his free hand.

We climbed a steep staircase and into a mammoth train terminal. The closest thing to it was the Bronx Botanical Gardens. Like a greenhouse it was, what with the glass roof. We headed to a ticket booth. Civilians lined up in front of us, but when they saw the airman they stepped aside and let us cut in front. If you want my opinion, the English are a little too polite for their own good.

"Golly, gee," I said. "I don't have a dime on me."

Fritz began rummaging through his overcoat pocket, pulling out a small waterproof canister. I looked when he opened the lid: a few matchsticks and a flint, nutritional capsules and a chocolate bar, a signal mirror and a small wad of English pounds. The Luftwaffe thought of everything.

"Three for Dover Priory, miss, no return," said the airman, taking the money Fritz offered him. "Second-class, if you please."

A one-way ticket to Nazi-occupied France, I thought.

I took my chances. "Mister, this man is an escaped pilot of the German Luftwaffe. And he's got a gun." The airman looked down at me, squinting an eye.

"Don't make a scene," he said.

I wiggled my elbow out of Fritz's clutches and started screaming my head off. People looked over and shook their heads, thinking I was a kid misbehaving in a public place and deserving of a spanking. Turning on my heels, I headed in the direction of a sign that read *WAY OUT*, knocking into a lady dressed like a grizzly bear and carrying several shopping bags.

"Would you control your boy?" she shouted, but by then my back was to her and I was moving like Jesse Owens in the Berlin Games.

I heard the sound of heel taps running behind me, catching up. As I pole-vaulted over a railing, I caught sight of the airman following close behind. Fritz hesitated and then turned in the opposite direction, running toward the train platforms. When I tried to skid around a corner, the soles of my sneakers gripped the marble floor and I stumbled forward. The airman snatched the back of my overcoat and swung me around. My feet were dangling a few inches from the floor.

"Now, now, son—no running off," he said, like a father disciplining his unruly child. He threw me behind a pillar, out of sight, and pinned me against a toothpaste billboard. Then, as he slammed the magazine end of a shiny Enfield service revolver against the back of my head, I could've sworn he said, "*Auf Wiedersehen.*"

CHAPTER TWENTY-SEVEN

Someone placed smelling salts under my nose. I opened my eyes to find a vision hovering above me. It was love at first sight. A second time for me.

"Am I in heaven?" I said.

"You darling boy," said the nurse. "Don't get up!"

I could've laid there all day looking up into her crystal clear green eyes. Her hairdo had come loose and a platinum blonde curl tickled my cheek. I was making ready to kiss her when them gorgeous lips were replaced by a doggone-ugly policeman's.

"Where's the nurse? I need medical attention!" I said.

"I'm right here, sweetie." The nurse took hold of my hand. "Tell me where it hurts."

Just then I came to my senses. "They're getting away!"

"Who is getting away?" asked the policeman.

"The two Nazis!"

"Concussion, I suspect," said the nurse. "Disorientation, confusion, and flights of fancy—those are classic symptoms."

"Did a ruffian attempt to rob you, son?" asked the

policeman. He wanted me to describe the assailant. "A pickpocket was he?" It seemed they'd been having a problem with that recently.

I tried to explain the situation: about the escaped Luftwaffe pilot, dressed like a fly-fisherman, and another Nazi dressed in a RAF navigator's uniform. "They're boarding the train for Dover," I said in a panic. I sat up, rubbing the bump on my head—it was going to be a doozy.

"Where's your mum?" asked the nurse.

I knew they weren't going to buy anything I told them, and I didn't have time to waste. I said, "Would you please take me to a pay phone. I need to call my brother. We got separated."

"Now he's talking sense," said the policeman. He gave me a hand up. The nurse put her arm under mine. She smelled like chocolate. Her hand was soft as a marshmallow. Her lips were the exact color of maraschino cherries. They walked me over to a row of phone booths. The policeman wedged himself into one and made the operator connect him free of charge. *I'll have to remember that,* I thought. He placed the phone to his chest and asked where I wanted to be connected. I thought for a second.

"Mrs. Harriet Wigglesworth, Culross Street." I wasn't thinking clearly, hoping my brother would answer a nonexistent phone.

He tapped his foot while he waited. "The operator says there's no such listing. Try another?"

"RAF Rochford, please. Ask for Flight Lieutenant

Jack Mooney, 121st Eagles, sir."

Just then, a loudspeaker announce that the train to Dover was departing from track five. I began protesting, but the nurse put her finger to my mouth stopping me. "Best to remain calm," she said. "Now let's sit down on this here bench and take a look at that cranium of yours." Once we were seated, she placed her kit bag on the floor and removed a bottle of Mercurochrome. I nuzzled up to her, leaning my head against her ample bosom. I watched as the policeman stood making hand gestures in the phone booth.

"The skin is hardly broken. However, the bump is formidable," she said, once she examined the wound. "Now aren't you a brave lad."

The policeman stuck his head out of the booth. "The flight lieutenant can't be reached, but I have a Warrant Officer Noble on the other end of the line. Says she wants a word with you."

Geraldine.

I stood up too fast and felt like I was on a merry-go-round. The nurse's arm held me up. "What's your name?" I asked, as we wobbled over to the phone booth.

"Judy," she said. I should've known it. Just like Judy Garland, the movie star.

The policeman folded down a little chair and stepped out of the booth, making me sit before handing me the receiver.

"Geraldine, is that you?" I said.

"Tommy! My God, we've been worried sick. Where are you?"

I launched into the story with gusto. She stopped me mid-sentence. "I have Tommy on the line!" she said to someone near her. I heard Daphne say, "Give me the phone," then, "Thomas Robert Mooney, where in blazes are you?"

I began crying right there in the train station, the nurse looking on. "Daphne, I've had an awful time. It's not like in the movies at all. Well, maybe a little bit."

"What?"

"I was abducted by a Nazi. It's not as fun as they make it seem in Hollywood. It scared the bejeebers out of me, Daphne." I started shaking then, and my teeth began chattering. I felt cold suddenly, like a wind had picked up even though we were inside. Shock has a way of coming on you when you least expect it.

"Thomas, where are you? We're coming straight-away. Are you safe?" It figured Daphne would be worried about me. I was her future brother-in-law, after all.

"I'm standing next to a copper," I said. "I think he's a real one."

The policeman took the receiver from my hand. "Let me speak to the lady," he said to me. Then to Daphne: "Ma'am, he'll be waiting over at the police house, the one what's right outside Charring Cross train station. You just look for the blue lamp. Name's Sullivan. I understand…I'll keep both eyes on the boy…Yes, ma'am, I have the necessary apparatus." He looked down at his belt, with a billy club hanging from it.

"Can I have the phone, sir?" I asked.

"Make it snappy," said the policeman.

I took the receiver. It was Geraldine on the line again. "Look Geraldine, get the MPs on the horn. You must've heard already from Mrs. Wigglesworth. We have two Nazis on the run, bolting for Dover on a train that just left Charring Cross station. They plan to lift a fishing boat…That's right, they're planning to nick a boat and row over to France. If Daphne comes with her drawing pencils I can help her make a mug shot—"

"That's enough," said the copper, taking the phone from me. (*Copper* being the English equivalent of *cop*.) He hung the receiver in its cradle. I tried to duck under his elbow, but he grabbed my collar. At the same time, he unclipped a pair of handcuffs. He gave me the evil eye and said, "Turn around with both hands behind your back."

What choice did I have? I was trapped in the phone booth and the copper had a blunt instrument swinging from his belt. The club looked like it came straight out of the Imperial War Museum. I swear, all over the battered wood was the dried blood of ancient Celts.

Next thing you know, I was sitting in a tiny police station, one of my wrists cuffed to the arm of a hard wooden chair. The worst part of the deal was when my dream girl excused herself to meet her husband. In my free hand was what you call a consolation prize: a *Beano* comic book featuring Dennis the Menace. The entertainment was provided courtesy of Police Constable Sullivan, who was seated behind an oak desk making notes into a ledger book.

"I'm an Irishman myself," I said, hoping to butter him up.

"You sound like a Yank to me."

"I'm first-generation American. My ma and da are straight-off-the-boat Irish."

"Fascinating." He looked up at a wall clock, the kind that ticks like a time bomb.

We'd been waiting for almost an hour. By now the Germans were halfway to Dover. But no amount of pleading would convince Sullivan to unleash me. My only hope was that Geraldine would send the military police after them. The problem was I forgot to give her a good description. It would be like looking for a downed Spitfire pilot in German-occupied France. I kept one eye on the comic and one glued to the glass door leading out to the road. Once Daphne arrived I'd be freed from my bondage and able to talk her into going in pursuit of Fritz and his accomplice. With any luck, Jack would show up with her—and in that case, the Nazis wouldn't have a hope in heaven.

Imagine my shock when in walked Lord and Lady Sopwith, my guardians for the duration.

"I might have known something of this nature would result from a simple holiday," said Lord Sopwith, taking a cigar from his mouth.

"Good God, young man," said Lady Sop, stopping herself mid-sentence so she could huff and puff all over me.

"Is he under arrest?" asked Lord Sopwith, lowering

his glasses for a good look at Sullivan.

"Do say it isn't so!" said Lady Sop, looking in a compact and dabbing power on her shiny nose. "He's already missed one day of tutoring, he can't afford to miss another."

"You wouldn't be this whippersnapper's father, sir?" said the constable, blown over by the idea that I'd sprung from the loins of this hoity-toity couple.

Lady Sop was the one to speak up: "We are his legal guardians—this here is Thomas Octave Murdoch Sop-with and I am his wife. This boy is, in fact, the progeny of people who reside in New York. Or rather, the suburbs of New York. I am in communication with his mother. She won't be pleased—that much you can be sure of."

It was almost like she was blaming Sullivan. I had to love Lady Sop.

"I told you my folks were straight-off-the-boat Irish," I reminded Sullivan.

Sullivan looked Lord and Lady Sopwith up and down. The only boat they'd gotten off of was *Endeav-our*, a world-class racing sailboat. "Very well," he said. "If you would please sign here." He motioned for them to approach the desk. "And I'll need to see your papers, sir. Just a formality, you understand."

"Of course, my good man. Can't go giving boys away to any passerby."

"I doubt anyone, unless they absolutely had to, would lay claim to this one," said Sullivan looking my way. Lord Sopwith took a fountain pen from the sat-in pocket inside his overcoat. Sullivan turned the ledger book around and pointed to the place he was to put his John Hancock, although I doubt they called it that in England.

"Might I have the key, Constable, so that this child might be loosed?" said Lady Sop.

Sullivan went through his pockets coming up empty. He moved things around on his desk, looking under the ledger, then bending down and searching the floor. "I'm afraid, ma'am, the key has gone AWOL."

"We can pick the lock with one of your hairpins," I told Lady Sop.

"Quite right, Tommy. You are full of ingenious ideas." She removed a hairpin from her bun and handed it to me. "I feel confident you are more skilled in this craft than I. If that doesn't work, we'll try a hatpin." I eyed the hatpin stuck near a yellow feather. It was topped with a fat diamond with two little rubies on either side. Before I could ask for it, the glass door swung open.

And there stood Daphne. No introductions were necessary—she and Jack had once spent a weekend at Warfield Hall, the Sopwith place.

"My dear," said Lady Sop, kissing her cheek. "You look a fright. Please have a seat." Lady Sop rushed to an empty chair, took a hankie from her pocketbook and wiped the seat. She made Daphne sit down.

"I got here on the first train out of South-end-on-Sea," said Daphne. She was breathing hard like she'd run the whole way. "Thank you so much for coming to his rescue, your ladyship."

"Call me Phyllis. Please."

"Well, Phyllis, when I called Warfield Hall last night, hoping that Thomas had returned home, I was told that you were in London at your sister's. Mr. O'Reilly was good enough to give me the telephone number."

"No trouble at all," said Lady Sop. "We were having a rather uneventful evening, sitting before the fireplace with dreadfully dull books, nothing whatsoever on the wireless. This certainly livened things up nicely." She clapped her hands gleefully.

"You are *too* good," said Daphne.

"Now that's done, let's not keep Duncan waiting," said Lord Sopwith, recapping his pen. "I insist that we drop you home, Daphne. You look unwell, my dear. East End, is it?" He said the destination with some trepidation. They'd come in the Rolls and the East End was the equivalent of the Bowery, no place for a luxury car. The car had a 6½ liter engine—there was still a chance of getting to Dover before Fritz.

Lord Sopwith, being the gentleman he is, opened the door for the ladies. When he seen I was still sitting in the chair, he said, "Come along now, boy."

I rattled the chains, so to speak, and he got my drift. I said, "Daphne, mind picking this lock? You promised to teach me."

"Watch carefully, then," said Daphne. Everyone crowded in, as she took a hairpin from her Victory roll hairdo. First she blew on the tip, warming it no doubt. I was counting the seconds, waiting for the sound of freedom. Six seconds flat—that's how long it took her.

"Well, I never," said Sullivan. "Who would have

guessed a nice young lady like yourself?"

Lord Sopwith held my elbow as we made our way to the car. On route, we passed a bun shop. The aroma made me dizzy again. "Sir," I said, "my ribs are starting to stick out. I haven't had anything but chewing gum since breakfast. Please—may I have a cinnamon bun?"

"Good God. You sound like Oliver Twist," he said, reaching for his wallet. Raising his voice, he called after his wife, who was walking ahead of us, arm and arm with Daphne. "Phyl," he said, "we must feed our young charge here."

"Oh, we mustn't," said Lady Sop, looking at the bun shop with utter contempt. She glanced at her diamond encrusted platinum wristwatch. "What do you know? It's teatime! But really dear, we mustn't eat refreshment room food. Not when the Savoy is right up the street."

"You make an excellent point, what? The Savoy it is!" Lord Sopwith raced over to the Rolls, jumping in the front. He didn't even give Duncan time to open the door.

CHAPTER TWENTY-EIGHT

THINGS WERE SPINNING out of control. I saw it all: us sitting in gilded chairs sipping Earl Grey tea from gold-rimmed cups, while Fritz rowed his way to Calais, a spanking new Messerschmitt waiting for him. But I was roughhoused into the waiting Rolls by Daphne, stuck in the back seat between her and Lady Sop.

"The Savoy, Duncan," said Lord Sopwith, sliding the partition window shut.

"They do an excellent job with finger food," said Lady Sop. "Really—first rate."

Nigel Duncan moved the car from the curb, gliding along the Strand toward the Savoy Hotel. I had about one minute to talk them into changing direction. Honest to God, I was starving. But duty called. "You've got to listen to me!" I begged. "There's a Luftwaffe pilot making his way to Dover with the help of a Nazi secret agent dressed as an RAF navigator. And I'm the only living human being who can identify them. We shouldn't be eating crumpets at a time like this!"

Lord Sopwith slid open the glass window that divided our sections. I started to repeat myself. "I'm telling you—"

"I heard every word you said, Tommy. Now you can take it down an octave or two." He turned his head toward Daphne. "What do you make of this outburst? Is there even a germ of truth in what the boy is saying?"

"I'm afraid, my lord, that there might just be," said Daphne. "You see, it's true that a Luftwaffe pilot was shot down—by my Jack, I'm proud to say—and that he's on the run. Jack and the whole base are out searching for him as we speak. And there was evidence found"—she bit her lip—"evidence pointing to the possibility that Tommy had been in the vicinity of the pilot. You see we found—"

"A marble, a photograph of my ma and da, a one-leafed clover, and a postcard from the Empire State Building. Near a Luftwaffe pilot's jacket. I threw everything from my pocket when he kidnapped me and Beatrix at gunpoint."

"Beatrix? *Beatrix?*" asked Lady Sop with wide eyes. "You don't mean little Princess Beatrix of the Netherlands? I thought the family was safely in Canada?"

Daphne explained that Beatrix was a nurse who had gone missing from the base. "And then there's the Polish pilot who was shot and found near the—"

"Postcard!" I said.

"And this Beatrix? Tell me she wasn't gunned down as well," said Lady Sop.

"I bet she's still holding onto the pharaoh's toe," I said. "At least, that's the last I seen—I mean *saw*—of her. Just before the Luftwaffe pilot forced me to take him to his grandmother in Mayfair. Mrs. Wigglesworth is her name. She's A-Okay."

"My head is spinning," said Lady Sop. "Please slow down." She meant me, but Duncan misunderstood and pulled the Rolls to the curb.

Lord Sopwith stopped me speaking again. "Let me think in quiet for just one confounded second."

"Oh, *do* let's go to Dover!" said Lady Sop, wiggling the rings on her finger anxiously. "I relish the idea of a chase. So thrilling!"

"Dear, *p-lease*," said Lord Sopwith, drawing out the last part until he was out of breath. It was so quiet in the car you could hear the tick of the dashboard clock and the sound of traffic dulled by thick tinted windows. Lord Sopwith knit his eyebrows. He looked at me, "You would recognize these men?"

"Where's the Bible, sir. I'd know their mugs anywhere. And—"

"That will be all," he said, slamming the glass partition shut.

As Duncan pulled the car from the curb, the three of us in the backseat leaned toward the glass, watching Lord Sopwith's lips. He spoke one syllable.

"Hip-hip-hurrah!" said Lady Sop.

Daphne moaned. She leaned back in the glove leather seat and closed her eyes. Once the car was rolling, Lady Sop looked at her and said, "My dear, are you well? You look a fright."

"She was just in the hospital," I said.

"Should you be out, then? Whatever is the matter, my dear?"

Daphne opened her eyes slowly. "I'll be fine. I'm recovering from some sort of poisoning. The doctor says all I need is rest and plenty of liquids from this point on. And besides, there's a shortage of beds at the hospital. They put me in a room with an awful bore—she kept going on and on about her silly Jack Russell terriers. I think I know everything there is to know about their bowel movements. Truth be told, I took the IV out of my hand and snuck out without telling the nurses. I've had a little nurse's training, you know."

"Take some brandy then, my dear." Lady Sop opened a cabinet by her knees—low and behold, in there was a minibar. But Daphne waved her off, her not being a drinker. Lady Sop poured herself a shot. "Was it food poisoning, dear?"

"No one can be certain what caused it," said Daphne, wore out. "But it had the earmarks of hemlock poisoning—paralysis and all that."

"Like Socrates!" said Lady Sop, who was up on Shakespeare and Greek philosophers.

"Precisely," said Daphne. " 'By all means, marry. If you get a good wife, you'll become happy; if you get a bad one, you'll become a philosopher.' "

"You were quoting Socrates as you passed out?" I asked.

"That's right, Thomas. He was killed by means of hemlock poisoning. It's one of my favorite quotes. I plan on having it recited at the wedding."

"Very apropos," said Lady Sop. "Quite. Usually people choose Corinthians, chapter 13."

So Daphne suspected even then—back when she

fell off the bicycle—that it was hemlock poisoning. She said, "Yes. I'd put two and two together, you see. The paralysis and then the fact that there is hemlock growing rampant in the yard at the manor house where I'd been having tea. I'm sure it must have been a simple mistake. There's chamomile growing right beside it. And lavender. It will be such a lovely garden come spring."

"I think I touched the hemlock!" I said. "Lady Sheffield made me wash my hands afterwards. She must've known." I examined my hands, worried that I didn't washed them good enough.

"Well—it could have been hemlock, anyway," said Daphne. "I hadn't had anything to eat at the base, not with so many people coming down with food poisoning."

"Why would someone want to poison you?" I asked.

"Jealousy," said Lady Sop, slapping her knee. "Can I venture a guess and say you were with a group of single women 'in want of a husband,' as Jane Austin says."

"Jealousy is one of the seven deadly sins, and one of the big ten, too," I said, rolling out my Bible knowledge. *Blanche*, I thought. She was always the one going on about wanting to marry a handsome pilot.

"It's true I was at the billet of a group of single WAAFs," said Daphne "And yet, I'm certain that no one intentionally poisoned me. Jealously? Maybe—but to go to that extreme? No, I can't see it. I mean, it's true Jack is the most handsome man on the base—maybe in the entire RAF—but there are plenty of others nearly as dashing."

"I can think of one or two—the king, being one," said Lady Sop. "He is stunning when he dons his uniform, you must admit. But I'm afraid the queen hasn't kept her figure, sadly."

We were nearing the edge of the city, which was taking forever because of fallen bricks and rubble in the road. Some streets were blocked off where a bomb blew. But traffic was finally getting thinner, just as houses got more rundown. Nigel Duncan drove the Rolls into a gas station. The glass partition slid back.

"We need petrol," said Lord Sopwith. "And besides, I think it would be wise to alert the authorities. It will take but a moment. Meanwhile, if anyone must use the WC, *Carpe Diem*, as the Romans said. We won't want to stop again."

"I could use a leak," I said.

"Thomas! Where are your manners?" said Daphne, finally getting color in her cheeks. Duncan opened the door for us. He bowed from the waist.

"Hurry along, my dears," said Lady Sop, scooting us out of the car. "We must make haste. And Daphne, dear—the facilities are bound to be filthy. Be sure not to touch anything."

Lord Sopwith walked over to a phone booth and the women were directed to the bathroom by a grease monkey. Duncan handed the attendant a ration book and then the two of us stood by the fender, doing our business. Just as I finished buttoning up my pants, Lord Sopwith called me to the telephone. "Describe the two fugitives to the Detective Chief Inspector, Tommy." He put the receiver in my hand and I stood on my tippy-toes to reach the mouthpiece.

"The Luftwaffe pilot is not much more than seventeen-years-old...." I gave a blow-by-blow description, remembering Fritz's pathetic attempt at a Hitler mustache and the secret agent's beak nose. "They're armed and dangerous," I said.

When we hung up the phone, Lord Sopwith removed his solid gold Patek Philippe pocket watch from a watch pocket on his vest, popping open the lid. The watch was attached to a gold chain, making it impossible to steal.

"What could be taking the ladies, I wonder?" he said, like this was a first.

"Can I sit in front with you and Duncan, sir?"

"Want to be with the menfolk, do you? All right, hop in."

By the time we got back on the road, the sun was getting low. Duncan ignored the posted speed limit signs. He even went through a couple of stop signs. At one red stop light, he blew the horn and drove straight through. Since Lord Sopwith wasn't complaining, I guessed it was at his instructions. Duncan usually wasn't such a daredevil. I was glad to be up front. We stopped only once, to let a shepherd cross the street with his flock of goats; they were taking forever, but the babies sounded awful cute with their ba-ba-bas.

"We are to go straightaway to the police station in the town center, Duncan, where Tommy will identify the fugitives. Victoria Avenue, wouldn't you know. I've already spoken to the DCI. He'll be waiting for us. So make haste while the day—"

"Meaning the Jerries 'ave been apprehended, your lordship?" asked Duncan.

"No, no. As far as we know they are still on the run. And we've been sternly instructed not to approach the fugitives ourselves. We're not armed, you see."

"Why, your lordship," said Duncan. "We've got the Webly in the glove box. Just in case of stickups, if you remember?"

"So we have. So we have. Yet, better to leave these matters to the professionals."

"But you're professional soliders!" I said, knowing already that they'd both served in the Great War, and that Duncan was Lord Sopwith's batman before he was his chauffeur—the solider who cleans an officer's boots, presses his uniform, and polishes his buttons.

"That's right, Tommy. I were his lordship's driver then, too." Duncan patted the steering wheel. "As such. But that were near the end, after so many fell. And what with all the drivers needed for the Ambulance Corp."

"For dear sakes, ol' chap," said Lord Sopwith. "We were on home soil the entire show. Building biplanes."

"Still, it were an important job, sir. 'Em two-winged birds won us the war, didnit? I practice from time to time with the Webly. Keep it oiled, too. In case of armed bandits on the road."

"You mean Robin Hood and his gang?" I said.

"That's it, exactly—Robin Hood. Like to burgle the rich and give to the poor, don't they?" Duncan laughed and then gunned the engine.

"Harrumph," said Lord Sopwith. "More like rob the rich and line their own blasted pockets."

Lady Sop slid the glass partition open and said, "My dear—please refrain from the use of profanity around the child. We are here to set the example."

"Quite right," he said. "—line their own *confounded* pockets, I meant."

CHAPTER TWENTY-NINE

Somewhere in Dover, England

SPECIAL AGENT Charles "Charlie" Ellis consults a small spiral notebook before pushing open a gate. He notices a wooden plaque attached to the gate: *Seamstress Within, Alterations, Expert Tailoring*, it says, even though what he is looking at is a simple cottage—well-kept, with a Victorian era cast-iron table and chair set placed under a barren tree. He removes his hat before knocking on the door.

A woman, her hair hennaed but the roots gray, comes to the door. Ellis can see her behind the lace curtains in the sidelight. He expects the door to open, but instead hears a voice say, "Who's calling?" while the door remains closed.

"Charles Ellis, ma'am. I've been sent down from London. I believe you are expecting me."

There is no reply. He sees the woman shuffle to a telephone, lift it from the table and return with it to the door.

Finally, "How'd I know it's you? You 'ave identification, do you? I'll want to call your office and make sure you aren't an impostor." She lifts the receiver; with the same hand she gets ready to dial.

Ellis reaches into his jacket pocket, coming out with a billfold, which he opens and presses to the side-light. He sees the curtain move aside.

"Let me get me reading glasses," says the woman, he assumes to be Mrs. Sanders.

Who, to date, has lodged twenty-six reports of ene-my agents present in Dover. He's read through every one of the reports in preparation for this interview.

A few minutes later, Mrs. Sanders appears at the door, now wearing half-rim glasses perched on the end of her nose. Ellis positions his identify card so that it is level with her eyes. The door is opened and he is invit-ed to step inside. The phone call to London will not be necessary, it seems.

"Mrs. Sanders, I believe," he says. "Might I have a word with you? Concerning a report you made about a suspicious fishing boat."

"It's about time," she says.

CHAPTER THIRTY

We were passing through Canterbury, with about half an hour to go, when Lord Sopwith began reciting *The Canterbury Tales*, a book that babbled on in Middle English, written by a fella named Chaucer. He'd once made me slog through the thing, and I'd thrown the illuminated vellum book against the library wall after only three pages. For that, I was sent to bed without supper. Lord Sopwith had studied what they called "The Classics" at school and couldn't get enough of the stuff. He deepened his voice so he sounded like Boris Karloff in *Frankenstein*:

> "This frere bosteth that he knoweth helle,
> And God it woot, that it is litel wonder;
> Freres and feendes been but lyte asonder.
> For, pardee, ye han ofte tyme herd telle
> How that a frere ravyshed was to helle
> In spirit ones by a visioun;
> And as an angel ladde hym up and doun…"

I could barely understand Lord Sopwith when he was speaking plain English, now it was impossible.

Duncan was speeding through Canterbury, a regular kind of guy like me and not a fan of Chaucer. I could tell by the way he tapped his thumbs against the steering wheel as Lord Sopwith recited his poem.

I'd never been to Dover. Only seen the cliffs once, and that was from Lord Sopwith's speedboat, when Daphne and me made our way to Belgium to rescue Jack. I remembered seeing a silhouette of the medieval castle that night. I'd wanted to visit the place, but we were on a rescue mission not a sightseeing tour. The castle was set up on a hill. Haunted, for sure. So imagine my joy when the castle loomed in front of us. It was straight out of *The Count of Monte Cristo*—I'd seen all three movie versions: the first one was silent, the second two were talkies.

"Slow down, Duncan," said Lord Sopwith, tapping the leather dash. "We want Tommy here to make a reconnaissance of the place. Pay attention, boy."

"My eyes are peeled, sir."

The Rolls rolled into town, passing row after row of whitewashed buildings, all facing the sea. Loads of them had been demolished by German bombs. Workers, wearing face masks to keep the dust out, shoved bricks into baskets, then carted off rubble in horse-drawn wagons. The front had come right off one building and we looked into a child's bedroom. A teddy bear dangled from an exposed beam, like it was holding on for dear life. Fritz would get goose bumps looking at that.

Along the seaside were dozens of fishing boats, something Lord Sopwith made note of: "Most of the sportsmen have moved their crafts elsewhere—to safer harbors. Ireland, often." He shook his head sadly. Lord Sopwith loved nothing better than sailing.

"We're only twenty-two miles from occupied Europe," I said. "A mother once swam across, we're that close to France."

"She was a champion swimmer, Thomas," said Daphne. "Don't you dare try it." After saying that I shut my mouth, embarrassed that I couldn't even dog-paddle well.

"We should stop and walk along the docks," I said. "The Luftwaffe pilot might be looking for a boat right now. Besides, this will be a good spot to get fish and chips, not that I like fish." I kept one eye open for a shop, the other eye for Nazis. I'd had nothing to eat since Mrs. Wigglesworth stomach-popping breakfast. My ma said I had the appetite of a killer whale and it was proving to be true.

"My guess is they'll wait until the cover of dark to nick a boat," said Daphne. "After all, that's what we did, Thomas. I mean, who would be so brazen as to nick a boat in broad daylight?"

"Let's change the subject," said Lady Sop, quickly. "My husband has an ulcer and you know how mention of the Chris-Craft upsets him. We don't want him on a diet of milk and cauliflower again." Lord Sopwith was still sore about us taking his speedboat to Belgium. It was a beaut, too.

But he let his hand go limp at the wrist, meaning that nothing bothered him; that all was forgiven; that he was happy to contribute to rescuing an RAF pilot; that he'd already forgotten about the Chris-Craft boat and why mention it now? I loved the man, I really did. He was what you called a *good sport*, a straight shooter, an all-around good guy. I leaned into him on a turn so's he'd know how I felt. He patted my knee in response. He said we must "push on" to the police station "with all due haste." After all, maybe they'd captured Fritz already. We didn't want to waste our time scoping out the docks when we could be chowing down on French fries.

"DCI Harris," said the head detective, shaking Lord Sopwith's hand. *Detective Chief Inspector.* "A pleasure to make your acquaintance. I'm a big fan of the Hawker Hurricane. May I say that the nation is grateful."

"The Spitfire has surpassed it," said Lord Sopwith, taking a stab at humility.

"I'm sure you have something even better than the Spit waiting in the wings." He laughed at his own humor. "Waiting in the wings!"

"Have you caught the Germans?" I asked, taking a look around. An oak paneled hallway led to offices, all with name plaques on the doors. If I wasn't mistaken, there was a bloodstain on the floor.

"I'm afraid not," said the DCI. "But we have all hands on deck. Ha! All hands on deck! Why, my men are searching the docks as we live and breathe."

"No boats have been reported missing?" asked Daphne.

"None that we know of thus far," said the DCI. "Of

course the coast is littered with rowboats, tethered to rocks with no one keeping an eye on."

I wondered if it was even possible to rowboat to France. I remembered the size of the waves on the Channel—scary even in a high-speed Chris-Craft motorboat. "Daphne's right, sir," I said. "They are hiding out and waiting till it's pitch dark. Meanwhile, they're probably holed up at the castle or in one of those tunnels I've heard about. Maybe I can—"

"Highly unlikely," said the DCI. "The Royal Air Force has that place on lockdown. Very highest security. But we should say no more."

"*Loose lips, sink ships*," said Lord Sopwith, his favorite phrase. Mostly he just used it to shut me up.

"I have to sit down," said Daphne. "Do you mind?"

The DCI took one look at her and rushed into his office. He brought over a rolling desk chair. "Where are my manners?" he said, hitting his forehead. "May I offer you something to drink?"

"A stiff scotch wouldn't be refused," said Lord Sopwith.

"I wouldn't mind a little tipple myself," said Lady Sop, giggling.

"Water, please," said Daphne.

I looked around for a Coke machine. They had them in police stations on Long Island. I'd been just a few feet from one once, stuck behind bars, unjustly accused of a petty crime. The proximity had been tormenting.

The DCI filled us in on the manhunt. He had undercover cops watching the train station and the streets surrounding it. Two trains from London had already arrived and there'd been no suspicious characters aboard—at least, none the undercover cops were able to identify.

"Not less than an hour ago," he told us, "we had a tip-off from a very reliable source. I'll say no more. Very highest in the land." He leveled a hand above his head. "Be sure of it—a certain fishing boat won't be leaving the pier tonight."

I mentioned that Daphne was a trained artist and suggested the two of us get to work on a wanted poster, the kind they had up in post offices when Bonnie and Clyde were on the run from the Feds back in 1934.

"I'm game," said Daphne. "Just bring me a pad of unlined paper and a pencil."

The DCI shouted over to a lady dressed in plainclothes and she went in search of the materials. The two of us were shown to an empty office, where the same lady cleared the desktop for us. Meanwhile, my guardians were having cocktails in the DCI's office.

"Let's start with Fritz," I said. "Since I'm most acquainted with his mug. His real name is Peter Albert Loehlein. Picture Mickey Rooney, only taller and with a narrower face."

Daphne began sketching away. "Like this?"

"His cheekbones are higher." I motioned across my face. She took an eraser and redrew the cheeks. "Now put some freckles on them and on his nose—that's it. Now the eyes need to be larger and darker. Think Rudolf Valentino… Yeah, and with long black eyelashes."

"You got a good look at him, did you?"

"I'm a master observer, Daphne. You should know that by now. Treasure hunters and budding Egyptologists got to be." I asked her to put a tweed cap on Fritz's head and to draw fuzz over his lip. She drew the shoulders of his overcoat so it looked a few sizes too small. When she showed me the drawing, I nearly fell over. "You could get a job as one of them characterture artists who work the Coney Island boardwalk. Gee, you're good."

She drew the other man in profile, because what I remembered best was the shape of his beak nose. Everything else was a blur, seeing that he'd knocked me out before the details could solidify in my mind. Daphne seemed satisfied though: "It looks like a portrait of Lorenzo de' Medici, who ruled Renaissance Florence."

"Make sure you draw him with a gold tooth."

"Now he looks like Lorenzo de' Medici snarling."

We took the two drawings into the DCI's office. "You say this is a good rendition?" he asked me, laying down his tumbler.

"Spitting image."

"Then I'll have my girl take this to the printers to make facsimiles on the mimeograph machine." He looked at me: "And that might be the perfect job for you, young man—handing them out, posting them in shop windows, on telephone poles and whatnot." He called out for the lady. "Run these over to Henderson's, would you? Ask for a hundred copies. Have him typeset WANTED NAZIS as a banner. And add these notes to the bottom of the page." He tore a piece of paper from a pad.

"Is there a reward, sir?" asked the lady.

"Tea with the queen," said Lady Sop.

"That will be all, Smith. Now, chivvy along," said the DCI.

The lady saluted and raced from the office. The rest of us sat there like lumps on a log.

"Shouldn't we join the manhunt?" I said.

"You've told us that at least one of the men is armed," said the DCI.

"The Luftwaffe pilot has already shot one man," said Daphne. "A pilot with No. 303 Polish Fighter Squadron, on loan to a Czechoslovakian squadron." The details were wrong, I knew, but I didn't correct her.

"Are they on *our* side?" asked Lady Sop, looking concerned. "I thought the Nazis had Eastern Europe?"

"They do, dear," said Lord Sopwith patting her knee, "but some managed to escape in '39 and join the Allies."

"Marvelous!" she said, clasping her hands together. "At this rate, we'll win the war before Christmas."

"One can only hope," said Lord Sopwith, raising one eyebrow. He'd heard that Christmas line before and wasn't buying it.

Daphne told us that Ciesielski, the Polish pilot, was alive—but just barely. He'd lost plenty of blood before someone spotted my postcard and went searching through the cornfield. You could say I saved his life. I mentioned to them that the secret agent, disguised as an RAF navigator, also had a revolver. Lady Sop swooned.

"An Enfield service revolver, you say?" said the DCI. "And an RAF uniform… My guess is the Gestapo took it off one of our downed men."

"Ghastly!" said Lady Sop. "Tragic. And no one to give him a proper C of E funeral." (C of E meant *Church of England*, as opposed to the Holy Roman Catholic Church, which didn't have an abbreviation.)

"It's likely the RAF navigator, from whom the uniform was stolen, is in a German prison camp, my dear," said Lord Sopwith.

"This dreadful war," said Lady Sop.

"Aren't downed airmen supposed to get out of their uniforms as soon as they crash?" I asked. "Maybe the navigator evaded capture but the Gestapo found the uniform he left behind."

"Well, that's a positive spin on things," said Daphne. "I do love your optimism."

"Not to put a damper on the subject," said Lord Sopwith, "but downed airmen, hoping to evade capture, are instructed to bury or burn their uniforms. If there's time, that is. I'll have to inform our intelligence people of this new ploy—the RAF uniform, I mean. Brilliant, what? To think the enemy agent would be given preferential treatment wherever he went. One can only hope he wouldn't be given access to RAF bases wearing the uniform."

"There's one detail I forgot about," I said. "Tell your intelligence friends that the Luftwaffe pilot's jacket had Jagdgeschwader Mölders embroidered on the sleeve. That's what made it so terrifying."

"Play them at their own game," said the DCI. "That's the idea!"

"Good thinking," said Daphne, before passing out on the floor.

Lady Sopwith loosened the top button of Daphne's blouse, fanning her face with a manila folder she'd taken from the DCI's desk. "Back away and give her air," she told us.

"In the movies, they slap the person's face," I said.

"You watch too many movies, Thomas," said Daphne, coming to and resting on her elbows.

"My dear, you should be in bed," said Lord Sopwith, asking the DCI to recommend a good hotel. "At least three stars, what?"

My hopes were soaring as they spoke. I came to learn that the Royal Navy had taken over one hotel and were calling it HMS Wasp. Meanwhile, the Burlington Hotel was a bombed out shell. The Grand Hotel got a direct hit too, leaving it in rubble. "Sixteen people killed that day and scores wounded," said the DCI, leading us in a moment of silence where everyone looked down at their shoes and shook their heads.

I wanted to break in with, "There's always the castle," but I knew to keep quiet.

Finally the DCI said, "Oh, the futility of war," shaking his head. "But no use crying over spilt milk. Seems to me that we have Jerry on the run finally."

"Let's stay in the castle," I said.

"I'd prefer to sleep in the Rolls," said Lady Sop.

"Castles are so drafty."

"The castle is being used as a military installation," said the DCI. "As well as the underground tunnels. I'm afraid the whole place is off-limits to civilians due to—'

"*Loose lips*," said Lord Sopwith.

"Maybe they'll make an exception for us," I said. "Being that I'm the brother of an RAF pilot and Daphne here is a fiancée. And let's not forget that Lord Sopwith builds airplanes."

"And where does that leave me?" asked Lady Sop, genuinely perplexed.

"In the Rolls. With Duncan," said Lord Sopwith.

After some pondering, the DCI recommended a guesthouse run by a Mrs. Hill, a lady friend of his. He said she served a "bang-up breakfast," whatever that was. For another thing, Mrs. Hill kept the paraffin heaters running night and day. We piled into the Rolls and drove around the block, parking in the gravel driveway of a Victorian brick house. Lady Sop said it reminded her of her great-aunt's house.

Mrs. Hill was a white-haired thing about my height but a hundred pounds heavier. She greeted us like her long-lost relatives. "Been ever so busy since the Grand was hit. My feet are run off. One good thing to come out of this—not that I'm happy what the Jerries did to the Grand, mind you. They served a lovely tea. On Saturday afternoons in the summer they'd have a four-piece orchestra playing."

"Must've seemed like the Titanic the day the bomb dropped," I said, remembering the eight-piece orchestra that played as the ship sank, hoping to calm the passengers.

Mrs. Hill only had two rooms available. Lady Sop insisted on sharing a room with Daphne so she could watch for signs of another faint. That left me with Lord Sopwith. Mrs. Hill showed us to adjoining rooms. She opened a windows to air the place out and left to find a chamber pot. The bathroom was down the hall, she said. The boiler was old, so we'd best space out our baths, she told us.

"Fine with me," I said, "I don't need one."

"You do too," said Daphne before heading to her room.

"She'll be fighting for that bathroom with the riff-raff," I said.

"Now Tommy, don't become a snob," said Lord Sopwith, sitting down on the bed nearest the door. I threw myself horizontally onto the other bed. The springs made it like a trampoline. A salty breeze came through the open window.

"So what's the plan, sir? You don't mean for us to come all this way and stay out of the action, do you? And now it's dark out, the German's will be looking for a boat."

"There *is* a plan, Tommy. And unfortunately it must include you." He looked troubled, rubbing the red marks on the bridge of his nose after removing his glasses.

"Swell. Lay it on me, sir."

Turned out Lord Sopwith's plan was to sneak out without alerting the ladies. He explained that Daphne needed rest, obviously, and that he didn't want his wife caught in the middle of crossfire. He was being chivalrous, one of the things he was best at. He always opened doors for ladies and stood whenever one entered a room. On top of that, *whilst* walking on a sidewalk, he took the place closest to the curb in case a car came along and splashed into a puddle. I imagined him throwing his coat over the puddle and letting the lady step right on it. He had a book in his library called *Rules of Etiquette For Gentlemen.*

My stomach rumbled like the San Francisco earthquake. I said, "We might need food first. To build up our manly strength."

"I'm a bit peckish myself," said Lord Sopwith.

There was a pad and pencil laying on a small desk. He made me write a note that said, *Taking a rest, please do not disturb.* I still had tape stuck to my trousers and we used some of it to attach the note to the bedroom door. Then we tip-toed down the hallway and descended a service staircase that led to the kitchen. Mrs. Hill was there putting food on a tray.

"Where are you two off to?" she asked. "Your wife asked me to bring up a tray. I have the remains of a nice bubble and squeak for you. And then there's my Wartime Banoffee Pie—you'd never know it was made with substitutes."

"Sounds delightful," said Lord Sopwith. "But I've promised the boy fish and chips. And a gentleman never goes back on his word." I followed him out a back exit. He turned and said, "And, Mrs. Hill. You'll keep that to yourself, won't you?"

"Like I wasn't even a fly on the wall. And if you're still here tomorrow night, I'll prepare for you the best fish and chips in the entire Empire. It's only that I don't have potatoes that I don't offer now."

"Capital," said Lord Sopwith.

CHAPTER THIRTY-ONE

I ASKED IF IT WAS TRUE we were going for fish and chips.
Lord Sopwith said a gentleman never lies. I thought
about the note he'd just dictated to me.

"Taking a rest are we?"

"In a matter of speaking," he said.

Duncan was waiting around the corner with the
car, reading the sports section but on the lookout for
our arrival. He opened the passenger door for us, even
though I tried to beat him to it. We piled into the front
seat again, me in the middle.

"There's been a slight alteration to the plan, Duncan." Turned out that Duncan was already in on "The
Plan." Lord Sopwith spoke in a whisper, even though
the windows were rolled up. "We will first stop off at a
chip shop. We'll take it in a package and eat on the go,
what? Not too heavy a meal, because we may be called
upon to swim."

The Rolls pulled up in front of a fish and chip stand
across from the seafront. Me and Duncan went to place
our order. I had to make sure they didn't put vinegar
on my chips. I asked the cook to slobber on the tomato

sauce, because he wouldn't know what ketchup was. My vocabulary was becoming more British every day. My ma wasn't going to like it one bit. Ever since Jack swore allegiance to King and Country, she'd been making donations to the Irish Republican Army.

Back in the Rolls, with greasy bags sitting on our laps, we ate our supper while Lord Sopwith outlined "The Plan." You call a plan like his a smoke out.

Same as me, Lord Sopwith had a sharp eye. When we first drove into town, he noticed that most of the boats were tethered to the docks—in clear view of pedestrians strolling along the waterfront or sitting out at a restaurant or pub. The idea was to rent the most seaworthy boat. Lord Sopwith was a champion World Cup yachtsman and would have no trouble operating it. We'd move the boat over to a deserted part of the seafront, somewhere with a lot of bomb damage, *hence*, where most people didn't want to be strolling, afraid they'd step on an unexploded shell. We'd leave the boat unattended and then find a hiding spot that gave us a good view and a clear shot. The Nazis would be looking to steal a boat, and ours would "suit their purposes to perfection."

"It's a good plan, your lordship," said Duncan. "And am I right to assume I'll be the one holding the Webley? Being I'm the one been practicing."

Lord Sopwith winked at Duncan. I started to protest. But to tell you true, I wouldn't know a Webley if it hit me on the head. I wished now I'd brought along my slingshot. Marbles might have come in useful, too. Even a yo-yo would've been better than nothing.

"You are the sentry," said Lord Sopwith, speaking to me. "A very crucial position. But in no instance are you to involve yourself beyond that."

"What are you playing, sir," I asked.

"I am the ship's captain, and your commanding officer." I stood at attention and saluted. Duncan did the same. We followed our chief to the boat docks.

It didn't take long to pick the right vessel. She was a tugboat with a small cabin up-front. The hull was painted green and the top half of the boat was white. It stood out in the moonlight. Little Union Jacks were strung from the mast to a ladder at the back. Lord Sopwith made a deal with the owner, who told us he'd fallen on hard times ever since the war started, what with German U-boats patrolling the Channel and preventing him from going into the deep waters. He was happy to get a wad of British pounds and Lord Sopwith's pledge to replace the boat if anything *catastrophic* happened to it.

"I'm off to the pub for a nip," said the tugboat owner, patting his wallet. "The one what's not a pile of bricks."

"Cheerio," I said.

We waded over to the boat in nothing but our drawers. Lord Sopwith and Duncan climbed into the boat while I turned the crank that raised the anchor.

"She's a bit of a rust bucket," said Duncan. "Not like *Endeavour.*"

"Don't be a snob, Duncan," said Lord Sopwith. "She shall suit our purposes to perfection." When Lord Sopwith got the boat started, she belched black smoke from a stack on top of the cabin. Once she got going though, she chugged along just fine. The perfect spot turned out to be right in front of what was once Dover's fanciest hotel. Now it was a heap of rubble. We dropped anchor about fifty yards from the shore, where the water was still deep—alongside a long pier that jutted out to the sea. I might've been able to leap to the boardwalk pillions and climb to the top, staying bone-dry. Only I didn't want to abandon my two comrades, who were older and might need my help. I'll admit that my heart raced as I jumped into the water, pointing my toes and keeping my arms pressed to my side, hoping not to belly flop. My body was like a torpedo, my feet hit the bottom of the sea and I pushed off, forgetting about the cut in my foot until it was too late; salt water stung it worse than rubbing alcohol. For a minute there—under the dark waves, water up my nose, swallowing a mouthful of brine—I panicked. But I didn't see my life flash before my eyes and I knew I'd make it. I surfaced, gulped air, and then got the idea to float on my back, pushing backwards like a retreating dolphin. It was a struggle, what with the tide going out instead of in. And the water was ice-cold. Lord Sopwith and Duncan were waiting for me at the shore.

"Now back to the Rolls where we will reclothe ourselves," said Lord Sopwith. He'd worked out all the details.

"If you'd told me the plan sooner, I would've brought along those fluffy towels with the hotel name embroidered on them," I said. "They were laying on our beds."

"I'll never keep you in the dark again, young man,"

said Lord Sopwith, shivering.

Duncan drove the Rolls closer to where we'd left the boat, while Lord Sopwith and me got back into our clothes. Then Lord Sopwith walked over to a phone booth and called the DCI at his home exchange.

"Jolly good news," he said when he hung up the receiver.

"Shucks," I said, stamping my foot. "They've caught them already?"

"Don't lose heart, young man. We may have a crack at them yet. Two men, meeting the exact description of Daphne's drawing, were earlier this evening spotted in a Dover pub having a pint of beer and four orders of bangers and mash. The barmaid is 100% certain they were the very Germans whom we seek. The devil, dressed as an RAF navigator, attempted to flirt with the barmaid, if you can believe it. The other man, who she mistook for his son, didn't say a peep—had his head in the plate the whole time. I'd say this is your Fritz character, the Luftwaffe man. There's one point that's troubling the Detective Chief Inspector. And I must say, it is disturbing news."

"They popped someone!"

"No, Tommy, they *seduced* someone. You see, the barmaid later watched as the German succeeded in wooing a WAAF into the booth. She was then seen leaving the pub in the company of the two men." He shook is head. "If you want my opinion, morals have declined since the start of this war. It's all this improper fraternizing between men and women—in the factories, in the services, in public houses. Why, before the war it would have been unheard of for a decent English girl to go into a pub unescorted and walk out with two Nazis."

"She may be a hostage, your lordship," said Duncan. "If they show up with the lass, what are we to do?"

"By golly—rescue the silly girl of course!" said Lord Sopwith, raising his palms. "Now, more than ever, it's of paramount importance that we keep our wits about us."

The obvious place to hide was up on the pier. There were little gazebos built along the wood boardwalk, which would provide the perfect cover. We'd have a clear view of the boat and, if need be, one of us could climb down to the water in seconds flat and stop Fritz and his accomplice from escaping. I made my suggestion to Lord Sopwith.

"Roger that," he said.

That's when Lord Sopwith began doubting the idea of having me along for the stakeout. He started saying I was too young, should be in bed, that Lady Sop was going to have a conniption because he'd let me along this far. He even brought my ma into the equation. I had to swear to stay hidden out of sight if there was even the slightest trouble. I wasn't allowed to "engage the enemy." Not even to save Lord Sopwith and Duncan. And if I disobeyed orders, I'd never get another pence of allowance or a bite of Mrs. Balson's delicious pudding. We crept to one of the gazebos, keeping low so that the railing and benches blocked our view from the seashore.

"We should've brought your high-powered binoculars, sir," I said.

"We'll see them if they make a move towards the boat. As fate would have it, they've picked a bright night to make an escape."

An hour flew by while we watched solitary pedestrians walking along the seashore and the road that fronted it. Duncan was the first to spot a man, making his way down the pier. As he came closer to our position, we could see he had a billy club in his hand.

"I don't recognize the fella," I whispered when he was about ten feet from us.

"Are you certain?" asked Lord Sopwith.

With the man five feet from us, I said: "100%. For one thing, he's wearing a police uniform."

"Who goes there!" shouted the copper. "Come out and present yourselves immediately." We stepped out from the gazebo and he shined a flashlight in our faces, making sure we saw the club he was wielding.

"Thomas Sopwith, at your service. Am I correct in saying that you report to DCI Harris?"

The copper put the club under his armpit and shook Lord Sopwith's hand. "Joining in the search, are you? Seen any suspicious activity?"

Lord Sopwith assured him we had everything under control, mentioning that he worked with the Air Ministry and that both he and Duncan were trained for this kind of operation. "Now, Constable, be so good as to let us get back to our post," he said.

"Carry on, gentlemen," said the copper, who turned around and left the pier.

We sat on the floor inside the gazebo, all eyes on the

seashore. Another hour or two passed by with nothing to break the boredom. Then, when the moon was right overhead, we spotted a car driving from a side street and heading toward the pier. The headlights were off, but that didn't mean anything—the blackout was in effect.

"It could be two lovers, out for a rendezvous," said Lord Sopwith.

The car stopped and we watched as a woman stepped from the driver's side, leaning against the hood of the car. She lit a cigarette. It was too dark, and we were too faraway, to get a good view of her as she gazed out to sea. After a minute or two, she tossed the cigarette butt into the sand, got back into her car, and drove back down the same side street.

"Well, that was exciting," I said.

More time passed, just as action packed. The three of us were having trouble keeping our eyes opened. Duncan suggested we take turns napping—two on duty, one resting. This way we'd save our energy for the chase. Lord Sopwith supported the plan and I was chosen to nap first.

"Wake me up if you see anyone approaching," I said.

And they promised to do it.

CHAPTER THIRTY-TWO

I WAS SOUND ASLEEP when the air-raid sirens woke me, not sure how much time had passed. The first thing I saw when I opened my eyes was Lord Sopwith and Duncan shaking themselves awake. I jumped up to see if the tug-boat was still there bobbing on the Channel waters.

It was.

"We'll have to find a bomb shelter, I'm afraid," said Lord Sopwith. "This position is too exposed."

I figured we had about five minutes to find cover before bombs began dropping. We ran to the Rolls and Lord Sopwith gave the order to head back to the guest-house. He wanted to make sure Daphne and Lady Sopwith were safe. We found them in an Anderson shelter in the backyard. "Plenty of room for everyone," said Mrs. Hill, making space for us. "And refreshments provided at no extra charge."

"Very thoughtful of you," said Lady Sop.

It was dark in the shelter. I sat on the ground, taking no particular notice of the man sitting next to me. "Good to see you, kiddo," he said, slapping my back.

Mrs. Hill lit a candle so I was able to get a good

look at my brother Jack. Daphne was sitting on his lap. Squadron Leader Kennard was sitting next to Jack, and Sel Edner was opposite me.

"Sel— you're alive! Gee, I'm glad."

"The Eagle rises again," he said, tapping his head. "Most of the boys are back in the saddle now. The Jerries can't keep us down, no siree."

Turned out that Lady Sopwith decided to call my brother, telling him where we were. She wanted Daphne's parents' number, too, just in case she didn't wake up from her nap: next of kin.

Kennard said, "Jack and I deserved a little holiday after three weeks on. Not that going in chase of a downed Luftwaffe pilot is much of a holiday. Edner here was corralled into joining the posse as we filed our flight plan. Technically, he's still on medical leave."

"I can't think of a finer way to spend my vacation," said Jack, squeezing Daphne.

A bomb dropped close enough to shake the ground. Mrs. Hill screamed and grabbed onto Squadron Leader Kennard. Lady Sop began singing a patriotic song, while she unpacked a basket full of snacks. She was a great sport.

"What news, Tommy? And don't think for a second you're off the hook for leaving us behind in that way—it was beastly wrong," said Daphne.

"I am to blame for the subterfuge," said Lord Sopwith. "You needed your rest, my dear." The ground shook again. The noise was deafening.

"I hope the Spits survive," said Jack. "We left them

sitting out on the tarmac."

Mrs. Hill passed around a plate of cheese—Kent made, she said—scones with strawberry jam, and apples. Daphne asked me to leave something for the rest of them, but turned down a scone when I offered her a bite of mine. "I'm still a bit wobbly," she said.

"My dear," said Lady Sop to her husband, "did you know someone tried to poison Daphne?"

"If it's true, I'll tear them limb from limb," said Jack.

"I really don't think it was intentional," said Daphne, naïve as usual. "It's just that the symptoms were so like hemlock poisoning. The plant is all over the yard at the WAAF billet where I'd just had tea. But for heaven's sake, the whole idea is insane—who would want to kill me?"

"About a dozen women I can think of off the top of my head," said Jack.

The shelter rumbled as another bomb exploded. My ears rang.

"That might have been the neighbor's house," said Mrs. Hill eventually. "It sounded *that* close, wouldn't you say?"

BOOM, BOOM, BOOM! The Germans were right overhead, having a field day. It was too loud to keep talking, so I got to thinking. Racking my brain, I pictured the kitchen in the WAAF billet, just as it was on Sunday afternoon when I'd finished up the yard work and found Daphne having teatime with her friends. I remembered that Geraldine was there and so was Blanche. With Blanche there was the jealousy motive. Or maybe it was a German husband who put her up to it. Dot was there, too—on my list of suspects. Then there was Alice. But I couldn't remember if she'd been there having tea. I didn't like the woman, but Lady Sheffield vouched for her and I trusted Lady Sheffield. I'd seen her son's grave with my own eyes. And besides, there was her Star of David necklace.

"Jack," I said, first break in the action. "This morning when Mrs. Wigglesworth called you, what did she say?"

"Mrs. Who?" asked Jack.

"Mrs. Wigglesworth—you know, the Luftwaffe pilot's English grandma."

"He has an English grandmother?" asked Kennard. "Are you serious?"

"It was Geraldine that she reached," I said. "When she called the base to tell you I was being held hostage by her grandson."

"But, Thomas," said Daphne. "I saw Geraldine this afternoon and she said nothing about a phone call."

My head began spinning, trying to put the pieces together. "Are you saying no one gave you the message—the message from Mrs. Wigglesworth asking you to come and rescue me in Mayfair?" It was dawning on me that my brother and Kennard didn't get the message. And yet, I was dang-tootin' sure Mrs. Wigglesworth was telling me the truth when she said she'd spoken to Geraldine. "How well do you know Geraldine?" I asked.

"Who is Geraldine?" asked Lady Sop. "Do I know the woman?"

"No, Warrant Officer Geraldine Noble," I said.

"You're not suggesting it was Geraldine who poisoned me?" said Daphne.

"And tripped the squadron giving Sel here a concussion. And poisoned the food in the base kitchen. And put hemlock in your tea, Daphne. And also made it so your Spitfire would catch fire, Jack."

"That's preposterous," said Daphne.

"I think, bub, you're barking up the wrong tree," said Jack. "Geraldine wouldn't hurt a fly. She's a swell gal. She's dating a buddy of ours."

Daphne was still protesting. Squadron Leader Kennard piped in, defending Geraldine's "stellar" reputation. Sel chimed in and said he thought she was a swell gal, too. I was alone in my suspicions, but I was sticking to my guns. Mrs. Wigglesworth *definitely* spoke with Geraldine. I said:

"So, how did you know I was a hostage? How did you know we were headed for Dover? Are you telling me you never came to rescue me from Mrs. Wigglesworth's house in London? Are you telling me you didn't read the note she left behind for you?"

"Who is Mrs. Wigglesworth again?" asked Lady Sop. "I'm having trouble keeping up."

The all-clear siren went off and we exited the shelter. The first thing we did was to follow Mrs. Hill to the fence that divided her property from the neighbor's. We heard a fire truck came to a stop in front of the house; or what once was a house, anyway. Little bonfires dotted the lawn. Two women dressed in Home Guard uniforms jumped out of a jeep.

Jack and the other men hurried next-door to help, while Daphne held onto the back of my collar. We watched as a lady from the Home Guard rescued a cat.

Mrs. Hill escorted a sobbing family from their shelter to her kitchen. "Tea is in order," she said. Everyone agreed.

Everyone but me. I sat in the corner of the kitchen, taxing my brain again. Everyone else gathered around the unlucky family, offering their support and making mean comments about Adolf Hitler. I looked over at my brother. His arm was around Daphne. I was viewing him in profile. It was that view of my brother's Clark Gable nose that triggered the memory. That and Daphne's arm resting next to his.

"There was a WAAF in the car with the Nazi!" I shouted.

"What child?" said Lady Sop. "What car? What Nazi?"

I made them all listen as I described the two-tone maroon and black car that passed the Crossley as Fritz drove Mrs. Wigglesworth and me away from her house in Mayfair. Better late than never: I could swear on a stack of Bibles that the RAF airman driving the car was the same airman—navigator, to be exact—who offered us chewing gum in the subway, and the same navigator who was helping Fritz make an escape. I'd seen the sleeve of a woman in a blue uniform, together with the man in the car—headed to Mrs. Wigglesworth's house. And I'd bet a million bucks she was the very person, a Nazi secret agent, who answered the phone at RAF Rochford when Mrs. Wigglesworth called trying to get in touch with Jack. The note she left behind gave them just enough information to catch our trail as we headed out of London for Dover. They must've been right behind us when Fritz crashed into the taxicab. And then the phony navigator followed us into the Tube station. While the woman, meanwhile—

"We have to find the car!" I shouted. Sometimes a kid has to yell to be taken seriously.

"The boy might be onto something," said Lord Sopwith, knitting his eyebrows, one eye half-closed. "Mrs. Hill, may I use your telephone to ring the DCI?"

"I hate to bring this up," said Duncan, "but could that 'ave been the lass we saw smoking a cigarette by the pier earlier? Did either of you notice what color 'er car was?"

"Good God!" yelled Lord Sopwith.

"The tugboat," I said, hoping it wasn't too late.

CHAPTER THIRTY-THREE

I WAS THE LAST MAN to reach the Rolls. Lord Sopwith slammed the door in my face, lowered the window and said, "Not this time I'm afraid, Tommy."

"Sorry, chief—hard luck," said Jack, who was sitting in the back seat with Squadron Leader Kennard and Sel Edner. Daphne came alongside me, put her arm around my shoulder and patted my back. The Rolls pulled out of the driveway, headed back to the pier.

"Let's get some sleep while it's still dark," she said. "That's been quite enough action for one night."

I went upstairs to the bedroom I shared with Lord Sopwith, with no intention of staying put. The door adjoining my room to Daphne and Lady Sop's was thin enough for me to hear the two of them talking. Daphne said, "I'd like to stay up a minute and read—that is, if you don't mind the light on."

"No problem at all," said Lady Sop. "The proprietress has kindly supplied me with slices of cucumber—so good in preventing wrinkles and with the added benefit of blocking out light."

The window in my room was still opened. It was easy enough to shimmy down a rain gutter. Before I could say Jiminy Cricket, my sneakers landed on gravel. The pier wasn't far from the guesthouse. I began hoofing it in that direction. The streets were so dark I tripped over a sandbag, ripping my jeans at the knee and getting a scrape that burned like the dickens. I limped over to a parked car, putting my foot on the fender so I could get a better look at the damage. Already my foot was throbbing and I knew that two of the stitches had come undone. In the moonlight, I could make out a stream of blood, soaking my jeans. Flecks of dirt and brick chips stuck to the mincemeat flesh. If it weren't for my foot on its fender, I would have passed by the two-tone maroon and black car without noticing it. I said a prayer of thanks to Saint Simon of Cyrene, who must've intervened on my behalf.

There was no one on the street, so I peeked into the car windows. Something furry was laying on the driver's seat. *A long-haired dog?* When I knocked on the window there was no movement or sign of life. The doors were locked, every one of them. But one of the back windows was down a crack. If only I'd had a coat hanger.

I tried the trunk and got lucky. Looking left and right, I hesitated for a second before jumping in and closing the trunk behind me—smart enough not to let the thing shut all the way. I'd been in trunks before, when Jack snuck me into the drive-in movies on Long Island. I was dead tired. Before I could stop myself, I let loose a yawn that sounded like a lion mating call. Suddenly, the hood popped open and there was Daphne, standing with one hand on the trunk and the other on her hip.

"I should have known you'd run off," she said. "Get out of there this second!" Her full skirt gave me something to hold onto as I yanked her into the trunk and brought the lid down behind her. She kicked me in the shin and said, "Are you out of your mind, Thomas?"

"Look, just give it a minute or two, would you? This is the car I saw the two Nazis driving. Back in London."

"How can you be certain?"

I mentioned my photographic memory. My arms were around Daphne's waist and she was struggling to get free—still too weak to put up much of a fight. We both heard a noise at the same time. Daphne's body went slack.

Footsteps running toward the car.

The driver's door creaked open and the car rocked as someone got into the seat. Daphne made a move to escape, but I rolled her over so her body was away from the trunk lid. I clapped my hand over her mouth. The engine started and we rolled down the road. She slapped me across the cheek, but quietly.

"We can jump out anytime we want," I whispered.

"I'm not jumping from a moving vehicle," she said. "And why must I always allow you get me into these predicaments?"

" 'Cause I'm your man of honor?"

"Because I'm balmy is more like it. Couldn't you just once listen to your elders?"

We didn't get far when the car came to a stop and the engine was killed.

"I betcha we're at the train station," I said. "At this

hour there won't be many people there. Give them a ten-second lead and then we'll follow. At least we'll get a good look at them." I counted to ten and then popped the lid, leaping from the car and looking around for a sign of the escaping Nazis. We weren't at the train station after all, but near the castle. Down the street was a gate leading into the military installation. In the dark we saw a woman, her back facing us. We stalked her, hiding behind a mailbox as she showed her identification to a sentry. She was wearing a knee-length gray wool overcoat over a blue skirt and flat heels. A scarf was tied around her head. Sneaking from the bottom was dark brown hair, almost black. Even though it was still night, she was wearing sunglasses.

"Too thin to be Blanche," I said. "And the brown hair—I can't see clearly, but that narrows it down to Geraldine or Dot."

"Dot, then," said Daphne, not wanting to incriminate her friend. "And the problem is we can't get into the base. But like you say, we've narrowed the search down and that's—"

"Shush," I said, as the sentry let the woman pass. He looked at his watch, yawning and stepping away from the gate. Probably to take a leak.

"I can climb that fence, no problem," I said. Before Daphne could stop me, I was racing to the gate, sticking the toe of my sneaker in the chain-link fence. When I leapt from the top I saw Daphne right behind me, making her way like a monkey climbing a stepladder. She was always good in a pinch.

Floodlights came on just then. A man perched somewhere to the left and above us shouted from a megaphone. We ducked behind a building and then sprinted in the direction we'd seen the woman go, slowing once we spotted her in front of us. She was entering a door marked *DRESSING STATION*—a door, glory to God, that led into one of the underground tunnels above the castle. The door was just about to shut when Daphne reached it, holding it open for me. I looked behind, seeing nothing but an empty pathway that led back to the front gate. So far, no one was following us.

"Let's keep behind her, but close the gap until we can get a good view," said Daphne. We were walking downwards through a narrow, arched tunnel. The woman opened another door and we followed about forty steps behind. When we opened the door ourselves, we saw her exiting another door on the far side. Cots lined both walls. As we passed, several men called out to Daphne, thinking she was a nurse.

"Begging your pardon, so sorry," she kept saying as we sped past. A wounded man reached out for Daphne's hand, pulling her to him and causing her to crash into a wheeled cart. Medicine bottles shattered on the floor. A bedpan—full, of course—crashed to the ground, splattering my sneakers.

A nurse shouted, "Whoa there!"

Opening the far door, we heard the sound of the German's heels, slamming the stone floor and echoing down a long, vaulted corridor. Bare lightbulbs, less than ten watts each, were strung at intervals overhead. She slowed under a dark patch, swinging her face in our direction. A bulb right over our heads gave her a clear view. Dashing down the corridor, she made a turn.

"That's it." I said. "She's seen us. Let's nab her!"

Daphne shouted: "We know you're a German agent, whomever you are!"

We picked up speed, making the turn without slowing. In front of us was a stone staircase, leading upwards. I caught a glimpse of the woman's shoe as she turned onto a landing.

She was fast, I had to give her that. The Germans trained her well. Down another corridor, up another staircase, around a bend—we were gaining on her, but just barely. We passed several rooms. I caught a quick look through glass windows into banks of equipment. Women—all in uniform—manned the instruments, pushing and pulling cords out of huge switchboards that looked like something out of *Flash Gordon*. It came to me that we were in an RAF radar station. It figured they'd put one in the tunnels—tunnels 22 miles from Nazi-occupied France. They were looking for German bomber squadrons heading for England. Would they spot a small tugboat, making its away in the other direction?

Daphne was winded and stopped short, putting both hands on her knees. A WAAF swung a door open and came into the corridor. "Can I help you?" she said, and not too nicely. She looked at me. "You're not permitted to be here. This is a restricted area. Come with me, young man. And you too, miss—"

"I'm not sure I can do this, Thomas," said Daphne, breathing heavily, all the blood drawn from her face. "And I don't want you running after her alone. It's not safe—she could be armed. Why we didn't alert the gate attendant in the first place, I don't know. I could slap myself." She turned to the WAAF, "Listen—"

I widened my stride.

"Stop," said the WAAF. "I'm calling the MPs straightaway!" Her voice echoed off the stone walls, "way—way—way."

I heard the tap-tap of Daphne's toes behind me; she ran like a ballet dancer. If I let her get too close, she'd grab onto my shirt. I bent down for a sprint like I was trained to do in gym class. A door slammed above me. I took three steps at a time, bounding up another staircase. Opening a door at the top of the stairs, a cold wind blew in my face. In front of me was a long grassy field sloping downhill. The castle loomed off to the left, the sea and the White Cliffs of Dover to my right. Waves crashed below. A foghorn sounded from a lighthouse across the harbor.

The woman was now far in front of me. She stopped short, whipping her head left and right, not sure which way to make an escape. I prayed she'd head toward the castle. I wanted a chase through the ancient ruins. It would've made a better story.

She headed toward the cliff, instead.

If she had a gun, she would've used it by now. The door behind me creaked open and crashed closed. Daphne came stumbling toward me.

"She's headed toward the cliffs," I said, without waiting for her to choke out a protest.

A hazy moon was going down below the sea's horizon, taking away what little light there was. Stepping into a hole, I twisted my ankle. Tears came to my eyes when I took the next step. But I knew this was my big shot at a medal. I pushed myself forward by picturing the king pinning it onto my chest. I visualized President Roosevelt handing me a trophy—a bowling trophy, funny enough. Blinding pain messes with your head.

It wasn't until I was sliding on my bottom—wet grass soaking through to my underwear—that I noticed it was raining cats and dogs. A boulder got in between me and the cliff edge. That was the good news. The bad news was that I slammed into it, breaking my arm.

My back was to the sea—resting against the cold, hard, rock—when I saw the shape of a woman cutting her way through the fog toward me. I couldn't even raise my good arm to fend her off. Any second and I'd be flung into the hungry sea. Right then, I wished I had a parachute. I wished I knew how to swim. I kicked my legs in the air, aiming for her knees.

"For crying out loud, Thomas. It's me," said Daphne.

She gave me a hand up, which I shook off. Instead, I tore along the cliff edge in the direction I was sure the Nazi agent had run.

"You can't escape, fräulein!" I yelled into the powerful wind, not sure if the woman could hear me.

"Please stop, Thomas!" yelled Daphne coming after

me. "The cliff edge isn't stable." Just as she said that, a big chunk of grass and white sand crumbled from under my right foot, falling to the sea below.

I seen three Spitfires flying out of the fog, low over the cliffs, and headed out to the sea. The sun was coming up behind the castle, shedding just enough light to let me see the woman up ahead, as she skirted around the cliff edge. Her scarf had come down onto her shoulders. Wet hair flew around her head, blinding her. Her hand reached up to swipe strands from her eyes. Frustrated, she pulled off a soaking wet wig, heaving it over the cliff edge. Underneath was dishwater blonde hair.

Just then, one of her shoes got stuck in mud. Heavier fog—this like potato soup—moved in from the Channel, making it impossible to see even my own nose. I lost sight of the woman, afraid to move forward and not sure where to put my foot. My aching, twisted, gashed foot. Daphne came up behind me, holding onto my sleeve: the one that held my broken arm. I yelled out in pain.

Another scream drowned out my own. At first the sound was booming, then grew fainter and fainter, taking the voice down, down, down, until the roaring of the sea muffled the voice, and the voice and the sea became one angry roar.

Me and Daphne stood straight, silent, and still. Like the mirror statues of Ramses at Abu Simbel, only colder.

I crossed myself. "God forgive me. Do you think it's my fault she fell? Is her blood on my hands, you think?" I looked down at my opened palms. They were muddy, but not bloody. Daphne began to weep—big sobs with little spaces in between for gulps of air. "I don't think it was Geraldine," I said, figuring it was the idea of her double-date friend's death that upset her most.

"I thought I'd lost you back there, Thomas. What would have happened to Jack? He'd never have gotten over it. Never. Why"—big sob—"I never would have gotten over it myself."

I turned around and threw my one good arm around Daphne, clinging to her. A shiver went down my wet body, building in force until I was shaking and my teeth were chattering in my head. Two MPs made their way to us. Out of the fog, I saw they both had rifles pointed at our chests.

"Get back from the edge," said one of them. "Raise your hands above your heads," said the other soldier.

"One of my arm's broke, sir. Mind if I raise just one?"

"It's only a kid," said the first soldier.

"And a girl," said the other.

They helped us make our way back up the slippery slope. We didn't mention the broken body laying—I was sure—in a pool of blood somewheres below the White Cliffs of Dover. First things first.

"Any chance you fellas have some hot cocoa brewing?" I asked.

"Tea," said a soldier. "That's the best we can do."

They patched me up at the tunnel dressing station, while the MPs interviewed me and Daphne. They already knew about the three Nazis loose in Dover and were on the hunt themselves. A pretty nurse made a plaster cast for my arm, and another wrapped my ankle in an ACE bandage. She restitched my foot using black thread. They even found some sugar to put in my tea.

"Do you need me to identify the body?" I asked.

"No!" cried Daphne. "She'll be a hundred shattered pieces. It's no sight for a child."

Daphne was shown to a phone and connected with the Dover RAF airfield. Jack and the other two pilots had just gotten back from their mission. As I suspected, it was their Spitfires we'd seen flying above us. Within a short time, they joined us at the dressing station.

"What happened?" I wanted to know.

The three men looked at each other without speaking.

"I'm twelve and a half! Stop babying me."

"You? A baby?" said Jack. Daphne shot him a look and shook her head. For once Jack ignored her. "We got to the seaside and saw the tugboat was missing."

"No sense going after them in a rowboat," said Squadron Leader Kennard.

"Too slow," said Sel Edner. "So we drove back to the airfield, to our Spits. A WAAF on duty phoned the radar station and a minute later they called back to say they'd spotted a tiny blimp, heading southwest about seven miles across the Channel.

"It wasn't one of ours," said Kennard. "Of that, they were certain."

"Six of one, half a dozen of the other," said Sel.

"One way or another—"

"So, we headed out," said Jack. "It was a piece of cake finding the boat. The tug was like a sitting duck. The sun was up then and we buzzed it low—wing to wing—getting a good look. It met Lord-What's-His-Name's description: white with a green hull."

"Union Jack flying nobly from the top mast," said Kennard.

"Two men on the deck saw us buzz over and ran into the cabin," said Sel.

Fritz and the phoney-bologna RAF navigator. I didn't have to say it.

Kennard radioed to my brother, who was the flight lieutenant: number two guy. They debated what to do. Technically the boat wasn't an enemy craft. And Fritz was a downed airman: regulations said not to shoot on him in cold blood. I breathed a sigh of relief, not because I was pally-pal with the Luftwaffe pilot, but because I'd be the one who would have to break the news to his grandmother if he died. Her, I liked.

"Then out of the sea—what should arise?" said Jack.

"Like a whale," said Sel.

"A German U-Boat!" I said, my eyes bugging out.

"Bingo," said Jack.

"They would have been better off heading straight for France in the tugboat. Stupid, if you ask me," said Sel.

"The two men had just jumped in the water and were swimming for a ladder up to the U-Boat deck," said Jack. "The hatch was opened and a sailor waited for them to hop onboard. Thing was, the moment he got a lookie-lookie at us, the hatch slammed tight. Next thing you know, they got the anti-aircraft guns working. So, all bets were off."

"I gave the order," said Kennard.

"Our cannons don't make much of a dent on a submarine," said Jack, "but the little tug got caught in the crossfire. Blown to smither—"

"No!" cried Daphne. She put her hands over her ears. Mine were sticking 90 degrees from my head.

"That's our job, honey. No two ways about it."

"Maybe they're good swimmers," said Kennard with a shrug of his shoulders.

I was going to have to break the news to Mrs. Wigglesworth, after all.

CHAPTER THIRTY-FOUR

THE MPs FOUND HER BROKEN BODY on a path under the cliffs and alongside the seashore. I didn't have to see the body to know who she was. An MP came into the dressing station carrying a suitcase.

"Do you recognize this? Found it in the boot of the maroon vehicle."

"I recognize it," I said.

"What's in here, bricks?" he asked.

I recognized the stickers. Pasted all over the battered leather case: Ceylon, India, New Zealand, and all the other British colonies. As they say in England, *The sun never sets over the British Empire.* It was a brilliant idea to disguise the case to make it look like it belonged to an English girl.

I tried to remember whose room I'd first seen the suitcase in. Dot and Alice's—that was it. Under one bed was the suitcase and under the other were nothing but dust balls and a pair of pink quilted slippers.

"You might say I'm an intrepid traveler," she'd said.

So it wasn't Geraldine who answered the phone when Mrs. Wigglesworth called the base. It was someone *claiming* to be Geraldine. Promising to send a rescue party to save me, when it was Fritz she was meaning to help.

"Daphne, can you break the case open?"

She removed a pin from her wet hair and felt around in the left lock. I pulled another pin from her hair and got to work on the right side lock. One after another the two clasps sprung open.

"I'll be a monkey's uncle," said Jack, when we all peered into the case.

Two WAAFs came into the dressing station just then. One pulled a power cord from the suitcase and plugged it into a socket. She flicked on a switch and consulted a cart that was taped inside the lid. Then she turned a few dials. "Let's take it outside," she said. "We'll get a better signal."

I was given a pair of crutches. We filed out the door and into the fog, Jack carrying the suitcase. He laid it on the ground and opened the lid again. An extension cord was run from inside the building. The WAAF pulled the earmuffs from the suitcase and attached them to her head. Another WAAF took a set of folding rabbit ears from a specially made compartment and set up the transmitter. The radio operator turned the dials this way and that. All we heard was a crackling sound coming from the transmitter. She began tapping out a message.

"She's trying to transmit using German code, I think. You see the chart inside the lid?" said a woman standing next to me. I looked close and saw that the markings on the instruments were in English. "Done so that if your landlady has a peek, she shan't go running to the Home Guard."

"No wonder the U-Boat knew precisely where to meet the tug," said Squadron Leader Kennard.

The radio operator said, "They're sending a message back in code. I think we may have Hamburg on the other end."

"Anyone have a message for Hitler?" I said.

Everyone had a message—but none that can be repeated.

CHAPTER THIRTY-FIVE

Back at MI5 Headquarters,
Wormwood Scrubs, East London

THERE IS A KNOCK ON THE DOOR, three quick taps. "If you have a moment, sir," says Agent Ellis, craning his head around the door. "Thought I'd bring you up to date on the Rochford Ring."

"Is that what we are calling it now, the *Rochford Ring?*" says Brigadier A.W.A. Harker, Deputy Director General of MI5. He has yet to make eye contact with his subordinate. He opens a desk drawer and shuffles things around to no purpose.

By now Ellis is impervious to these hints. Uninvited, he steps into the office and takes a seat. "I interviewed the lad, that American boy responsible for uncovering the Rochford Ring."

Hacker looks up finally. "Two Nazi spies do not make a ring, Ellis."

"There might be others, sir, planted deep in our ranks. RAF Command is seeking ways to tighten base security. There's an effort on to reconfirm the identity of all personnel—both civilian, auxiliary, and military—

make it impossible for the Abwehr to infiltrate one of our military installations again. Won't be at all surprised if these new measures extend to the entire British Armed Forces. The whole affair has caused quite a shake-up."

"Well, I should hope so," says Hacker. "I mean, letting a twelve-year-old boy onto an Royal Air Force base during wartime! Unheard of."

"Clever lad that one. I should warn you, sir, that the chaps over at the Ministry of Information have got wind of the story and think it might be of value…to encourage civilian vigilance and what have you. Of course, I told them that I'm not at liberty to discuss the case without your express permission, sir." He taps his pen against his notepad and leans forward expectantly.

Hacker grips the arms of his desk chair until his knuckles turn white. He loosens his necktie and runs a finger around his starched collar. No one but his wife— and their family physician—knows that he suffers with ulcers. He finds a bottle and spoon in his desk drawer and mixes a teaspoon of powder into a glass of water.

"Vitamins," he says.

Ellis reads *Sodium Bicarbonate* on the bottle's label.

"Well then…shall I let the Ministry of Information see the file, sir?" Ellis lifts a manila folder. On the tab is penned THOMAS R. MOONEY/ROCHFORD RING. "The lad's brother is with the Eagle Squadron, you see. So, naturally, the Ministry of Information is chomping at the bit. They've suggested asking Pathé to make a newsreel. Issue the lad a citation, what have you. Have him meet the king and the princesses. The Americans will love this, they say. Just the story, they suspect, for *Life* magazine. I should mention, sir, that 10 Downing has heard rumors."

"The prime minister? Good God!"

"I'm afraid that one of our secretaries mentioned it to one of his. We've issued her a strong reprimand."

"Give me the file, Ellis. I'll take this from here."

Ellis reluctantly hands over the folder. He has a strong suspicion that it will not be forwarded to the Ministry of Information.

"That will be all," says Hacker. "*Do* shut the door as you go."

He waits for the click of the latch before flinging the folder into a rubbish bin.

EPILOGUE

LORD AND LADY SOPWITH insisted I come home with them. "Your studies," explained Lady Sop. So it was only later that the whole mystery was explained to me.

Back at RAF Rochford, Henry Wilson came forward and confessed. Turned out he'd been standing beside the staircase the morning Jimmy Donavon came flying down the stairs and fell, causing the rest of the squadron to trip over him. Wilson'd seen a broom laying on the stair, but didn't say anything. He was sick and tired of Jimmy ribbing him about being a lowly mechanic. No one blamed Wilson. All the guys agreed that Jimmy's stabs were out of line. Squadron Leader Kennard did an about-face and recommended Wilson to RAF Command. He was leaving for flight training in Canada, not that he needed it. Dot's fancy-pants family stuck up their noses when they met him. Even though their future son-in-law would be a Spitfire pilot and an officer, to boot.

The blindfold—that chichi silk pilot's scarf—belonged to Dot. She'd left it in the mess hall by mistake. Soon as she got it back, she stuffed it into a "Dear John" letter and mailed it to the Millionaire pilot stationed in

Egypt. I didn't feel too sorry for him. He'd probably find the tomb of Nefertiti before I had my shot at it.

Jack cornered a cook in the base kitchen and got a confession from him. The kidneys had been left out overnight by mistake. But when the cook smelled them the next morning he judged them to be A-Okay. Problem was, he was coming down with a nasty head cold and his nose was stuffed. When I started snooping around, he got the jitters and threw me into the Frigidaire while he got rid of the evidence. The refrigerator wasn't cold enough to kill me, he said, and he'd meant to let me out eventually.

The box of spark plugs I'd seen while snooping around Alice's closet turned out to be little German explosives, made to replace airplane spark plugs. They were designed to blow up when the engine reached a certain temperature. One of them spark plugs almost murdered my brother, which justified chasing Alice off a cliff.

Blanche, it turned out, had a long list of dream husbands penned into her prayer book, "It is a *prayer* book, after all," she explained. "I had a thing for that German chap before the war. So tall he was, and ever so debonair. I suppose I ought to cross his name off the list."

And Alice? The church in Bramhope where she claimed to hail from is called St. Giles, *not* St. Nicholas. St. Nick, it turns out, is the big cathedral in Berlin. If only I'd known my churches better. And her name wasn't Skinner, even though it said so on the identity card found soaked in her blood. Daphne put herself in the line of fire by letting on that she knew the real Alice

Skinner, a WAAF from RAF North Weald, who was last seen boarding a train for Glasgow, visiting home before reporting for her new assignment at RAF Rochford. A little more hemlock in Daphne's tea and…I can't even write it.

In the end, everything we knew about that awful, blaspheming woman—who, on top of everything, was stingy with the chocolate—wouldn't fill a teaspoon.

Lady Sheffield would never get over the shock of learning that her son's fiancée was a Nazi agent and likely his murderer. She wept an ocean of tears when she learned the truth. It wasn't fair. But then again, not much in this crazy war is.

Take my case, for example. I'm still waiting for the Victoria Cross, preferably cast in solid gold. So far, all's that's happened is a visit from the British Security Service: a man identifying himself as Agent Charles Ellis.

My brother rewarded me though—in the form of a burger and fries at the American Eagle Club in London. The fries came with real American Heinz ketchup. On top of that, I got a genuine Coca-Cola straight out of a chilled glass bottle. That's something, anyway.

And we never did figure out who hit my brother on the head in the pub up in Garsington. Could've just been a mean drunk.

Or maybe…

The Series Continues!

LETTER VIA PARIS

By Cate M. Ruane

PROLOGUE

THE FÜHRER, A MAN OF MIDDLING HEIGHT, leans over a marble-topped conference table, running his stubby hand over a blueprint that is spread out before him, pressing down on the curled edges. "Bring me a paperweight!" he shouts.

His secretary hurries toward a set of colossal oak doors; an Ardabil carpet silences her steps. With the brunt of her weight, she pushes the doors open. Her eyes fix on the golden eagle perched above the doorframe. Outside can be heard the shuffle of jackboots against a marble floor. Whispered voices, eager to obey, echo down a quarter-mile long reception gallery:

"The führer requires a paperweight!"

"Which paperweight?"

"Any paperweight!"

Within seconds, heels click together and the sought-after paperweight is produced, balanced upon an outstretched palm, biceps straining to hold up the cast bronze object.

The führer continues to examine the blueprint, having forgotten his request.

At his shoulder, but a step behind, stands a tall and lanky architect, his hands grasped behind his back, his fingers opening and closing nervously. "Well, put the paperweight down, you fool," says the architect, slamming his hand on the table. *Contain yourself, Albert*, thinks the architect, immediately regretting the outburst, which still rings from the stone walls. *I ought to have specified mahogany paneling*, he thinks, surveying the 1312 square foot office. The echo fades, replaced with library-like silence.

Then finally the verdict: "You are a genius, Speer," says the führer, patting the architect's forearm.

"No, *mein Führer*," says Speer. "The genius is yours. The Führermuseum will be your crowning achievement, the greatest art collection since the destruction of the Alexandra Library."

"Greater than the Louvre," says the führer.

"Greater than the Hermitage or the Metropolitan Museum of Art," says Speer.

The führer pauses. A smile lifts below his square mustache. He motions to his secretary, "Bring me an inventory for both the Moscow and New York museums."

"Very wise, *mein Führer*," says Speer. "Perhaps we ought to add two more wings to the Führermuseum?"

The führer leans over the blueprint again, taking up a pencil and drawing an X. "Here is where we will hang my centerpiece."

"Ah, the Vermeer, *mein Führer*," says Speer. "And

where is it now? Here in Berlin, I hope?

"Somewhere safer, Speer. Never you mind," says the führer.

CHAPTER ONE

England

CLINCHING MY TEETH and crossing my fingers did no good at all. The airplane was descending with too much velocity. Its fuselage tilted at the wrong angle and it wasn't banking tight enough. The wing grazed a pillar, and I flinched. The nose tilted downward and the plane went into a tailspin.

The phone rang right then. O'Reilly, the butler, stepped into the path of the spiraling aircraft. I crossed myself. There wasn't time to shout a warning. The airplane hit O'Reilly square in the head. He screamed at the top of his lungs:

"Tommy Mooney, you rascal!"

I crouched behind the banister, four floors up the spiral staircase. Peering between the railings, I saw O'Reilly crane his neck. "Homework, my foot!" he said. At his feet were dozens of paper airplanes, all failed experiments.

The course was called *The Principles of Aviation Mechanics*, and I was the only student. Lord Thomas Octave Sopwith—my reluctant guardian—was my tutor.

He was an aviation pioneer and owner of Hawker Aviation, manufacturer of fighter planes and light bombers. "Safer to learn the principles with paper models, what?" he said after our first lesson, in a real airplane. I wouldn't pass until I designed a paper airplane able to descend like a vulture going for a wounded rabbit, circling the floors without hitting the railings and landing belly down. Lord Sopwith wanted the results of each launch recorded in a notebook: wingspan, fuselage length, and aileron configuration—also the paper's weight, as seen on the watermark. This way, once I hit on a successful design, it could be reproduced. *Mass production,* Lord Sopwith called it: the secret to getting an air fleet built fast enough to keep up with the German Luftwaffe.

I was crouched behind the banister and making notes when O'Reilly shouted, "Tommy! You are summoned to the telephone!"

At first I thought it was a trick to get me out of hiding. But I looked down and saw that he was holding the receiver in his hand. As I slid down four flights of waxed banister, I wondered who could be calling me.

Maybe it was my ma calling from New York to tell me she'd found a way to get me over the *Kriegsmarine*-infested Atlantic Ocean. I ran away from home on Long Island two months earlier, first bicycling to the Brooklyn Harbor before stowing away on the Sopwith's yacht. Later I made my way to Daphne, my brother's fiancée in London, and onward to occupied Europe, where together we rescued Jack, who was missing in action until we found him. Now I was back in England, with my ma missing me like a kid missing his front teeth.

If the Nazis didn't surrender soon, I wouldn't be home for Christmas. Ma said not to worry, she'd mail me a box of my favorite Christmas cookies: gingerbread men with maraschino cherry eyes. But it killed me to think my sister Mary would be the one licking the beater and bowl. She'd probably pick the cherry eyes out before my ma went to mail the box to England.

I couldn't remember my ma's voice, only that it sounded like an Irish jig. She sent me regular letters, written in cursive and sprinkled with apple blossom body powder. Pressing the paper to my nose was like getting a hug. Even if I *was* too old for that mushy stuff.

By the time my feet hit the marble landing, I was bracing for a disappointment. A transatlantic call would bankrupt the family, what with Da still taking odds-and-end jobs but finding nothing steady. It must be my brother Jack, I figured, which was just as good. He knew how to butter up a WAAF—The Women's Auxiliary Air Force—so'd she let him use the phone at the Royal Air Force base. My brother was a Spitfire pilot and the target of every dame in the British Empire, which stretched from British Columbia clear around the globe to Singapore. Jack had the pick of the litter, and was about to marry the cat's meow.

I grabbed the phone out of O'Reilly's white-gloved hand and yelled into the receiver. "Jack! Is it you?"

"No, it's Daphne," said my brother's fiancée, the cat's meow herself.

O'Reilly wasn't budging. He stood one foot from

my toes, looking down at me with that Frankenstein face of his. "Give a fella privacy, won't you?" I said.

"Make it snappy and do not tie up the line," he said. "His lordship might receive a call at any moment—one of importance to the Nation."

"Thomas? Hello? Are you there?" said Daphne's crackling voice, coming from the earpiece.

I put the receiver against my flannel jacket and said to O'Reilly, "Don't you have anything more important to do? Counting bed sheets or wine tasting or something? Doesn't the silver need polishing?"

O'Reilly growled, but backed away. "No more than two minutes, you hear?" He pretended to inspect a flower arrangement, when the whole time he had one eye on a pocket watch.

"Daphne. Talk fast," I said.

"We've a letter from Paris," she said. "A very odd sort of letter."

"We?"

"Addressed to the both of us, and sent to my address in London. From the postmarks, it looks as if it was mailed from Vichy France." That, I knew, was the part of France occupied by the Germans just a week or two before, but in cahoots with the Nazis from the get-go. Daphne went on: "Maybe the sender entrusted the letter to someone traveling to the south of France? Amazing that it got through the censors. Why, they've put their swastika stamps all over it."

"Did the censors black out parts? Maybe cut parts out using a razor blade?"

"Actually, the odd thing is all that's in the envelope is a blank piece of paper with no marks of any sort."

"Smell it, would you? Does it smell like Coca-Cola?"

I knew without asking that the letter was from my friend Juliette. As I was leaving Paris for the escape over the Pyrenees Mountains with Jack and Daphne, I told her to write to me using invisible ink. Coke was the perfect fluid: it dried invisible. But once you heated up the letter the writing became visible again. Anything acidic will do the trick.

"It smells like salad dressing," said Daphne. "Vinegar, to be exact."

"One and a half minutes remaining," said O'Reilly, swinging his watch from the chain.

Rapid-fire, I said, "Holdtheletteruptoalamp!" hoping Daphne could keep up.

"Hold the letter up to a what?" she said.

"A lamp! Then watch carefully. If I'm right, a message will appear like magic. Only, don't let the letter touch the light bulb or it will catch on fire."

"One minute," said O'Reilly, tapping the toe of his spit-shined shoe.

Daphne started hyperventilating. "Someone has written, *Help! Sophie is missing.* Oh, my, it's signed... *Juliette!* Why this is dreadful, Thomas. What could have happened to Sophie?"

Sophie was Juliette's big sister, and Daphne's best friend. We holed-up at their place in Paris while we searched for my brother. I owed the Doumer family big-time. They fed me and everything; gave me a roof over my head; Madame Doumer even took me to see a guillotine. If they were in trouble, I was gonna help.

Heavy breathing come over the line. Daphne moaned.

I considered the situation from every angle and said, "My guess is Sophie ran away to work for the French Resistance and then got herself caught. The Nazis are probably torturing her. Those dirty rotten sons-of-female dogs, those low-life—"

O'Reilly was making his way back to the phone. "Thirty seconds," he said, tapping the face of his pocket watch. I gripped the receiver with both hands.

Just then, Lady Sopwith peeked her head out from the drawing room. "O'Reilly. Oh, there you are," she said. "May I have a moment of your time? I need help with the radiator. It's leaking over the parquet floor again. The boards are warping. Come and see what can be done. The village plumber has been called up, you know, but you're just as handy in a pinch."

Thank Jesus, Mary, and Joseph for Lady Sop. She'd saved me out of more than one fix. It was her idea to invite me to hole-up at Warfield Hall while I was stranded in England. If it'd been up to O'Reilly, I would've been given a blow-up raft, a loaf of wheat bread, a jar of Marmite, and one oar.

Meanwhile, Daphne was sobbing on the other end of the line. "My dear Sophie. Oh dear, dear, darling Sophie! Oh Thomas, I hope it isn't as you said."

"Look Daphne, sorry I said what I said," I said.

"You know how my imagination gets going. Maybe she *did* join the Resistance but had to go underground." I liked the idea of having another friend in the Resistance. They were my heroes, after all. Right up there with the Royal Air Force and the U.S. Army Air Forces.

"Be off that telephone by the time I return," said O'Reilly as he goose-stepped to the drawing room.

Daphne was hiccuping now. I said, "I betcha Sophie ran off with some fella. Probably one of them Frenchies who pose buff for her paintings." Sophie was an artist. Her paintings were what my ma would call indecent: fellas with everything hanging loose. I added, "She probably eloped to the Riviera wearing one of them berets and forgot to leave a note. Heck, Daphne. Would you stop crying already?"

"Perhaps you're right," said Daphne, all drawn out, like she was trying to buy my story. I helped her along:

"Something like that is how my ma ended up in New York. Her big sister was supposed to go and work as a maid, but ran off with an Irish farmhand the night before the boat was sailing. Didn't tell anyone. My ma sailed in her place and had to work her fingers to the bone to send money home to Ireland. And all 'cause her sister disappeared with some farmhand."

Static electricity filled my ear while Daphne got herself together. Meanwhile, I let my wheels spin. I figured that my first guess was the right one: Sophie was in tight with her sister Juliette and with her ma—who she called *Maman*. She wouldn't've run off without telling them.

"Wouldn't she have left a note?" said Daphne, reading my mind and making a good point. Even I'd left a note when I ran off—in my ma's top dresser drawer where she hid a secret stash of chocolate mints. But Sophie was practically a grown-up, eighteen-years-old. If she wanted to elope she'd invite her family along, her maman to bake a three-story cake, Juliette for a flower girl, Daphne for maid of honor.

It was obvious. The Nazis had her.

People in Paris were getting carted off left and right. Alvar Lidell talked about it on the BBC news, which the Sopwiths tuned into every night. Hitler's plan was to wipe out Jews, socialists, Gypsies, and jazz musicians. And Sophie was the artsy type, dressed like a Gypsy, listened to jazz, and hob-knobbed with socialists. You can't go around wearing berets and smocks without the Gestapo noticing. Not in occupied Paris, anyway. And her best friend, Daphne, was half-Jewish on her mother's side.

I was the first to pipe up. "We're got to act fast before the trail grows cold."

"But whatever can we do, stuck here in England?" said Daphne.

"There's an airline flying from Whitchurch to Lisbon, Portugal," I said. "I read about it in the paper. The Luftwaffe tried to shoot the plane down the other day."

"And you want us to book tickets?"

"From Lisbon it's an easy train ride to Paris. I'll round up maps tonight and work out a route. Lord Sopwith has ones he keeps in the library."

"Thomas Robert Mooney, we are not going back to occupied Europe again. My parents were frantic the whole time I was over there, not that they knew where I was at the time. They thought I'd run off and eloped." She laughed. "If I'd had any idea how desperate the situation was over there, I never would have let you talk me into going. I'm not nearly as naïve now. So get the idea out of your head."

"Okay," I said, ignoring her. "Then we have a plan. Meet me at Whitchurch Airfield tomorrow morning at sunrise."

"Thomas Rob—"

As luck would have it, just then O'Reilly ripped the phone out of my hands and slammed the receiver down. As he grabbed my elbow, pulling me to a table full of tarnished tea sets and jars of polish, we heard the phone ring again.

"No need to answer," I said. "You know how girls can rattle on—all chatty when a fella wants a little peace and quiet."

O'Reilly sneered. "At your suggestion, I've decided it's time to polish the silver. Lady Sopwith is in full agreement." After a snicker he said, "It's high time you pay back for the food you consume. So get to work young man, and no dilly-dallying. Give it elbow grease."

End of Sample.

THE ADVENTURE BEGINS:
Telegram For Mrs. Mooney

With only a telegram to guide him, Tommy Mooney leaves his Long Island home in search of his big brother Jack—a RAF Spitfire pilot missing in action somewhere in Nazi-occupied Europe.

His first stop is London, where he'll enlist the help of Daphne Clarke, Jack's British fiancée.

Hope turns to foreboding as it begins to look as though the two are being deceived by the Gestapo—used in a plot to expose a Resistance network created to help downed airmen evade capture. "What a bleeding conundrum," says Daphne, as it becomes clear that by continuing the search for Jack, they risk the lives of many like him—as well as their own.

THE ADVENTURE CONTINUES:
Letter Via Paris

Daphne receives a letter from Paris, written in invisible ink. The letter is from Juliette, begging Tommy and Daphne to return to Paris and help find her sister, Sophie, who has gone missing. There is no way that Daphne is returning to German-occupied Europe—unless, that is, Tommy can find a way to drag her there. A mystery involving a stolen masterpiece, communist Resistance members, and a foolhardy attempt on the life of Hermann Göring, leader of the Luftwaffe.

Message For Hitler is a work of fiction, but some of the characters are loosely based on real people who lived and died during World War II.

Tommy is based on my own da, Thomas Robert Mooney, who was a child when his oldest brother, Flight Lieutenant John "Jack" Mooney, flew with the RAF Eagle Squadron.

Jack was a twenty-one-year-old Spitfire pilot, engaged to marry a seventeen-year-old London girl named Daphne. About all I know of the real woman comes from a newspaper article quoting a letter that she'd written to my grandmother when Jack was missing: "I've put away the trousseau for a while but I'll be taking everything out again soon as I know he'll be back." The character of Daphne is built entirely from that one line.

Thomas Octave Murdoch Sopwith (who was appointed Commander of the Most Excellent Order of the British Empire in 1953, and was not actually a "Lord") was an English aviation pioneer and yachtsman. His *Endeavour* challenged the America's Cup in 1934 and 1937. Warfield Hall is in Berkshire. I have taken the liberty of relocating it to Hampshire.

In September 1942, the Eagle Squadrons were

transferred from the RAF to the Eighth Air Force of the U.S. Army Air Forces. In *Message For Hitler* I've delayed the transfer by a few months. And, on another subject, after having written this book, I learned that Wormwood Scrubs was bombed and MI5 had been relocted during the time this novel is set: It's hard to keep up with the Luftwaffe!

At the Imperial War Museum in London, you can ask to view a two-second film shot from Jack's Spitfire as he fires upon a German minesweeper.

And, while you're in London, drop by the building that once housed the Eagle Club: 24-28 Charing Cross Road. There just happens to be a fantastic burger shop on the ground floor. Raise a glass and toast the American RAF Eagle Squadron.

ABOUT THE AUTHOR

Cate M. Ruane spent years working as a copywriter and art director at advertising agencies in New York City and San Francisco. Born and raised on Long Island, she now lives in Asheville, N.C. She is also the author of *Telegram For Mrs. Mooney.* And since writing this book, she has added two more to the series: *Letter Via Paris and Ticket to Manhattan.* Some days she wakes up thinking it's 1943.

www.catemruane.com

ABOUT THE AUTHOR

Cate M. Ruane spent years working as a copywriter and art director at advertising agencies in New York City and San Francisco. Born and raised on Long Island, she now lives in Asheville, N.C. She is also the author of *Telegram For Mrs. Mooney*. And since writing this book, she has added two more to the series: *Letter Via Paris and Ticket to Manhattan*. Some days she wakes up thinking it's 1943.

www.catemruane.com

Fonts used in this book

The headline and subtitle font is LD Telegram,
by Inspire Graphics, licensed from LetteringDelights.com.

The text font is Adobe Caslon Pro.
Englishman William Caslon (1672-1766) first cut his
typeface Caslon in 1725.
His major influences were the Dutch designers
Christoffel van Dijcks and Dirck Voskens.

www.ingramcontent.com/pod-product-compliance
Lightning Source LLC
Chambersburg PA
CBHW070652180626
46817CB00006B/2343